DUI / DWI

DUI / DWI

THE HISTORY OF DRIVING UNDER THE INFLUENCE

DAVID N. JOLLY

Outskirts Press, Inc.
Denver, Colorado

DUI / DWI
The History of Driving Under the Influence
All Rights Reserved.
Copyright © 2009 David N. Jolly
v3.0

Cover Photo and Cover Design © 2009 Robert F. Jolly and JollyDesignInc.com

Cover Design:
Robert F. Jolly
Jolly Design Inc., Calgary, Canada.
www.JollyDesignInc.com

Cover Photography:
Maria Tchalakova
www.FDPstudio.com.

Outskirts Press, Inc.
http://www.outskirtspress.com

ISBN: 978-1-4327-4622-3

Library of Congress Control Number: 2009934642

Outskirts Press and the "OP" logo are trademarks belonging to Outskirts Press, Inc.

PRINTED IN THE UNITED STATES OF AMERICA

This book is dedicated to my wife, Janean and son, Christopher.
Thank you for your patience, love, and support.

*A special thanks to my parents, Dr. Clive and Dianne Jolly,
and my Grandparents, Robert and Bethia Millar.
Thank you for providing me with direction,
guidance, and opportunity.*

Animo et Fide

Those who cannot learn from history are doomed to repeat it.
—George Santayana

Contents

Introduction

Driving under the influence is a serious offense and carries with it severe consequences and a social stigma. The governmental data is staggering. According to statistics provided by the United States government, in 2008, 11,773 individuals lost their lives in motor vehicle accidents in the United States involving a driver with a BAC of 0.08 or higher. *Traffic Safety Facts: 2008 Traffic Safety Annual Assessment - Highlights*. NHTSA. DOT HS 811 172 (June 2009) Further, the financial cost in the United States of alcohol-related accidents totals more than $51 billion annually. Blincoe, L, Seay, A, Zaloshnja, E, Miller, T, Romano, E, Luchter, S, et al. *The Economic Impact of Motor Vehicle Crashes, 2000*. Washington (DC): Dept of Transportation (US), National Highway Traffic Safety Administration (NHTSA) (2002) The criminal impact is also extreme as 1.4 million drivers were arrested for driving under the influence of alcohol or narcotics in 2007. Department of Justice (US), Federal Bureau of Investigation (FBI). *Crime in the United States 2007: Uniform Crime Reports*. Washington (DC): FBI (2008) Whether the statistics accurately convey the dangers of driving under the influence or not, the simple fact is that the problem is significant enough for the government to dedicate billions of dollars to the study, prevention, and punishment of the crime. Yet, driving under the influence has only been taken seriously for a relatively short period of time.

Driving under the influence (DUI) combines two primary activities, the consumption of alcohol (or intake of drugs) and driving a motor vehicle. The great majority of DUIs are alcohol based and as such will remain a significant problem in those countries that are accepting of the use and consumption of alcohol in a social environment. Beverage alcohol plays a central role in most societies from dinners with family and friends, cocktail parties, sporting events, fraternity parties, and any number of other public settings. Besides the social acceptance and encouragement of alcohol consumption, alcohol is also regularly used for the reduction of tension, guilt, anxiety, frustration and many other regular activities.

The acceptance of alcohol consumption in western society is easily observed. The alcohol industry aggressively advertises on television and at sporting events and suggests that alcohol is connected to positive cultural symbols and psychological needs. Jacobson, Michael, Atkins, Robert, and Hacker, George. *The Booze Merchants: The Inebriating of America.* Washington, D.C.: Center for Science in the Public Interest. (1983)

While alcohol can serve as a social lubricant and actually enhance the lives of many it is equally true that alcohol is associated with many personal and social problems and with much human misery. A study from the early 1980s by the U.S. Department of Health and Human Services found that "one in three Americans surveyed . . . felt that alcohol caused problems in his or her family." *Fifth Special Report to the U.S. Congress on Alcohol and Health from the Secretary of Health and Human Services* (December 1983)

This social acceptance of alcohol combined with the western world's love affair (and arguably, need) with the automobile has caused a potentially dangerous cocktail. The car has become a symbol of social status and life-style and for many the vehicle even serves a psychological need for power, aggression, fantasy, and control. Meyer, J., and Gomez-Ibanez, J. *Autos, Transit and Cities: A Twentieth Century Fund Report.* New York: Twentieth Century Fund (1981) Additionally, the lives of most in the western world necessitate the need for transportation for work and the world has evolved around that need with infrastructure enabling those with automobiles to commute great distances.

Historically, as the need for the automobile increased so did drinking and driving. Over the last century law makers have attempted to keep up. Laws were enacted at the beginning of the 20th century that made driving under the influence illegal but law enforcement needed a way to prove someone was indeed committing the crime. Initially crude physical testing was conducted that had little or no scientific credibility to support the findings. Physical testing and observations led to the invention of primitive breath testing devices that have subsequently evolved over the years to relatively accurate, although far from perfect, breath testing units. The crude field sobriety testing has also evolved into "standardized" field sobriety testing that law enforcement trusts and relies upon in most DUI cases.

The past century and in particular the last thirty to forty years, has also seen the practice of driving under the influence condemned by society. Organizations have been created with the specific goal of advocating against the crime of driving under the influence and have strongly lobbied governments into enacting stricter conditions and penalties to those individuals convicted of the offense. Further, politicians have run campaigns for election on platforms based on harsher penalties for those convicted of DUI.

The criminalization of driving under the influence will "celebrate" its 100th birthday (in the United States) in the year following the publication of this book. Since the first DUI law was enacted in 1910 in New York, the criminalization of DUI has evolved and embraced new technology and has supported stiffer penalties and lower tolerance. The law is not static however and the next 100 years will undoubtedly see continued evolution. In all likelihood the laws and mechanisms employed in the practice of DUI in the distant future will bear little resemblance to the laws in place in 2009. It will be an interesting journey indeed that will see conflict, controversy, billions of dollars of government funding, and great tragedy, not unlike the first 100 years of driving under the influence.

This book is divided into chapters that individually examine the history of a particular area of the practice of DUI law. Therefore, the chapters include a general history of the crime and its involvement with the motor vehicle, the changing laws, and the advancement in technology; the history of alcohol; the history of drugs; the history of law enforcement; the history of DUI investigations; the history of determining blood alcohol concentration; the history of alcohol and drug evaluation and treatment; the history of DUI organizations; the history of prevention and reoccurrence programs; and a brief look into the future of driving under the influence.

The book attempts to remain largely objective and provide the reader with both sides of each issue presented. Therefore the book is primarily fact based, not opinion based. Throughout the book the phrase "driving under the influence" is used to simplify the genre, although admittedly terms such as "driving while intoxicated," "operating a vehicle while intoxicated," "operating a vehicle while intoxicated," "drunk driving," and "drink driving" are readily used in different jurisdictions. Similarly, the acronym "DUI" is consistently used in this book to refer to "driving under the influence," although admittedly DWI ("driving while intoxicated"), OVI ("operating a vehicle while intoxicated"), and OMVI ("operating a motor vehicle while intoxication") are also commonly used. Additionally, the term "BAC" is used interchangeably with "BrAC" for simplification and consistency.

CHAPTER 1

The History of DUI Laws

*[History] is little else than a picture of human
crimes and misfortunes.*
—Voltaire

The combination of consuming alcohol and operating modes of transportation has occurred for thousands of years. The use of animals as transportation was most certainly done under the influence too many times to chronicle. It was probably unwise and led to many a disaster but prior to modern times it was never illegal. Moreover, this type of activity rarely endangered anybody or anything other than the operator and the animal.

Many famous historical figures were well known for their consumption of alcohol. Alexander the Great's death remains a mystery but many have theorized that he died of alcohol poisoning. Regardless of the actual cause of death, the consensus is that he indulged liberally in alcohol. Further, this consumption undoubtedly led to many rides on horseback while under the influence of alcohol. Similarly Attila the Hun also allegedly died from alcohol poisoning (on the night of his marriage). Regardless of the true determination of death, Attila did consume alcohol in copious amounts and was rarely off the back of a horse. Like Alexander, it can be safely assumed that Attila the Hun often rode a horse while under the influence of alcohol. Additionally, in ancient Rome many chariots must have been powered by an intoxicated driver. So ancient history is not immune from this activity, although such an activity was not criminal.

In more modern times the Industrial Revolution introduced the world to motorized transportation, namely locomotives and the great railroad movement. This is really genesis in regards to operating a motorized form of transportation under the influence of alcohol. Locomotives traveled at great speed carrying many passengers and there was real danger of serious tragedy if something went wrong. This issue became more severe if the train engineer was operating while under the influence of alcohol. To that end, in the United States in 1843 the New York Central Railroad prohibited drinking by employees while on duty. Borkenstein, Robert F. *Historical Perspective: North American Traditional and Experimental Response.* Journal of Studies on Alcohol, suppl. 10:3-12 (1985) In 1904 the *Quarterly Journal of Inebriety* editorialized, with a hint of things to come, that "the precaution of railroad companies to have only total abstainers guide their engines will soon extend to the owners of these new motor wagons. . . .With the increased popularity of these wagons, accidents of this kind will multiply rapidly." Crothers, T.D. M.D, Editor. *Quarterly Journal of Inebriety.* Hartford, MA. (1904) However, such conduct as operating a vehicle while under the influence of alcohol was not yet a crime.

The automobile was not invented by one single individual but instead its history reflects an evolution that took place worldwide. It is estimated that over 100,000 patents created the modern automobile. Bellis, Mary. *The History of the Automobile.* http://inventors.about.com However, it is fair to say that along the way there were many "firsts." Historical figures such as Leonardo da Vinci and Isaac Newton both tinkered with plans for a motorized vehicle that predated any actual working model. *Id.*

There is much debate over the exact date the automobile was born, but the general consensus is that the first modern automobile as we know it, that is to say a vehicle that used an internal combustion engine as its power source, was the Benz Patent Motorwagen, invented by Carl Benz in 1885. The vehicle Benz designed was awarded German patent number 37435 in November, 1886 and was officially unveiled to the public on July 3, 1886 in Mannheim, Germany. Smil, Vaclav. *Creating the Twentieth Century: Technical Innovations of 1867-1914 and Their Lasting Impact.* Oxford University Press. (2005) The vehicle was a three-wheeled automobile with a rear-mounted engine constructed of steel tubing with woodwork panels. The wheels were steel-spoked with solid rubber tires and the engine had a single-speed transmission. For vehicles with internal combustion engines, this was indeed genesis.

At first Benz, along with another German automobile company Daimler, made money and sustained their business by licensing their patents and selling their engines to other motor vehicle manufacturers. The first actual "manufacturers" in the world of actual automobiles en masse were believed to be Panhard & Levassor in 1889 (using a Daimler engine) and Peugeot in 1891. *Id.*

Although the Benz vehicle may indeed be the first internal combustion powered vehicle, this was not the true beginning of motorized personal transportation. Steam-powered self-propelled vehicles are believed to have predated the Benz design by more than one hundred years. Frenchman Nicolas-Joseph Cugnot exhibited his experimental steam-driven artillery tractor, the *fardier à vapeur*, in approximately 1770. Unfortunately for Cugnot this design proved to be impractical and potentially dangerous. In fact, this vehicle may have been involved in the first automobile accident when in 1771 it went out of control and knocked down part of a wall. Renaud, Jean. *Un siècle de Tracteurs Agricoles. De la vapeur à l'électronique.* 2nd Ed. France Agricole Editions (2003)

By 1784, Scottish engineer and inventor William Murdoch had built a working model of a steam carriage, and in 1801 English (Cornish) inventor Richard Trevithick, Murdoch's contemporary, built a full-size steam road locomotive named the "Puffing Devil." Chan, C.C. and Chau, K.T. *Modern Electric Vehicle Technology.* Oxford Science Pub. Page 16 (2001) The problem was that these vehicles could not maintain sufficient steam pressure over long periods of time and were thus not practical.

There were other steam vehicles that later proved to have moderate commercial success. However, these relatively large and fast vehicles did cause much concern among the general public and English lawmakers. As a result, the Locomotive Act of Great Britain was passed in 1865 which required that such self-propelled vehicles being used on public roadways in Great Britain be preceded by an individual on foot waving a red flag and blowing a horn. This law was not repealed until 1896, although the need for the red flag was removed in 1878. Stephens, J.E.R. *Highway Cases, Together With All the Principal Statutes relating to Highways, Bridges and Locomotives.* The Sanitary Publishing Company, Ltd. London. Page 186 (1903)

The United States was not far behind in the development of the automobile. The first automobile patent in the United States was awarded in 1789 to Oliver Evans. www.gm.ca This steam-powered "automobile" was first demonstrated by Evans in 1805 and was not only the first successfully self-propelled vehicle in the country but also the first amphibious vehicle. This vehicle was able to travel on land using its wheels and on water using a paddle wheel.

Steam powered vehicles were not the only motorized form of transportation being introduced. Thomas Davenport of New Hampshire built a carriage that ran on rails using a non-rechargeable battery. Chan, C.C. and Chau, K.T. *Modern Electric Vehicle Technology.* Oxford Science Pub. Page 16 (2001) This was followed by Scotsman Robert Davidson, who built an electric locomotive in 1838 that allegedly reached a breathtaking top speed of 4 miles per hour. *Id.* However, it was not until the 1890s that Americans paid much attention to the growing technology of electric power, namely rechargeable battery power.

The last decade of the 19th Century saw considerable advances in the rechargeable battery powered automobile. One of the earliest manufacturers was the Electric Carriage & Wagon Company owned by Morris and Salom of Philadelphia. This company successfully built a fleet of electric powered taxis in the mid-1890s that were used in New York City. *Id.* The turn of the twentieth century saw electric vehicles being produced by Anthony Electric, Riker Electric Baker

Motor Vehicle, Detroit Electric, Woods Motor Vehicle and others, and at one brief moment these vehicles actually outsold gasoline-powered vehicles. In England the London Electrical Cab Company began in 1897 with 15 taxis and in France rechargeable battery cars, trucks, buses, and limousines were manufactured from 1899 to 1906. *Id.*

But the few years of glory quickly ended for the electric powered vehicle and the vehicle powered by the internal combustion engine took over. In the years ahead the electric powered vehicle may take back its briefly enjoyed mantle from the internal combustion engine, but then again, the hydrogen engine shows promise utilizing the world's most abundant resource and emitting only water as its emission.

The legal system reacted to this new fangled mode of transportation and the trouble that followed. In fact the first known law regarding operating a motor vehicle while under the influence was passed in England in 1872. This law, enacted before the invention of the "modern" motor vehicle, made the operating of a steam-powered vehicle while intoxicated illegal and convictions could lead to a prison sentence. http://www.scienceservingsociety. com

The first law directly related to drinking and "driving" was enacted in 1872 and it was not for another twenty-four years that England saw its first drunk driving fatality. This is largely due to the fact that there were very few modes of motorized transport, few roads capable of serving such a machine, and that the automobile as we know it was not even invented until 1885. However, the day would invariably come when a tragic event involving an automobile would occur.

In 1869 well known Irish scientist Mary Ward became the first automobile accident fatality. During this period the development of steam powered vehicles was all the rage and one such vehicle was developed by William Parsons and his sons. In 1869 Mary and her husband were traveling in the Parsons vehicle in Ireland with the Parsons boys and their tutor when Mary was thrown from the vehicle while it was rounding a bend in the road. Mary fell under the steel wheel and apparently died almost instantly. A doctor lived near the scene of the accident and arrived shortly after the accident occurred and found Mary cut, bruised and bleeding from the ears. She died from a broken neck. *Profile of Mary Ward*. Irish Universities Promoting Science Group.

Twenty seven years later the world's second known traffic fatality involving the automobile occurred. On August 17, 1896, 44 year old Bridget Driscoll was killed while crossing the grounds of the Crystal Palace in Hyde Park, London. Bridget was with her daughter May, and was struck by an automobile owned by the Anglo-French Motor Carriage Company. The company was displaying its new creation and it was being used to give demonstration rides. Witnesses proclaimed the vehicle was traveling at a "reckless pace, in fact, like a fire engine," but the driver, Arthur James Edsall claimed to be travelling at only 4 miles per hour. History of Road Safety. Cardiff Council Road Safety Centre. http://www.roadsafety.cardiff.gov.uk/history. Controversially, Mr. Edsall's passenger, Alice Standing, claimed that the engine was modified to allow the vehicle to travel faster and possibly reach speeds as fast as 4.5 miles per hour! The matter proceeded to the civil courts and eventually to trial where the jury returned a verdict of "accidental death." The coroner, Percy Morrison said he hoped "such a thing would never happen again." Mr. Edsall was not criminally prosecuted. *Id*.

It was not long after Mrs. Driscoll's life was tragically cut short by the automobile when the world experienced the very first arrest for driving under the influence. Like Mrs. Driscoll's happening, the first DUI arrest occurred in London, England. On September 10, 1897, London Taxi cab driver George Smith (age 25) was arrested for driving under the influence when the taxi he was driving drove onto the pavement and collided with the building located at 165 Bond Street, London. Mr. Smith, who worked for the Electric Cab Company of Hackney, London, allegedly admitted to "having had two or three glasses of beer." He was later convicted and fined 20 shillings (no jail). www.history.com

The taxi cab company that employed Mr. Smith shortly thereafter was involved in a far more tragic event. Thirteen days after Mr. Smith's historic arrest, Stephen Kempton, aged 9, was crushed to death when the coat he was wearing got caught in the chain drive of the electric taxi after he had jumped onto the outside of a cab. The Electric Cab Company ceased trading in August, 1899 with all of its 77 vehicles being sold. A year later, the London Metropolitan Police stopped licensing this type of electric cab. http://www.encyclo. co.uk/calendar/September.php

The first known traffic fatality (non-alcohol related) in the United States occurred on September 10, 1899, in New York City. Henry Hale Bliss was disembarking a streetcar at West 74th Street and Central Park West when an electric-powered taxicab (Automobile Number 43) collided with him crushing his head and chest. *Fatally Hurt by Automobile.* New York Times article. (September 14, 1899) Henry died the next morning from his injuries. The driver of the taxi, Arthur Smith, was arrested and charged with manslaughter. He was later acquitted based on the defense that the conduct that resulted in Mr. Bliss' death was unintentional. Interestingly, the passenger in the taxicab was Dr. David Edson, the son of former New York City mayor Franklin Edson.

The location of this accident is memorialized with a plague, that reads:

Here at West 74th Street and Central Park West, Henry H. Bliss dismounted from a streetcar and was struck and knocked unconscious by an automobile on the evening of September 13, 1899. When Mr. Bliss, a New York real estate man, died the next morning from his injuries, he became the first recorded motor vehicle fatality in the Western Hemisphere. This sign was erected to remember Mr. Bliss on the centennial of his untimely death and to promote safety on our streets and highways. *Id.*

Prior to any laws in the United States making driving under the influence a crime, another great tragedy occurred involving drunk driving. In 1907 near Colorado City, Colorado, an accident occurred that killed the four passengers in the car driven by Albert Marksheffel, who survived the accident. Allegedly the accident occurred after the five friends had been drinking at a local Elks Club. After leaving the club Albert lost control of his speeding vehicle, hit some nearby railroad tracks and ended up in the ditch. Laden, Rich. *Sign of old Times / Colorado Springs history posted on streets all.* The Colorado Springs Gazette. (July 17, 2001)

This particular case was the cause for many states considering enacting driving under the influence laws. The story of Albert Marksheffel doesn't end with this horrific vehicle accident. The same year, 1907, Albert moved to Colorado Springs and managed the Western Automobile & Supply Company. The year following this DUI accident he opened his own automobile dealership, the Marksheffel Motor Company, and sold Chalmers, Dodge, Cadillac and Chevrolet cars. *Id.* He later co-founded the Colorado Springs Rotary Club and had, rather ironically, a local street named after him, Marksheffel Road. Id.; www.coloradospringsrotary.org

Although Great Britain enacted the first known law making "drinking and driving" illegal in 1872, the United States would not make this activity unlawful for another 38 years. However, prior to this enactment in the United States drinking and driving was in the news. The first reported news article regarding drinking and driving in the United States appeared in 1904 and the following years such activity appeared in newspapers and periodicals more frequently. Even still it was not until 1910 that New York became the first state to enact drinking and driving laws. To give some perspective, the Model T Ford was introduced in 1908 and by the time the first driving under the influence law was introduced, nearly 12,000 of Ford's Model T had been sold. Interestingly, Henry Ford did have an opinion about drinking and driving and his opinion was clear, to wit: "booze had to go when modern industry and the motor came in." Lender, Mark E., and Martin, James K. *Drinking in America: A History.* New York: Free Press (1982)

Following the enactment of New York State's driving under the influence law was enacted other states quickly followed, including California in 1911. Once the law put in place a system whereby a driver could be prosecuted for drunk driving there needed to be a way to measure the driver's level of intoxication. And thus the race was on to invent a machine to accomplish this task. Naturally, prior to the invention of such a machine there was no presumptive level of impairment because there was no way to validate such a level. http://www.borkensteincourse.org

The study of human breath is not a 20th century phenomenom. As far back as 1774 French chemist Antoine Lavoisier conducted studies regarding respiration, but his contribution to the field of breath testing involves his invention, the "gasometer." This invention was the first instrument to make relatively accurate measurements of respiration gases.

In 1803 William Henry formulated a chemical equation, later known as "Henry's Law," that has had significant impact on the measurement of human breath. Jones, A.W. *Physiological Aspects of Breath Alcohol Measurement, Alcohol, Drugs and Driving.* 6(2):1-24, Page 12 (1990)

Following Henry's impact and more than fifty years after Lavoisier's gasometer design, British and Australian physician John Hutchinson adapted the design and invented the first "spirometer," which was used for measuring the volume of a patient's breath. *The Spirometer, the Stethoscope and the Scale Balance.* London: John Churchill (1852)

In 1874, British physician Francis Anstie went one further and actually trapped human breath and applied colorimetric analysis to study alcohol in the body. Anstie, FE: *Final experiments on the elimination of alcohol from the body.* Practitioner 13:15 (1874)

In 1927 Dr. Emil Bogen reported measuring blood alcohol concentration (BAC) by analyzing a person's breath. Bogen, Emil. *Drunkenness, a quantitative study of acute alcoholic intoxication.* (1927) And, the breath testing device was nearly reality.

Also in 1927, Dr. Gorsky, a police surgeon in Britain, testified at an early "DUI" trial regarding the "drunkenness" of the defendant.

Mitchell, C. Ainsworth. *Science and the Detective*. The American Journal of Police Science (Northwestern University) 3 (2): 169–182 (March/April 1932) The defendant was convicted largely based on the evidence provided by Dr. Gorsky. *Id.*

The first "practical" breath testing machine was invented by Professor Rolla N. Harger in 1938. Called the "Drunk-o-meter" it was intended to be used by police and thereafter as evidence in courts of law. Holcomb, R.L. *Alcohol in Relation to Traffic Accidents.* JAMA, 1076-1085 (1938)

Also in 1938 The National Safety Council's Committee on Alcohol and Other Drugs (COAD) (formally known as the Committee on Tests for Intoxication) collaborated with the American Medical Association's Committee to Study Problems of Motor Vehicle Accidents to establish standards for defining the phrase "under the influence." COAD based these standards in large part, on research completed by Dr. R. L. Holcomb, a pioneer in DUI studies.

In 1939, a year after Harger's "Drunk-o-meter" invention became reality, his home state of Indiana became the first state in America to establish a presumptive alcohol impairment level of 0.15%. The enactment of "presumptive levels" shifted the focus in DUI investigations and trials from simply using officer observations to more "scientific" chemical testing.

The 1940s saw more development of the breath test machinery, with both the "Intoximeter" and "Alcometer" introduced in 1941. In 1944 the National Committee on Uniform Traffic Laws and Ordinances incorporated presumptive alcohol concentrations in the Chemical Tests Section of the Uniform Vehicle Code. In 1948, the CAOD collaborated with "Licensed Beverage Industries, Inc.," to fund a research project at Michigan State College to study breath-testing methods. This study examined the three most prevalent breath-alcohol testing instruments of the time, the Drunkometer, Intoximeter and Alcometer. Each of these instruments utilized wet chemical methods that analyzed breath samples based on chemical interactions between the alcohol molecules and a reagent. The study, effectively the first of its kind, determined that the three instruments could achieve results that were in "close agreement" with direct blood alcohol results. At the time these findings were perceived very favorably by the law enforcement community.

Immediately following World War II, the National Committee on Uniform Traffic Laws and Ordinances held the first national highway safety conference. http://www.ncutlo.org/ The government had become concerned with the dramatic increase in highway accidents involving injuries and deaths, due in large part to the higher number of vehicles on the road following World War II. An outcrop of the conference and subsequent studies was a recommendation setting a standard level for blood alcohol impairment at 0.15 %. This number would then become a "target" that states would aspire to in determining when a driver was presumptively impaired. This particular BAC level was also recommended by the American Medical Association (AMA) as an "accepted" level for impairment based on the AMA's own independent research.

In 1950 Stockholm, Sweden, hosted the "First International Conference on Alcohol and Driving." Twenty-two counties participated and the goal was to share information and research and take a substantial first step in making sense of the "problem of alcohol and road traffic." Wagnsson, K., Bjerver, K., Nelker, G., Rosell, S., and Akerbladh-Rosell. *Alcohol and Road Traffic. Proceedings of the First International Conference*. Stockholm: Kugelbergs Boktryekeri. (1951) Although it would appear that there were no definitive answers to the drinking and driving problem, important discussion occurred regarding chemical testing, medical opinions, witness statements, police reports, and how these issues relate to drinking and driving in the legal sphere. Presenters at this conference included authorities on the subject at the time, including L. Goldberg (who presented medical articles regarding the significance of tolerance), R. N. Harger, R. B. Forney and H. B. Barnes (who presented information regarding the estimation of the level of blood alcohol from analysis of breath), and a paper comparing breath analysis and the Widmark method of the determination of ethyl alcohol by K. Bjerver, R.K. Bonnichsen, and L. Goldberg. *Id.*

New York was the first state to adopt what has commonly become known as the "implied consent law" in 1953. This law was designed to force possible drunk drivers to submit to a blood, breath or urine test after the driver had been stopped by an officer and the officer then had a reasonable belief that the driver was impaired. The theory behind the practice of implementing implied consent laws (also known as informed consent) is that any driver who used the roads and highways implicitly consented to giving his or her permission for a breath or blood (and in some states, urine) sample that could be subsequently used as evidence at trial.

Over the years implied consent statutes have been attacked for a variety of constitutional reasons, usually unsuccessfully. This arena is ripe for litigation but courts have consistently held that the statutes do not violate a driver's Fourth Amendment protection from unreasonable search and seizure, or Fifth Amendment right against self-incrimination. The statutes usually are upheld on due process grounds, although courts have found statutes that permit the revocation of a license without a hearing unreasonable and unconstitutional.

In upholding the implied consent laws courts have generally looked to one of two theories supporting their validity. The first theory is that driving on public roads and highways is a privilege, not a right. To be entitled to this privilege a driver must adhere to state laws, including laws prohibiting driving while intoxicated. The second theory is that so long as the driver is afforded due process the implied consent laws are a reasonable regulation of driving pursuant to the state's police power. In hearing arguments that assert that implied consent laws are unconstitutional or unreasonable courts have weighed the interests of society against the interests of individuals, and have ruled that driving under the influence of alcohol or drugs is enough of a danger to society that a slight infringement on the liberty of individuals is justifiable.

The New York law enacted in 1953 enabled a driver to refuse testing but with the penalty of a license suspension of 12 months. Every state has followed the New York law and there is a license suspension or revocation of some length for refusing to provide a breath, blood or urine sample when lawfully requested in every jurisdiction.

Coinciding with the implementation of the New York implied consent law was the introduction of a new breath test machine. In 1954, Robert Borkenstein, a retired Captain in the Indiana State Police who had been the Director of the Police Laboratory, filed for US Patent Number 2824789, "Apparatus for analyzing a gas." He had invented the "Breathalyzer" breath testing instrument.

Coinciding with Borkenstein's invention, President Dwight D. Eisenhower successfully convinced Congress to approve the Interstate Highway System. Eisenhower was inspired by the German Autobahn when his troops occupied Germany during World War II, and more importantly, he understood the immense value to national commerce and travel such a system would create. The Interstate Highway System was authorized by the Federal-Aid Highway Act of 1956 and was popularly known as the National Interstate and Defense Highways Act of 1956. This highway system created changes in mobility for Americans that was unheard prior to the Eisenhower presidency.

The 1950s also saw further studies in the relation of alcohol to road accidents. A controlled study in Toronto, Canada, compared the blood alcohol concentrations of 433 drivers involved in accidents with 2015 other drivers. Lucas, G. H.W. et al. *Quantitative studies of the relationship between alcohol levels and motor vehicle accidents.* Proceedings of 2nd International Conference on Alcohol and Road Traffic. Toronto. Page 139 (1955) According to the research the danger of accidents became significant when the blood alcohol level was greater than 0.10, and when it rose above 0.15, the hazard was approximately ten times greater than when the concentration was below 0.50. *Id.* A further study in Baltimore, Maryland in 1957 examined 500 consecutive highway fatalities to drivers, passengers and pedestrians. It was determined that approximately one-third of the fatal accidents were associated with blood alcohol levels greater than .150 BAC and about half with levels greater than .50 BAC.

Freimuth, H.C., Watts, S. R. and Fisher R.S. *Alcohol and highway fatalities.* J. Forensic Sci. 3, 65 (1957) These figures seem to compare with those reported in a similar survey completed in Perth, in 1957. Pearson, A. T. *Alcohol and fatal traffic accidents.* Med. J. Australia. 2, 166 (1957) Another controlled study of drinking drivers involved in accidents was done in Bratislava, Czechoslovakia. Vamosi, M. *Experiences with non-alcoholic road traffic in Czechoslovakia.* Proceedings of Third International Conference on Alcohol and Road Traffic. London. Pages 79-82 (1963) The results of this study again stated that as a driver's BAC increased so did the hazard. Specifically, the study declared that the chances of being involved in a traffic accident were 124 times greater for a person with a blood alcohol level of over 0.150 than they were for a person with only 0.030. *Id.*

In 1958, the Symposium on Alcohol and Road Traffic at Indiana University declared that a BAC of 0.05 g/dL "definitely impairs the driving ability of some individuals." Levine, Barry. *Principles of Forensic Toxicology.* 2nd Edition. AACC Press (2006) Further, they claimed that as the BAC increases, an escalating percentage of individuals experience impairment, until the BAC reaches 0.10 g/dL, at which point all individuals are "definitely" impaired. *Id.* In 1960, the Committee on Alcohol and Drugs issued a statement recommending that DUI laws be amended to reflect a 0.10 g/dL BAC as presumptive evidence of guilt. The Uniform Vehicle Code was amended to reflect this recommendation in 1962.

Along with advances in the study of breath and the ability to capture and evaluate breath samples, further studies were conducted that concentrated on the study of driving under the influence. One of these pre-eminent studies was the "Grand Rapids Study" (Michigan) in 1964. This study examined vehicle accidents and their relation to alcohol use. The study concluded that there was a causal relationship between vehicle accidents and higher BAC levels. Moreover, and more alarmingly, the study showed that there was a higher chance of a fatality when the driver has a higher BAC reading. This report was a precursor to states implementing a lower

BAC level for drinking and driving. The first states to actually enact a lower BAC (lower than 0.15%) after the Grand Rapids Study was New York and Nebraska, which did so in 1972.

As the 1960s neared its end the Department of Transportation (DOT) and the National Highway Traffic Safety Administration (NHTSA) began to take a more active role in promoting stiffer legislation for drinking and driving. Their role played on the Grand Rapids study and involved the promotion of statistics proving the connection to fatal automobile accidents and alcohol. Important to mobilizing attention and resources to this perceived problem was the Highway Safety Act of 1966 which effectively federalized this issue by establishing the National Highway Safety Bureau, the precursor of the National Highway Traffic Safety Administration (NHTSA), and by authorizing the U.S. Department of Transportation's historic 1968 report "Alcohol and Highway Safety." The 1968 report found that "the use of alcohol by drivers and pedestrians leads to some 25,000 deaths and a total of at least 800,000 crashes in the United States each year." The report warned that "this major source of human morbidity will continue to plague our mechanically powered society until its ramifications and many present questions have been exhaustively explored and the precise possibilities for truly effective countermeasures determined."

In 1970 the federal government decided to solicit bids for research scientists in an attempt to develop a system of standardized "field sobriety tests." The idea behind the government's proposal was to provide police officers tools which would assist in their identification of DUI suspects and their subsequent arrest for suspicion of driving under the influence of alcohol. The National Highway Traffic Safety Administration (NHTSA), a division of the United States Department of Transportation, eventually supported a group of scientists at the Southern California Research Institute (SCRI). Dr. Marcelline Burns, and Dr. Herbert Moskowitz, were the primary authors of the study and the final product, completed in 1983, that resulted in NHTSA's "Standardized Field Sobriety Tests (SFSTs)."

The original "SFST Manual" was published in 1984 and was

very short and received little attention. Subsequently the NHTSA manuals have been updated over the years with new publications produced in 1987, 1989, 192, 1995, 2000, 2002, 2004 and 2007. These standardized field sobriety tests remain the subject of great debate regarding their validity and the manner in which they are conducted, nevertheless their role in the investigation of DUIs remains an important one. (More on SFSTs in Chapter 5)

In the 1960s and 1970s the public's view of drinking and driving was not, arguably, as harsh as it is now. The late Dr. Patricia Waller, a well known advocate for public safety and researcher in the area of drinking and driving, stated that in the past "[d]runk driving was considered more or less a "folk crime," almost a rite of passage for young males. Most adults in the United States used alcohol, and most of them, at some point, drove after doing so. This is not to say that they drove drunk, but many of them undoubtedly drove when they were somewhat impaired." Waller, P.F. Am J Prev Med 21(4, Suppl. 1): 3-4. (2001)

The laws over the years continued to evolve and the pressure on law makers to make DUI laws stricter was too much to ignore. In 1972, Nebraska and New York passed the first laws making driving with a 0.10 blood alcohol content "illegal per se." With this type of law the prosecution need not present any evidence of the driver's impaired ability to drive to support a conviction. These laws were instituted for "public safety" reasons and based on some studies that suggested that drivers were significantly less capable of operating a motor vehicle at this level. By the end of the decade, twelve states had set an illegal per se limit, all of them at 0.10% except New Hampshire which set that state's per se limit at 0.15%. Internationally, other countries enacted per se laws well before the United States. Such laws were introduced in Norway in 1936, Sweden in 1941, Australia in 1966, Great Britain in 1967, and Canada in 1969. Jones, A.W. *Fifty Years on – Looking Back at Developments in Methods of Blood and Breath Alcohol Analysis.* National Board of Forensic Medicine, Department of Forensic Chemistry. University Hospital, SE 581 85 Linköping, Sweden (2000)

A new component to DUI arrests was the "Administrative License Revocation" (also referred to as an "Administrative License Suspension") law and in 1976 Minnesota became the first state to enact such a law. This law had been previously recommended by NHTSA as a manner of suspending or revoking an accused DUI driver's driving privileges regardless of whether the accused had been charged criminally. The idea behind these administrative license suspension laws was that any driver who submitted to a breath test which resulted in a level equal to or greater than the state's presumed "impairment" level would be summarily suspended or revoked for a period of time. Typically the penalties for refusing the breath test were equal to or greater than the penalties imposed if the driver did take the breath test. These laws were civil or administrative in nature in order to avoid any double jeopardy issues.

In 1982 Congress looked to focus some of their attention on the perceived drunk driving problem by passing legislation designed to allocate $125 million to states over a three-year period. The bill was signed into law in December of 1982 and allowed for incentive grants to the states if they adopted the following three legislatively mandated provisions in 23 U.S.C. §101: 1) a 0.10% per se statute; 2) a 90-day license suspension upon probable cause for first-time DUI offenders or those who refuse to take a chemical sobriety test, and 3) a minimum 48 consecutive hours in jail or 10 days community service for subsequent DUI offenses within a five year period.

In addition to the three requirements the states were also mandated to provide increased law enforcement and education efforts designed at eliminating drunk driving. States were also eligible for supplemental funds if they met additional requirements in addition to the basic incentive grants. Although the specific criteria for funding would be determined by federal and state rules, the suggested requirements were that there be: adequate statewide record-keeping regarding drunk driving convictions and license suspensions, alcohol rehabilitation and treatment programs, vehicle impoundment for any person convicted of drunk driving, alcohol safety programs which are financially self-sufficient and locally coordinated, sentence-screening authority by courts, adoption of a 21-year minimum drinking age, and adoption of the recommendations made by the Presidential Commission on Drunk Driving.

Due to intense public pressure President Reagon appointed a National Commission on Drunk Driving, which issued a report recommending a number of ways to enhance the effectiveness of a national anti-drunk driving program. The most significant recommendations of the Commission included selective enforcement and judicially approved roadblocks; the abolition of plea bargaining; victim assistance and restitution programs; administrative per se license suspension; per se statutes; mandatory sentencing; the abolition of pre-conviction diversion; the strengthening of implied consent laws; and increased efficiency in court administration relating to DUI charges.

In 1984 the "Age 21 National Driving Age Law" was enacted to force states to increase the drinking age to 21. Failure to comply would cost those states millions of dollars in federal funds. Several states did initially resist but by 1986 all of the states had complied (Louisiana being the last state to comply).

In 1986 the American Bar Association (ABA) got into the act and formed a national committee to study how to deal effectively, legally and fairly with the drunk driving problem. The ABA National Committee on Drunk Driving was initially focused on the effectiveness, appropriateness and legality of the innovative sanctions and techniques proposed by the Presidential Commission, Mothers Against Drunk Driving (MADD), the National Highway Traffic Safety Administration (NHTSA), the insurance industry and other influencial parties. A special Drunk Driving Advisory Project was also formed to evaluate enforcement techniques and alcohol related traffic offenses. The Advisory Project compiled a report entitled, *Drunk Driving Laws & Enforcement: An Assessment of Effectiveness* (1986).

Areas that were examined by the Project Advisory Board included roadblocks, per se legislation, preservation of scientific evidence, mandatory jail sentencing and license suspensions, abolition of plea bargaining, a national means to track license suspensions, insurance industry problems, and preservation of due process guarantees in the trial of alleged drunk drivers.

Also in 1986 MADD began its first training of volunteers to support victims of drunk drivers and to serve as "victim advocates" in court proceedings and began to use their influence on a federal level. MADD was founded in 1980 by Candice Lightner after her own personal tragedy of losing her daughter to a DUI accident. MADD supports education, advocacy and victim assistance in the DUI legal realm and are strong advocates of maintaining the per se blood alcohol content level of .08%, stronger sanctions for DUI offenders, including mandatory jail sentences, treatment for alcoholism and drug dependency issues, the installation of ignition interlock devices, attendance at a victim impact panel (VIP), license suspensions, "sobriety checkpoints" and "saturation patrols," maintaining the legal age of drinking in the United States at 21 years of age, additional taxes on the purchase of beer, and even for lowering the per se BAC limit again to a figure less than the current and accepted limit of 0.08. Without question MADD has been a significant player on the DUI stage, although not without controversy and criticism. (More on MADD in Chapter 8).

Also around this time a similar organization to MADD was created in England. Campaign Against Drinking and Driving (CADD) was founded by John Knight and Graham Buxton who both lost children to drinking and driving accidents. www.cadd.org.uk

In 1986 the American Medical Association (AMA), who four decades earlier supported per se BAC levels of 0.15%, publicly supported a per se BAC level in the United States of 0.05%.

The "Drunk Driving Prevention Act of 1988" was then introduced in 1988 and authorized the Secretary of Transportation, over a period of three fiscal years, to award certain monetary grants to individual states "to improve the effectiveness of the enforcement of laws to prevent drunk driving". *23 USC 410* Under this act if a state adopted an enforcement program, it received a grant equal to 75% of the cost of implementation and enforcement for the first fiscal year, followed by 50% for the second fiscal year and 25% for the third fiscal year. To be eligible for the federal grant, certain conditions were required including, "an expedited driver's license suspension or revocation system" and "a self sustaining drunk driving prevention program".

In 1990 the United States Supreme Court leapt into action by ruling that "sobriety checkpoints" did not violate the United States Constitution's Fourth Amendment. An individual state was still permitted to protect its citizens from random searches and seizures under their state's constitution, but this was still a huge victory for advocates of roadblocks. *Michigan Dept. of State Police v. Sitz*, 496 U.S. 444, 110 S. Ct. 2481, 110 L.Ed.2d 412 (1990)

In the fall of 1992, the United States Department of Transportation (DOT) issued a report that recommended each state adopt a 0.08% BAC per se statute. The DOT Report concluded, among other things, that "[l]owering the BAC is likely to reduce fatalities....There is also evidence that lowering BACs, and publicizing the effort, can reduce alcohol related deaths at all BACs." In this regard, the Report notes that 80% of the 22,086 alcohol related fatalities in 1990 involved BACs in excess of 0.10%. Whitaker. *DOT Report Recommends States Adopt .08% BAC Per Se Standard.* 7 DWI Journal: Law & Science 1 1 (November 1992)

In 1993 the famous "Grand Rapids" study was revisited by a German study sponsored by the Center for Traffic Sciences at the University of Wuerzburg. H.-P. Krüger, H.P., Kazenwadel, J. and Vollrath, M. Grand Rapids Effects Revisited: Accidents, Alcohol and Risk. Center for Traffic Sciences, University of Wuerzburg, Röntgenring 11, D-97070 Würzburg, Germany (1994) This 1993 study addressed the perceived shortcoming in the Grand Rapids Study, namely the risk of causing an accident while the driver was under the influence. The authors of this 1993 study concluded that the 1964 Grand Rapids Study did not know whether the impaired driver was responsible for accidents.

The authors of the German study concluded that their "accident study" replicated the Grand Rapids Study and the "comparison indicates that driving under the influence of alcohol resulted in a greater accident risk in 1994 compared to 1964." Id. The authors also concluded that "simply changing the legal DUI limit from 0.08% to 0.05% is insufficient with respect to alcohol-induced accidents," a most interesting result which seemingly contradicts what MADD and the AMA advocates. Finally, the 1993 study which involved 4,615 accidents and an additional 13,149 motorists, conceded that "although drivers under the influence of alcohol are obviously at a greater relative risk than unintoxicated drivers, the magnitude of the risk to the larger community attributable to the presence of intoxicated drivers remains an unanswered question." Id.

In 1995 President Bill Clinton announced that all states needed to adopt the 0.08% per se BAC. Federal legislation was subsequently adopted in October, 2000 which threatened to withhold billions of additional federal dollars from states that did not enact new laws implementing the 0.08% per se BAC standard. Most states complied within the next two legislative sessions and in 2005 Minnesota became the final state to pass the law.

In 1998 Congress amended the alcohol-impaired driving incentive grant program which provided extra funding for states that meet certain legislative enactment criteria. In passing TEA-21 (Transportation Equity Act for the 21st Century) a state could qualify for a federal grant by meeting five of seven criteria. The criteria for the basic grant included a program targeting drivers with high BAC levels.

To qualify under the high-BAC criteria states must demonstrate the establishment of a graduated sanctioning system that provides enhanced or additional sanctions (punishments) to drivers convicted of DUI if they were found to have a high BAC. Further, the enhanced sanctions must be mandatory, must apply to the first (and subsequent) DUI offense, and may include longer terms of license suspensions, increased fines and treatment for substance abuse where appropriate.

In the last couple of decades drug DUI cases have been growing in number. More and more American motorists are taking prescribed or over-the-counter medications that cause negative and potentially dangerous effects on the driver. Furthermore, in the last 10 years or so, police officers have been trained on "drug recognition" techniques that assist them in identifying drivers who have taken drugs that impair motor skills.

Use of common non-prescription medicine such as aspirin, ibuprophen or acetaminophen can have an additive effect to a person's impairment from alcohol while many non-prescription drugs (ie. antihistamines) can impair a person who later consumes alcohol. This "combination" of alcohol and many types of medications, including prescription and illegal drugs, can drastically increase the impairment effects on a driver. In 2003, Nevada became the first state to pass DUI drugs laws setting presumptive impairment levels for a variety of contraband substances such as marijuana, followed in 2005 by a similar law in Virginia.

The criminalization of a DUI charge is now taking a different road by making a DUI offense a felony. Currently, thirty-seven states have DUI statutes that incorporate a felony charge if the driver has prior DUI convictions.

Although these statutes differ among states, there are some similarities, such as using two major factors to determine if the DUI will result in a felony. The first factor, used by all of the felony DUI states, is the number of prior DUI convictions at the time of the offense. The number required to raise a DUI to a felony ranges from the second to the fifth conviction, with the majority of states setting the limit at the third or fourth DUI conviction. The second factor, required by thirty states, is the DUI offender must have a specific number of prior convictions within a certain period of years before the current DUI conviction will be a felony. These time periods range from three to twelve years with the majority of states having either a five or ten year limit. Two states, Idaho and Kentucky, incorporate a third factor in the felony DUI determination. Both states use the BAC level of the driver at the time of the offense to define a felony threshold. These felony convictions also increase the potential jail time facing the individual accused of DUI.

CHAPTER 2

The History of Alcohol Consumption

*In analysing history do not be too profound,
for often the causes are quite superficial.*
—Ralph Waldo Emerson

Alcohol is a product that has provided a variety of functions for people throughout history. Historically, alcoholic beverages have played an important role in religion and worship and have also served as a valuable source of needed nutrients and have been widely used for their medicinal, antiseptic, and analgesic properties. The role of such beverages as thirst quenchers and social lubricants is obvious and they have played an important role in enhancing the enjoyment and quality of life.

The word "alcohol" probably comes from the *Arabic language*, although the exact origin of this word is not known. That being said, "al-" is Arabic for "definite article," but the second part may be derived from the word *al-kuhl*, the name of an early distilled substance, or perhaps from *al-gawl*, meaning "spirit" or "demon" and similar to liquors being called "spirits" in English. Similarly, names like "life water" have continued to be the inspiration for the names of several types of beverages, like Gaelic whisky, French eaux-de-vie and possibly vodka. Also, the Scandinavian akvavit spirit gets its name from the Latin phrase *aqua vitae*.

History indicates that alcohol consumption has existed for at least 10,000 years. Archeologists have discovered beer jugs from the Stone Age that actually established the very fact that purposely fermented beverages were developed by prehistoric man. The use of wine is liberally referenced in the Old Testament, including an early reference to when Isaac's son "brought him wine, and he drank" (Genesis 27:25). Oral tradition recorded in the Old Testament asserts that Noah planted a vineyard on Mt. Ararat in what is now eastern Turkey. (Genesis 9:20) The Old Testament suggests temperance when it warns "[f]or the drunkard and the glutton shall come to poverty" (Proverbs 23:21). The Old Testament is not alone in the religious references to alcohol. The Qur'an acknowledges positive effects, stating "[t]hey question thee about strong drink and games of chance. Say: In both is great harm and utility for men; but the harm of them is greater than their usefulness." (2:219) Alternatively, Islamic tradition came to forbid alcohol consumption to such an extent that the devout are to avoid medicines and toothpastes containing even a trace of it.

Egyptian pictographs from 4,000 BC have illustrated that wine was part of the Egyptian lifestyle. Further, the ancient Egyptians believed that the God Osiris invented beer, which was thought to be a necessity of life and was brewed by Egyptians in their own homes.

According to many account the ancient Egyptians made at least 17 types of beer and at least 24 varieties of wine. Not only were these beverages consumed by the locals but they were also deified and offered to the Gods. Alcohol played a large role in the ancient Egyptian community as it was used for pleasure, nutrition, medicine, ritual, economic and for funeral purposes (alcohol was stored in the tombs of the deceased for the afterlife). Although the use of alcohol was widespread in Egypt there is also ample suggestion that moderation was stressed and excessive use was discouraged.

The Egyptians of the ancient world were not alone in their belief that alcohol had its place. There is evidence that alcohol was produced in China as far back as 7000 BC. McGovern, Patrick E. *Ancient Wine: The Search for the Origins of Viniculture*. Princeton: Princeton University Press. Page 314. (2003) Wine jars have been found in Jiaha, which was the site of a Neolithic Yellow River settlement based in the central plains of ancient China, now modern Wuyang, Henan Province. These wine jars held beverages that were produced by fermenting rice, honey, and fruit.

The ancient Chinese used alcohol (known as "jiu") as a spiritual food rather than simply a physical food. There is much evidence to suggest that the use of alcohol in the ancient Chinese culture played a significant role in the local religious life and was consumed by the locals when offering sacrifices to the gods or their ancestors, before battles, celebrating victory after battle, and ceremonies for births, marriages, and deaths. In the Middle Ages, during the time of Marco Polo (1254-1324) alcohol was consumed daily by the average Chinese person and was allegedly one of the treasury's biggest sources of income.

The people of the Indus Valley Civilization (modern India) have also been consuming alcohol for thousands of years. Alcohol was in wide use from as far back as 10,000 BC where a beverage that was distilled from rice meal, wheat, sugar cane, grapes, other fruits and soma drink was popular among the peasant population and Kshatriya warriors. Spess, David L. *Soma: The Divine Hallucinogen*, Rochester, VT: Park Street Press (2000) These drinks were used for many purposes including medicinal, religious, and social. *Id.*; Peele, Stanton and Grant, Marcus. *Alcohol and Pleasure: A Health Perspective*. Page 102. Psychology Press (1999) Soma, which had hallucinogenic properties, was primarily used as a ritual drink and was prepared by pressing juice from the stalks of certain plants assumed to be amanita muscaria (fly agaric), blue lotus, and honey. Oldenberg, Hermann and Shrotri, Shridhar B. *Religion of the Veda: Die Religion Des Veda*. Motilal Banarsidass Publ. (1988)

The Babylonians enjoyed beer as early as 2,700 BC and according to many, worshipped a wine goddess and other wine deities. These alcoholic beverages were not only consumed by the peoples of this time but also used for religious purposes and offered to their gods. The famous Code of Hammurabi, enacted around 1,750 BC and discovered in 1901 by the Egyptologist Gustav Jéquier, devotes some attention to alcohol. The Babylonians through the Code of Hammurabi and their neighbors who enacted similar codes (including the Code of Ur-Nammu, (ca. 2050 BC), the Laws of Eshnunna (ca. 1930 BC) and the Codex of Lipit-Ishtar of Isin (ca. 1870 BC)) helped to develop the earliest system of economics through a recognized legal code. King, L. W. *The Code of Hammurabi: Translated by L. W. King.* Yale University (2005); Horne, Charles F. Ph.D. *The Code of Hammurabi : Introduction.* Yale University (1915) The Code dealt with the commerce of alcohol and the economic effects of such commerce. Alcohol consumption in Babylon was accepted and was not illegal, but by the same token evidence suggests that the Babylonians were critical of drunkenness.

There is also evidence of the ancients like of beer from the Sumerians as far back as 1800 BC. A prayer to the goddess Ninkasi known as "The Hymn to Ninkasi" serves as both a prayer as well as a method of remembering the recipe for beer in a culture with few literate people. Stuckey, Johanna. *Nin-kasi: Mesopotamian Goddess of Beer.* Matrifocus (2006)

The ancient culture of Greece has also participated in the production of alcoholic beverages for more than 2,000 years. The art of winemaking reached the Hellenic peninsular around 2,000 BC. However, the first fermented beverage to obtain widespread popularity was mead, which was made from honey and water. By 1,700 BC winemaking was commonplace in the region that is now Greece. Like many other cultures wine was used for social, religious, and medicinal purposes. There is evidence to suggest that the Greeks were a relatively temperate people, particularly compared to other ancient civilizations. Their rules stressed moderate drinking, the praise of temperance, and the general avoidance of excess. The one obvious exception to the rule of temperance was the Cult of Dionysus (Dionysus was the God of wine). The Cult of Dionysus has its origins in Minoan Crete and is strongly associated with, among other things, wine. The general belief, as it pertains to wine, is that intoxication brought people closer to their deity. Interestingly, the cult found its way into Rome around 200 BC and was called Bacchanalia

(Bacchus was the Roman God of wine). Originally the Bacchanalia were held in secret and attended by women only, but admission was eventually extended to men. Bacchanalia was prohibited in Rome and the practice of it brought severe punishment.

In addition to the Cult of Dionysus, the Macedonians also viewed the excessive consumption of alcohol as a sign of masculinity and were well known for their drunkenness. Moreover their King, Alexander the Great (356-323 BC), whose mother practiced the Dionysian cult, developed a reputation for his love of alcohol. This is interesting considering his childhood tutor and mentor, Aristotle, was outwardly critical of drunkenness.

Both Xenophon (431-351 BC) and Plato (429-347 BC) praised the moderate use of wine as beneficial to health and happiness, but both were allegedly critical of drunkenness, as were Aristotle (384-322 BC) and Zeno (cir. 336-264 BC). Hippocrates (cir. 460-370 BC) identified numerous medicinal properties of wine which had long been used for its therapeutic value.

The Roman Empire saw the widespread use of wine as a daily drink, typically with meals. It has been suggested that during the 2nd Century B.C. a large amount of wine from Rome began to be produced for domestic consumption and trade. Cunliffe, Barry W. *Greeks, Romans, and Barbarians: Spheres of interaction.* New York: Methuen, at 75 (1988). By around 100 B.C. wine in some form was thought to have become the daily drink of all Romans regardless of their socio-economic position. Younger, W., *Gods, Men, and Wine*, London: Food and Wine Society, Page 169(1966); Hyams, E.. *Dionysus: A Social History of the Wine Vine.* New York (1965) Thousands of ceramic wine vases (amphorae), drinking cups, and other evidence of frequent drinking, from all social economic groups, have been found throughout the Mediterranean and more northern provinces. These archeological finds suggest the wide availability of wine during the Roman expansion and domination. Cunliffe at 71-78; Younger, at 151-226.

Most of the studies and research involving the Roman Empire and alcohol consumption suggest that wine was the primary beverage of the Mediterranean (except Egypt) and Roman world. Wine, and in particular mature vintage wine, was considered an integral part of civilized life. Vineyards were also considered essential to the economics and culture from the early Republic through the end of the Empire and into the early Middle Ages. Even today many western European vineyards can trace their origins to ancient Rome.

Wine taverns and cafes were common throughout most of Roman history. These establishments, along with wine shops, were found in urban areas and along country roads from this period until the end of the Empire. Younger at 166-167. Many remains from these establishments, particularly in Pompeii and Herculaneum, have been uncovered and studied.

Although it is clear that wine was very much a part of everyday Roman life, the primary drinking culture was probably one of moderation, similar to the Greeks. Younger, Chapt. 4. To avoid intoxication wine was usually mixed with water and generally consumed with meals.

Although wine was the preferred drink of the Romans, beer had an important role in northern cultures. Beer was spread through Europe by Germanic and Celtic tribes as far back as 3000 BC, though it was mainly brewed locally. *Prehistoric brewing: the true story*. 22. Archaeo News. (October 2001) The early European beers often contained ingredients that included fruits, honey, numerous types of plants, spices and other substances such as narcotic drugs. Nelson, Max. *The Barbarian's Beverage: A History of Beer in Ancient Europe*, Routledge (2005). However, what they did not contain was hops, as that was a later addition—first mentioned in Europe around 822 by a Carolingian Abbot, and again in 1067 by Abbess Hildegard of Bingen. Unger, Richard W. *Beer in the Middle Ages and the Renaissance*. University of Pennsylvania Press. Page 57 (2004); Max Nelson, *The Barbarian's Beverage: A History of Beer in Ancient Europe*. Routledge. Page 110 (2005)

Beer produced before the Industrial Revolution continued to be made and sold on a local level, although by the 7th century AD beer was also being produced and sold by European monasteries.

During the Industrial Revolution, the production of beer moved from local and traditional manufacturing to industrial manufacturing. As a result local manufacturing lost most of its significance by the end of the 19th century. Cornell, Martyn. *Beer: The Story of the Pint.* Headline (2003) The development of hydrometers and thermometers changed brewing by allowing the brewer more control of the process and greater knowledge of the results.

In other regions of the world different alcoholic beverages had their support. Uniquely Japanese, the actual origins of sake is unclear, although the earliest written reference to use of alcohol in Japan is recorded in the *Book of Wei*, of the Records of Three Kingdoms. Zhang, Xiuping et al. *100 Books That Influenced China: Sanguo Zhi.* Nanning, Guangxi. Renmin Press. (1993) This 3rd century Chinese text speaks of the Japanese drinking and dancing. Sake is also mentioned several times in the *Kojiki*, Japan's first written history, compiled in 712 AD.

History suggests that the first alcoholic drink in Japan may have been *kuchikami no sake* ("mouth-chewed sake"), which is made by chewing nuts or grains and spitting them into a pot. The enzymes from the saliva allow the starches to saccharify (convert to sugar), and then ferment. This method was also used by Native Americans (see cauim, chicha and pulque), and inscriptions from the 14th century BC mention Chinese millet wine being made the same way.

Regardless of the actual origin, by the Asuka period (approximately 528 to 710 AD, although the exact dates are unknown), true sake —made from rice, water, and kōji mold—was the dominant alcohol in Japan.

On the other side of the world from both Europe and Asia, the native civilizations of the Americas were also developing their own alcoholic beverages. Many versions of these ancient beverages are still produced today in some form or another.

One such beverage is a traditional native beverage of Mesoamerica called pulque (also called octli) and is made from the fermented juice of the maguey. The Maguey (Agave americana) is an agave originally from Mexico but cultivated worldwide as an ornamental plant. If the flower stem is cut without flowering, a sweet liquid called agua miel ("honey water") gathers in the heart of the plant. This may then be fermented to produce pulque, which may then be distilled to produce the alcoholic drink, mezcal. The pulque and maguey fibre (another by-product of the plant) were important to the economy of Mexico before Europe invaded. Pulque is depicted in Native American stone carvings from as early as AD 200. The origin of pulque is unknown, but because it has a major position in religion, many folk tales explain its origins.

Another alcoholic drink originally from pre-Columbian Americas is Chicha. Chicha is a Spanish word for a variety of traditional fermented beverages from the Andes region of South America. It can be made of maize, manioc root (also called yuca or cassava) or fruits. During the Inca Empire women were taught the techniques of brewing chicha in Acllahuasis (feminine schools). Chicha de jora has been prepared and consumed in communities throughout in the Andes for millennia. The Inca used chicha for ritual purposes and consumed it in vast quantities during religious festivals.

The native populations of Brazil have consumed a traditional alcohol drink by the name of Cauim for many hundreds of years. Cauim is made by fermenting manioc (a large starchy root), or maize, sometimes flavored with fruit juices. The French explorer Jean de Léry made note of the native's use of this beverage in his account of his trip to Brazil in the 16th century. de Léry, Jean. *Voyage to the Land of Brazil (1577)*

The Medieval period saw great advances in the production of alcoholic beverages and a relative "modernization" of the process. Namely, distillation became more of a science. While distillation took advanced leaps in this era, there were early types of distillation known to the Babylonians in Mesopotamia (modern Iraq) from at least 200 BC, the peoples in northwest Pakistan from as early as 500 BC, and to the Greeks around the 1st century AD. Levey, Martin. *Babylonian Chemistry: A Study of Arabic and Second Millennium B.C. Perfumery*, Osiris 12. Pages 376-389 (1956); Russell, Colin Archibald. *Chemistry, Society and Environment: A New History of the British Chemical Industry.* Royal Society of Chemistry. Page 69 (2000); Underwood, Edgar Ashworth. *Science, Medicine, and History: Essays on the Evolution of Scientific Thought and Medical.* Oxford University Press. Page 251 (Arno Press 1975/1953). Simmonds, Charles. *Alcohol: With Chapters on Methyl Alcohol, Fusel Oil, and Spirituous Beverages.* Macmillan and Co. Ltd. Page 6 (1919)

Despite these early versions of distilling, the art of "pure distillation" did not occur until around the 8th century AD. This highly effective "pure distillation" process has been credited to Arabic and Persian chemists in the Middle East during this period. They produced a distillation process to isolate and purify chemical substances for industrial purposes, such as isolating natural esters (perfumes) and producing pure alcohol. Briffault, Robert. *The Making of Humanity.* Page 195 (1938) This distillation process eventually found its way into Europe around the 12th century AD.

The Black Death and subsequent plagues, which began in the mid-fourteenth century, dramatically changed people's perception of their lives. With no understanding or control of the plagues that reduced the population by as much as 82% in some villages, "processions of flagellants mobbed city and village streets, hoping, by the pains they inflicted on themselves and each other, to take the edge off the plagues they attributed to God's wrath over human folly." *Id.*

Some individuals during this period dramatically increased their consumption of alcohol in the belief that this might protect them from the mysterious disease, while others thought that through moderation in all things, including alcohol, they could be saved. It would appear that, on balance, consumption of alcohol was generally high. For example, in Bavaria beer consumption was probably about 300 liters per capita annually (compared to 150 liters today) and in Florence wine consumption was about ten barrels per capita annually. Understandably the consumption of distilled spirits, which was exclusively for medicinal purposes, increased in popularity. Austin, Gregory A. *Alcohol in Western Society from*

Antiquity to 1800: A Chronological History. Santa Barbara, CA: ABC – Clio. Pages 104-108 (1985)

As the end of the Middle Ages approached the popularity of beer spread to England, France and Scotland. *Id.* at 118-119. Beer brewers were recognized officially as a guild in England and the adulteration of beer or wine became punishable by death in Scotland. Monckton, Herbert A. *A History of English Ale and Beer.* London: Bodley Head. Pages 69-70 (1966); Cherrington, Ernest H. (Ed.) *Standard Encyclopedia of the Alcohol Problem.* 6 vols. Westerville, OH: American Issue Publishing Co. (1925-1930) Additionally, the consumption of spirits as a beverage began to occur during this time period. Braudel, Femand. *Capitalism and Material Life, 1400-1800.* Translated by Miriam Kochan. New York, NY: Harper and Row. Page 171 (1974)

During the Renaissance period religion played a big role in European society. Protestant leaders such as Martin Luther, John Calvin, the leaders of the Church of England, and even the Puritans did not differ substantially from the Catholic Church teachings. Simply, the attitude was that alcohol was a gift of God and must be used in moderation for pleasure, enjoyment and health. Intoxication however, was viewed as a sin. Austin at 170, 186, and 192.

During the Renaissance period beer and wine remained the choice of drink. However, during this period the production and distribution of spirits began to slowly grow, although drinking spirits was still largely done for medicinal purposes throughout most of the sixteenth century.

One particular beverage that made its debut during the seventeenth century was sparkling champagne. The religious influence continued and credit for the development of champagne goes primarily to a Benedictine monk, Dom Perignon. Around 1668, he used strong bottles, invented a more efficient cork (and one that could contain the effervescence in those strong bottles), and began developing the technique of blending the contents. Despite these innovations it would be another century before sparkling champagne would become popular.

Although the origins of the original grain spirit whisky is unknown, what is known is that its distillation has been performed in Scotland and Ireland for centuries. The first confirmed written record of whisky comes from 1405 in Ireland and the production of whisky from malted barley is first mentioned in Scotland in 1494, although both countries could have had distilled grain alcohol before these dates.

One distilled spirit that became popular immediately after the Renaissance was gin. This distilled spirit was generally flavored with juniper berries and called "jenever," the Dutch word for "juniper." The French changed the name to "genievre," which the English changed to "geneva" and then modified to "gin." Originally used for medicinal purposes, the use of gin as a social drink did not immediately become popular. In 1690, England passed "An Act for the Encouraging of the Distillation of Brandy and Spirits from Corn" ("corn" meant grain in general) to utilize surplus grain and to raise revenue, and the popularity of gin took off.

Gin soon became a favorite of the poor as it was relatively easy to distil, readily available, cheap, and soon the daily volume sold exceeded that of the more expensive beer and ale. Seedy shops advertised: "Drunk for one penny, dead drunk for two, clean straw for nothing." The straw was used to lie on while sleeping off a hangover. Many of the Industrial Revolution's poor remained permanently inebriated in their search for relief from the terrible factory conditions. To lessen the negative impact that gin was having on the population, an excise license of £20 was introduced in 1729 and a duty of two shillings per gallon was charged. Then in 1736 "The Gin Act" was introduced in England and decreed that a £50 license was required to sell gin, making it prohibitively expensive. This act by the government to outlaw the drink caused considerable social unrest and led to rioting. On the day before the Act was passed, mobs took to the streets determined to drown their sorrows in the last legal gin available. At the time of the Act approximately 11 million gallons of gin were produced in London annually, roughly the equivalent of 14 gallons for each adult male. Within six years of

"The Gin Act" being introduced, only two distillers took out licenses, yet over the same period of time production rose by almost 50%. The Gin Act, finally recognized as unenforceable, was repealed in 1742. Harris, R.W. *England in the Eighteenth Century*. London, Blandford Press (1963)

After its dramatic peak, gin consumption rapidly declined. From 18 million gallons in 1743, it dropped to just over seven million gallons in 1751 and to less than two million by 1758, and generally declined to the end of the century. Ashton, Thomas S. *An Economic History of England: The Eighteenth Century*. London: Methuen and Co. Page 243 (1955)

The reason for the decline can be attributed to the production of lower priced yet higher quality beer, rising corn prices and taxes which eroded the price advantage of gin, a temporary ban on distilling, a stigmatization of drinking gin, an increasing criticism of drunkenness, a newer standard of behavior that criticized coarseness and excess, increased tea and coffee consumption, an increase in piety and increasing industrialization with a consequent emphasis on sobriety and labor efficiency. Sournia, Jean-Charles. *A History of Alcoholism*. Trans. by Nick Hindley and Gareth Stanton. Oxford: Basil Blackwell. Pages ix-xvi (1990)

While intoxication was still an accepted part of life during the Industrial Revolution there was a slow change in attitude which came as a result of the increasing industrialization and the need for a reliable and punctual work force. Drunkenness would come to be defined as a threat to industrial efficiency and growth. Groups that began by promoting the moderate use of alcohol would ultimately form temperance movements and press for the complete and total prohibition of the production and distribution of alcoholic beverages.

In Eastern and Northern Europe vodka had found a significant following. The origins of vodka cannot be traced definitively but it is believed to have originated in the grain-growing region that now embraces western Russia, Belarus, Lithuania, Ukraine, and Poland. It also has a long tradition in Scandinavia. It was not originally called vodka but was called "bread wine" (khlebnoye vino). Pokhlebkin, William. *A History of Vodka*. Versa Pub. (1992) It was mostly sold in taverns and was quite expensive. Vodka in Poland has been produced since the early Middle Ages and in these early days, the spirits were used mostly as medicines.

The first written usage of the word vodka in an official Russian document appeared by decree of Empress Elizabeth on June 8, 1751, which regulated the ownership of vodka distilleries. *Id.* The taxes on vodka became a key element of government finances in Tsarist Russia, providing at times up to 40% of state revenue. Bromley, Jonathan. *Russia, 1848-1914.* Heinemann Advanced History. (2002) By the 1860s Russian governmental policy promoted consumption of state-manufactured vodka and as a result it became the drink of choice for many Russians. In 1863, the government monopoly on vodka production was repealed, causing prices to plummet and therefore making vodka available even to low-income citizens. By 1911, vodka comprised 89% of all alcohol consumed in Russia. *Id.*

The new world started life with more alcohol than water. The Mayflower left Southampton, England, full of Puritans and with more beer than water. Admittedly, the fact that the Mayflower transported Puritans with more beer than water does sound odd due to their general tendency to oppose the consumption of alcohol. However, at that time drinking wine and beer was safer than water - which was usually taken from sources used to dispose of sewerage and garbage. Also, alcohol was an effective analgesic and thought to provide energy necessary for hard work and enhance the quality of life. And finally, although the Puritans did not favor excessive consumption of alcohol they were not opposed to drinking alcohol in moderation. West, Jim. *Drinking with Calvin and Luther!* Oakdown Books. Page 68 (2003)

The early settlers to the Americas continued to drink beer and ale with dinner, like their brethren in the Old World. However, because importing a continuing supply of beer from Jolly Old England was expensive, the early settlers brewed their own. Yet brewing their own beer wasn't necessarily easy as it was difficult to make the beer they were accustomed to because wild yeasts caused problems in fermentation and resulted in a bitter, unappealing brew. As a result hop seeds were ordered from England and while they waited for an adequate supply, the colonists improvised a beer made from red and black spruce twigs boiled in water, as well as a ginger beer. *Id.*

Besides beer the colonists learned to make a wide variety of wine from fruits, flowers, herbs, and even oak leaves. Early on, French vine-growers were brought to the New World to teach settlers how to cultivate grapes. *Id.*

Spirits also quickly found their way into the lives of the Colonists. Rum was not commonly available until after 1650 when it was imported from the Caribbean. The cost of rum dropped after the colonists began directly importing molasses and cane sugar and then distilled their own. By 1657, a rum distillery was operating in Boston and the rum business became a highly profitable trade in New England. The Puritan minister and major colonial figure, Increase Mather, expressed the common view in a sermon against drunkenness: "Drink is in itself a good creature of God, and to be received with thankfulness, but the abuse of drink is from Satan; the wine is from God, but the drunkard is from the Devil." During the 17th century the first distillery was established in the colonies on what is now Staten Island, cultivation of hops began in Massachusetts, and both brewing and distilling were legislatively encouraged in Maryland. Austin, Gregory A. *Alcohol in Western Society from Antiquity to 1800: A Chronological History.* Santa Barbara, CA: ABC – Clio. Page 230 and 249 (1985)

Although rum was introduced to the world and presumably invented by the first European settlers in the West Indies, no one knows when it was actually first produced or by whom. By 1657, a rum distillery was operating in Boston. It was highly successful and eventually would become colonial New England's largest and most prosperous industry.

Alcohol was also introduced to another British colony in its infancy, Australia. The first English boat to arrive on Australian soil, the

Endeavour (captained by James Cook), contained beer as a means of preserving drinking water. On August 1, 1768 as Captain Cook was fitting out the Endeavour for its voyage, Nathaniel Hulme wrote to Joseph Banks (English Naturalist, botanist and part of Captain Cook's voyage to Australia on the Endeavour) recommending that he take:

"[a] quantity of Molasses and Turpentine, in order to brew Beer with, for your daily drink, when your Water becomes bad . . . [B]rewing Beer at sea will be peculiarly useful in case you should have stinking water on board; for I find by Experience that the smell of stinking water will be entirely destroyed by the process of fermentation." Chambers, Neil, Editor. *The Indian and Pacific Correspondence of Sir Joseph Banks. 1768–1820.* Pickering & Chatto Publishers (2008)

Although beer became a staple of Australian society and its most popular alcoholic drink, rum was the drink of choice for the first settlers and convicts. Unfortunately drunkenness was an enormous problem in early colonial Australia. As a means of reducing drunkenness, beer was promoted as a safer and healthier alternative to rum. Lord Hobart in a letter to Governor Philip King on August 29, 1802, stated:

"The introduction of beer into general use among the inhabitants would certain lessen the consumption of spirituous liquors. I have therefore in conformity with your suggestion taken measures for furnishing the colony with a supply of ten tons of Porter, six bags of hops, and two complete sets of brewing materials."

King family - Papers concerning Philip Gidley King and Phillip Parker King, 1786-1838. State Library of New South Wales, Archives (Acquired 1997) So, beer was officially encouraged in early Australia and the rest is history.

While drunkenness was still an accepted part of life in the

eighteenth century in Europe and parts of the new world, the nineteenth century would bring a change in attitudes as a result of increasing industrialization and the need for a reliable and punctual work force. King, Frank A. *Beer Has a History*. London: Hutchinson's Scientific and Technical Publications. (1947)

Self-discipline was needed in place of self-expression, and task orientation had to replace relaxed conviviality. Drunkenness would come to be defined as a threat to industrial efficiency and growth. Problems commonly associated with industrialization and rapid urbanization was also attributed to alcohol. Thus, problems such as urban crime, poverty and high infant mortality rates were blamed on alcohol, although "it is likely that gross overcrowding and unemployment had much to do with these problems" *Id*. at 21. Over time, more and more personal, social and religious/moral problems would be blamed on alcohol.

The production and consumption of alcohol continued its course until 1919 when it came to an abrupt halt in the United States. On January 16, 1919 the 18th Amendment to the United States Constitution was ratified by 36 states and took effect one year later. This law signaled the beginning of prohibition.

The first section of the amendment reads:

"After one year from the ratification of this article the manufacture, sale, or transportation of intoxicating liquors within, the importation thereof into, or the exportation thereof from the United States and all territory subject to the jurisdiction thereof for beverage purposes is hereby prohibited."

What the 18th Amendment effectively did was take the business licenses away from every brewer, distiller, vintner, wholesaler and retailer of alcoholic beverages in the United States in an attempt to reform an "unrespectable" segment of the population. Three months before it was to take effect, the Volstead Act, otherwise known as the National Prohibition Act of 1919, was passed and gave power to the "Commissioner of Internal Revenue, his assistants, agents, and inspectors" to enforce the 18th Amendment.

Although it was illegal to manufacture or distribute "beer, wine, or other intoxicating malt or vinous liquors" curiously it was not illegal to possess it for personal use. The provision allowed Americans to possess alcohol in their homes and partake with family and guests as long as it stayed inside and was not distributed, traded or even given away to anyone outside the home.

Prohibition became increasingly unpopular, especially in the big cities. On March 23, 1933, President Franklin Roosevelt signed an amendment to the Volstead Act known as the Cullen-Harrison Act, allowing the manufacture and sale of "3.2 beer" (3.2% alcohol by weight, approximately 4% alcohol by volume) and light wines. Upon signing the amendment, Roosevelt made his famous remark; "I think this would be a good time for a beer." The Cullen-Harrison Act became law on April 7, 1933. *Liquor: Liquor Milestone.* Time Magazine (December 11, 1933)

The Eighteenth Amendment was repealed on December 5, 1933 with ratification of the Twenty-first Amendment. *Id.* After the repeal of the national constitutional amendment, some states continued to enforce prohibition laws. Mississippi, which had made alcohol illegal in 1907, was the last state to repeal Prohibition, in 1966. Kansas did not allow sale of liquor "by the drink" (on-premises) until 1987. There remain numerous "dry" counties or towns where no liquor is sold, even though liquor can often be brought in for private consumption.

Despite the problems that have been associated with alcohol and its abuse current research suggests that the moderate consumption of alcohol may be medically preferable to abstinence. Studies have suggested that moderate use of alcohol appears to reduce the incidence of coronary heart disease, cancer, osteoporosis, and even increase longevity. Razay, G., Heaton, K. W., Bolton, C. H., and Hughes, A. O. *Alcohol consumption and its relation to cardiovascular risk factors in British women.* British Medical Journal. *304, 80-83 (1992);* Gavaler, Judith S. and Van Thiel, David H. *The association between moderate alcoholic beverage consumption and serum estradiol and testosterone levels in normal post menopausal women: relationship to the literature.* Alcohol: Clinical and Experimental Research. 16, 87-92 (1992) Moreover, in the words of the founding Director of the National Institute on Alcohol Abuse and Alcoholism,

"... alcohol has existed longer than all human memory. It has outlived generations, nations, epochs and ages. It is a part of us, and that is fortunate indeed. For although alcohol will always be the master of some, for most of us it will continue to be the servant of man." Chafetz, Morris E. *Liquor: The Servant of Man.* Boston: Little, Brown and Co. Page 223 (1965)

CHAPTER 3

The History of Drugs

We cannot escape history.
—Abraham Lincoln in Annual Message to Congress, Dec. 1, 1862

Drug use has existed as far back as prehistoric times. There is archaeological evidence of the use of psychoactive substances dating back at least 10,000 years, and historical evidence of cultural use over the past 5,000 years. Merlin, M.D. *Archaeological Evidence for the Tradition of Psychoactive Plant Use in the Old World.* Economic Botany 57 (3): 295–323 (2003) While it is clear that medicinal use has played a very large role, it has been suggested that the urge to alter one's consciousness has also been a primary motivator for the use of drugs. Siegel, Ronald K. *Intoxication: The Universal Drive for Mind-Altering Substances.* Park Street Press, Rochester, Vermont. (2005)

Drugs such as tobacco (Nicotiana), hemp (Cannabis sativa), opium poppy (Papaver somniferum), and other plants containing drugs have been chewed and smoked almost as long as alcohol has been consumed. *Id.*

One of the oldest records of medicinal recommendations is found in the writings of the Chinese scholar-emperor Shen Nung, who lived in 2735 B.C. He compiled a book about herbs, a forerunner of the medieval pharmacopoeias that listed all the then-known medications. Fulder, Stephen. *The Book of Ginseng and Other Chinese Herbs for Vitality.* Healing Arts Press. Rochester, Vermont.

(1993) Emperor Shen Nung found value in Chinese herbs and their medicinal use. He found many plants that had medicinal benefits such as Ch'ang Shan (helpful in treating fevers), Shun Chi (leaves of this plant contained antimalarial chemicals), and Ma Huang (now called Ephedra sinica, this plant contained a number of alkaloids, chief of which, ephedrine). *Id.*

Opiates

Opiates are the source of many drugs and are so named because they are derivatives of constituents found in opium, which is processed from the latex sap of the opium poppy, "Papaver somniferum." The major biologically active opiates found in opium are morphine, codeine, thebaine and papaverine. Synthetic opioids such as heroin and hydrocodone are also derived from these substances.

The use of poppies for medicinal or recreational drug use has been documented to prehistoric time with finds from Neolithic settlements in Switzerland, Germany, and Spain. The first known cultivation of opium poppies was in approximately 3000 BC in the Mesopotamia region by Sumerians who called the plant "Hul Gil," the "joy plant." Brownstein, M.J. *A brief history of opiates, opioid peptides, and opioid receptors.* Proc Natl Acad Sci USA 90 (12): 5391–5393 (June 15, 1993) Tablets found at Nippur, a Sumerian spiritual center south of Baghdad, described the collection of poppy juice and its use in the production of opium. Schiff, Paul L. Jr. *"Opium and its alkaloids".* American Journal of Pharmaceutical Education. (2002). Cultivation continued in the Middle East by the Assyrians, who also collected poppy juice in the morning after scoring the pods with an iron scoop; they called the juice aratpa-pal, possibly the root of Papaver. Opium production continued under the Babylonians and Egyptians.

Opium has had many uses including being used with poison hemlock to put people quickly and painlessly to death, while also being used in medicine (sponges soaked in opium, were used during surgery). Brownstein, M.J. (1993) The Egyptians cultivated opium thebaicum in poppy fields around 1300 B.C. and opium was traded from Egypt by the Phoenicians and Minoans to destinations around the Mediterranean Sea, including Greece, Carthage, and Europe. By 1100 B.C., opium was cultivated on the Mediterranean island of Cyprus, where surgical-quality knives were used to score the poppy pods, and opium was cultivated, traded, and smoked. Kritikos, P.G. and Papadaki, S.P. *The early history of the poppy and opium.* Journal of the Archaeological Society of Athens. (January 1, 1967) Opium was also mentioned after the Persian conquest of Assyria and Babylonia in the sixth century B.C. Schiff, Paul L. Jr. (2002).

The Islamic Empire, which followed the Roman Empire, also used opium for medicinal and social purposes. Further, Arab traders introduced opium to China. Trocki, Carl A. *Opium as a commodity and the Chinese drug plague.* (2002). The Persian physician Abu Bakr Muhammad ibn Zakariya al-Razi Rhazes (845-930 A.D.), the renowned ophthalmologic surgeon Abu al-Qasim Ammar (936-1013 AD), and the Persian physician Abu 'Ali al-Husayn ibn Sina (Avicenna) all used opium for medicinal purposes.

Opium was not well received by authorities in Europe during the middle ages and was stigmatized as a negative Middle Eastern influence. Despite this perception medical use of opium continued well into the nineteenth century. U.S. president William Henry Harrison was treated with opium in 1841, and in the American Civil War, the Union Army used 2.8 million ounces of opium tincture and powder and about 500,000 opium pills. Schiff, Paul L. Jr. (2002).

The increase in opiate consumption in the United States during the 19th century can be largely contributed to legal opiates prescribed by physicians to women with "female problems" (mostly to relieve painful menstruation). Between 150,000 and 200,000 opiate addicts lived in the United States in the late 19th century and between two-thirds and three-quarters of these addicts were women. Kandall, Stephen R. M.D.: *Women and Addiction in the United States—1850 to 1920.* Harvard Univ. (1996)

In addition to valid medicinal purposes opium has been used as a recreational drug for many hundreds of years. It was said that the use of opium was used to aid masculinity and strengthen a man's sex drive. Tobacco mixed with opium was called madak (or madat) and became popular throughout China and its seafaring trade partners (such as Taiwan, Java and the Philippines) in the seventeenth century. Zheng, Yangwen. *The Social Life of Opium in China, 1483-1999.* Modern Asian Studies 37 (1): 1–39 (2003). Madak was banned in 1729 but the smoking of pure opium in bamboo pipes became more popular.

Chinese emigrants in the eighteenth-century to the United States and England brought their manner of opium smoking with them. Opium use during the eighteenth century was also passed from one culture to another by sailors. *Opium degrading the French Navy.* The New York Times. (April 27, 1913); McCoy, Alfred W. *The politics of heroin in Southeast Asia* (1972)

In the United States opium was not initially illegal. In 1883, opium importation was taxed at $6 to $300 per pound, until the Opium Exclusion Act of 1909 which prohibited the importation of opium altogether. In a similar manner the Harrison Narcotics Tax Act of 1914, passed in fulfillment of the International Opium Convention of 1912, nominally placed a tax on the distribution of opiates, but served as a de facto prohibition of the drug. Today, opium is regulated in the United States by the Drug Enforcement Administration under the Controlled Substances Act.

Internationally, the International Opium Commission was founded in 1909, and by 1914, thirty-four nations had agreed that the production and importation of opium should be diminished.

The effects of opiates will be discussed in specific detail in the following pages, however suffice to say the combination of opiates and alcohol enhances the sedative effects of both substances and therefore increases impairment. Kissin, B. *Interaction of Ethyl Alcohol and other Drugs.* In: Kissin, B. and Begleiter, H. eds *The Biology of Alcoholism: Vol. 3.* Clinical Pathology. New York: Plenum Press. (1974)

Morphine

Morphine is a highly potent opiate analgesic drug and is the principal active agent in opium. Morphine is considered to be the prototypical opioid. Like other opioids (e.g. oxycodone, hydromorphone, and diacetylmorphine (heroin)), morphine acts directly on the central nervous system (CNS) to relieve pain.

Morphine was the first active principle chemically isolated from any plant. German pharmacist Friedrich Wilhelm Adam Sertürner first isolated morphine in the autumn of 1804 in Paderborn, Germany and he named it "morphium" after Morpheus, the Greek god of dreams. Widespread use did not begin until about 1853 with the development of the hypodermic needle. Morphine was used for pain relief, and as a "cure" for opium and alcohol addiction, which is unusual considering that it was later found to be even more addictive than either alcohol or opium.

The socio-economic development of morphine directly or indirectly lead to the manufacture of other opioids such as dihydromorphine, hydromorphone, nicomorphine, heroin, hydrocodene, codeine, and numerous other alkaloids.

The effects created by morphine include euphoria and the feeling of well-being, relaxation, drowsiness, sedation, lethargy, disconnectedness, self-absorption, mental clouding, and delirium. Couper, Fiona J., and Logan, Barry K. *Drugs and Human Performance Fact Sheets.* NHTSA. Page 76-77 (March 2004) When mixed with alcohol sedation, drowsiness, and decreased motor skills may occur. Laboratory studies have shown that morphine may cause sedation and significant psychomotor impairment for up to 4 hours following a single dose in normal individuals. Early effects may include slowed reaction time, depressed consciousness, sleepiness, and poor performance on divided attention and psychomotor tasks. Late effects may include inattentiveness, slowed reaction time, greater error rate in tests, poor concentration, distractibility, fatigue, and poor performance in psychomotor tests. Subjective feelings of sedation, sluggishness, fatigue, intoxication, and body sway have also been reported. According to NHTSA, in several driving under the influence case reports where the subjects tested positive for morphine, observations included slow driving, weaving, poor vehicle control, poor coordination, slow response to stimuli, delayed reactions, difficultly in following instructions, and falling asleep at the wheel. *Id.*

In the DUI context and field sobriety testing, horizontal gaze nystagmus, vertical gaze nystagmus, and lack of convergence are not present. Further, pupil size is constricted and there is little or no reaction to light. The subject's pulse rate, blood pressure, and body temperature are generally lower. *Id.*

While law enforcement relies on NHTSA produced studies, there is independent research that questions some of NHTSA's conclusions. One such study examined the driving implications of individuals who had consumed slow-release morphine sulfate tablets, and concluded that "long-term analgesic medication with stable doses of morphine does not have psychomotor effects of a kind that would be clearly hazardous in traffic." Vainio, A, Ollila, J, Matikainen, E., Rosenburg, P. and Kalso, E. *Driving Ability in Cancer Patients Receiving Long-term Morphine Analgesic.* Lancet. 346:667-70 (1995) Another study concluded that individuals exhibited only minimal impairment in one test after having consumed morphine sulfate. Hanks, G.W., O'Neill, W.M., Simpson, P. and Wesnes, K. *The Cognitive and Psychomotor Effects of Opiod Analgesics II, A Randomized Controlled Trial of Single Doses of Morphine, Lorazepam, and Placebo in Healthy Subjects.* Eur. J. Clin. Pharmacol. 48:455-460 (1995)

Heroin

Diacetylmorphine (better known as heroin) is another derivative of the opium poppy, and was synthesized from morphine in 1874 by C. R. Alder Wright, an English chemist working at St. Mary's Hospital Medical School in London, England. Wright had been experimenting with combining morphine with various acids and boiled anhydrous morphine alkaloid with acetic anhydride over a stove for several hours and produced a more potent, acetylated form of morphine, now called diacetylmorphine. Heroin was subsequently brought to market by the pharmaceutical giant Bayer, in 1898. Heroin is nearly twice as potent as morphine and as with other opioids heroin is used as both a pain-killer and a recreational drug.

Heroin, or Diacetylmorphine, as it was known exclusively at that time, only became popular after it was independently re-synthesized 23 years later by another chemist, Felix Hoffmann. Hoffmann, working at the Bayer pharmaceutical company in Germany, was instructed by his supervisor Heinrich Dreser to acetylate morphine with the objective of producing codeine, a constituent of the opium poppy, similar to morphine pharmacologically but less potent and less addictive. But instead of producing codeine, the experiment produced diacetylmorphine. Bayer would name the substance "heroin," probably from the word heroisch, German for heroic, because in field studies people using the medicine felt "heroic."

From 1898 through to 1910, heroin was marketed as a non-addictive morphine substitute and cough suppressant. Bayer marketed heroin as a cure for morphine addiction before it was discovered that it is rapidly metabolized into morphine, and as such, heroin was essentially a quicker acting form of morphine. Bayer was understandably embarrassed by this finding and it soon became an historical blunder for the company. Bayer lost some of its trademark rights to "heroin," as it did with aspirin (and other drugs), under the 1919 Treaty of Versailles following the German defeat in World War I. *Treaty of Versailles*, Part X, Section IV, Article 298. Annex, Paragraph 5. (June 28, 1919)

In the United States the Harrison Narcotics Tax Act was passed in 1914 to control the sale and distribution of opioids, including "heroin." This law permitted the drug to be prescribed and sold for medical purposes only. Then in 1924, the United States Congress passed additional legislation prohibiting the sale, importation or manufacture of the drug. It is now a Schedule I substance, and is thus illegal in the United States.

The effects created by heroin are very much the same as those created by the use of morphine and include euphoria and the feeling of well-being, relaxation, drowsiness, sedation, lethargy, disconnectedness, self-absorption, mental clouding, and delirium. Couper, Fiona J., and Logan, Barry K. *Drugs and Human Performance Fact Sheets*. NHTSA. Page 76-77 (March 2004) When mixed with alcohol sedation, drowsiness, and decreased motor skills may occur. Laboratory studies have shown that morphine may cause sedation and significant psychomotor impairment for up to 4 hours following a single dose in normal individuals. Early effects may include slowed reaction time, depressed consciousness, sleepiness, and poor performance on divided attention and psychomotor tasks. Late effects may include inattentiveness, slowed reaction time, greater error rate in tests, poor concentration, distractibility, fatigue, and poor performance in psychomotor tests. Subjective feelings of sedation, sluggishness, fatigue, intoxication, and body sway have also been reported. According to NHTSA, in several driving under the influence case reports where the subjects tested positive for heroin, observations included slow driving, weaving, poor vehicle control, poor coordination, slow response to stimuli, delayed reactions, difficultly in following instructions, and falling asleep at the wheel. *Id.*

In the DUI context and field sobriety testing, horizontal gaze nystagmus, vertical gaze nystagmus, and lack of convergence are not present. Further, pupil size is constricted and there is little or no reaction to light. The subject's pulse rate, blood pressure, and body temperature are generally lower. *Id.*

Methadone

Methadone is a synthetic opioid used medically as an analgesic, antitussive and as a maintenance anti-addictive for use in patients on opioids. The drug was developed in 1937 in Nazi Germany and although chemically unlike morphine or heroin, methadone also acts on the opioid receptors and thus produces similar effects. The drug was given the trade name "dolophine" from the Latin dolor meaning pain

After the war, all German patents, trade names and research records were requisitioned and expropriated by the allied forces. Methadone, and some other drugs were then brought to the United States and in 1947 it was given the generic name "methadone."

Since then, it has been best known for its use in treating narcotic addiction. To date, methadone maintenance therapy has been the most systematically studied, most successful and most politically polarizing of any pharmacotherapy for the treatment of drug addicted patients. Methadone is approved only for the treatment of opioid dependence.

Importantly and often forgotten by consumers of this drug, methadone treatment can impair driving. Giacomuzzi, SM, Ertl, M, Vigl, A, et al. *Driving capacity of patients treated with methadone and slow-release oral morphine.* Addiction 100 (7): 1027 (2005) Further, studies have shown that patients using methadone are more likely to be involved in serious automobile accidents. A study out of Queensland University in Australia produced data showing that 220 patients on morphine had been involved in car accidents killing 17 people, compared to a control group of other patients randomly selected having no involvement in fatal crashes. Sobering statistics, indeed. Reece, AS. *Experience of road and other trauma by the opiate dependent patient: a survey report.* Substance Abuse Treatment, Prevention, and Policy 3: 10 (2008)

The effects created by the use of methadone include drowsiness, sedation, dizziness, lightheadedness, mood swings (euphoria to dysphoria), depressed reflexes, altered sensory perception, stupor, and coma. Couper, Fiona J., and Logan, Barry K. *Drugs and Human Performance Fact Sheets.* NHTSA. Page 57-58 (March 2004)

The drug manufacturer cautions that methadone may impair the mental and/or physical abilities required for the performance of potentially hazardous tasks, and that the sedative effects of the drug may be enhanced by concurrent use of other CNS depressants, including alcohol.

In the DUI context and field sobriety testing, horizontal gaze nystagmus, vertical gaze nystagmus, and lack of convergence are not present. Pupil size is constricted and there is little to no reaction to light. Pulse rate, blood pressure, and body temperature are lower.

Oxycodone

Oxycodone is an opioid synthesized from opium-derived thebaine. It was developed in 1916 in Germany by Freund and Speyer of the University of Frankfurt, only a few years after pharmaceutical company Bayer had stopped the mass production of heroin due to addiction and abuse. It was hoped that a thebaine-derived drug would retain the analgesic effects of morphine and heroin with less addiction. The first clinical use of the drug was documented in 1917. Sunshine, A., Olson, N.Z., Colon, A., Rivera, J., Kaiko, R.F., Fitzmartin, R.D., Reder, R.F., Goldenheim, P.D. (1996). *Analgesic efficacy of controlled-release oxycodone in postoperative pain. J Clin Pharmacol* 36 (7): 595–603 (1996)

The drug was first introduced to the US market in 1939 and is the active ingredient in a number of pain medications commonly prescribed for the relief of moderate to severe pain, either with inert binders (e.g. OxyContin) or supplemental analgesics such as paracetamol (acetaminophen), (e.g. Percocet, Endocet, Tylox, Roxicet) or aspirin (e.g. Percodan, Endodan, Roxiprin). More recently, ibuprofen has been added to oxycodone under the name Combunox.

Unfortunately Oxycodone is a drug subject to abuse. The introduction of higher strength preparations in 1995 resulted in increasing patterns of abuse. Unlike Percocet, whose potential for abuse is somewhat limited by the presence of paracetamol (acetaminophen), OxyContin and other extended release preparations contain mainly oxycodone. Abusers crush the tablets to defeat the time-release "micro-encapsulation" and then ingest the resulting powder orally, intra-nasally, rectally, or by injection. It is notable that the vast majority of OxyContin related deaths are attributed to ingesting substantial quantities of oxycodone in combination with another depressant of the central nervous system such as alcohol, barbiturates and related drugs. *Summary of Medical Examiner Reports on Oxycodone-Related Deaths.* DEA Office of Diversion Control. United States Department of Justice. Common side-effects of oxycodone that may affect drivers include fatigue, dizziness, and anxiety.

Hydrocodone

Hydrocodone is a semi-synthetic opioid derived from two of the naturally occurring opiates codeine and thebaine. It is marketed, in its varying forms, under a number of trademarks, including Vicodin. Hydrocodone was first synthesized in Germany in 1920 and was approved by the FDA on March 23, 1943 for sale in the United States under the brand name Hycodan. http://www.fda.gov/

As a narcotic, hydrocodone relieves pain by binding to opioid receptors in the brain and spinal cord. Common side effects that drivers should be concerned about include dizziness, lightheadedness, nausea, and drowsiness.

Cocaine

Cocaine (benzoylmethyl ecgonine) is a crystalline tropane alkaloid that is obtained from the leaves of the coca plant. Aggrawal, Anil. Narcotic Drugs. National Book Trust, India. (1995) The name cocaine, comes from "coca" in addition to the alkaloid suffix "ine," forming "cocaine" and is both a stimulant of the central nervous system and an appetite suppressant.

For over one thousand years South American indigenous peoples have chewed the coca leaf, a plant that contains vital nutrients as well as many alkaloids, including cocaine. However, the isolation of the cocaine alkaloid was not perfected until 1855 by the German chemist Friedrich Gaedcke.

With the discovery of this new alkaloid, western medicine was quick to exploit the possible uses of this plant. The use of the drug varied but was typically used to treat such things as flatulence, was thought to be able to whiten teeth, was added to certain wines, and perhaps most famously, added to Coca-Cola. A "pinch of coca leaves" was included in John Styth Pemberton's original 1886 recipe for Coca-Cola, though the company began using decocainized leaves in 1906 when the Pure Food and Drug Act was passed into law. The specific amount of cocaine that Coca-Cola contained during the first twenty years of its production is unknown.

Other uses for cocaine include its use as a treatment for morphine addiction in the late 1800s. Cocaine was introduced into clinical use as a local anesthetic in Germany at about the same time. By the turn of the twentieth century, the addictive properties of cocaine had become obvious and the problem of cocaine abuse began to capture public attention in the United States.

Currently, cocaine is the second most popular illegal recreational drug in the U.S. (behind marijuana) and the U.S. is the world's largest consumer of cocaine. Central Intelligence Agency, *The World Factbook – Illicit Drugs*. (March 19, 2009)

The effects caused by the use of cocaine include euphoria, excitation, feelings of well-being, general arousal, increased sexual excitement, dizziness, self-absorbed, increased focus and alertness, mental clarity, increased talkativeness, motor restlessness, offsets fatigue, improved performance in some simple tasks, and loss of appetite. Higher doses may exhibit a pattern of psychosis with confused and disoriented behavior, delusions, hallucinations, irritability, fear, paranoia, antisocial behavior, and aggressiveness. Couper, Fiona J., and Logan, Barry K. *Drugs and Human Performance Fact Sheets*. NHTSA. Page 19 (March 2004)

According to NHTSA the observed signs of impairment in driving performance have included subjects speeding, losing control of their vehicle, causing collisions, turning in front of other vehicles, high-risk behavior, inattentive driving, and poor impulse control. As the effects of cocaine wear off subjects may suffer from fatigue, depression, sleepiness, and inattention.

In the DUI context as it relates to field sobriety testing, horizontal gaze nystagmus, vertical gaze nystagmus, and lack of convergence are not present. Pupil size is dilated and there is a slow reaction to light. Pulse rate, blood pressure, and body temperature are elevated.

Independent studies seem to contradict some of the findings by NHTSA. These studies have found that cocaine increases alertness, consciousness, energy levels, pulse rate, body temperature, and glucose availability (energy for the body), and has been found to counteract effects of fatigue and alcohol consumption. Rush, C.R., Baker, R.W., and Wright, K. *Acute Physiological and Behavioral Effects of Oral Cocaine in Humans: A dose response analysis.* Drug Alcohol Depend. 55. Pages 1-12 (1999); Stillman, R. Jones, R.T., Moore, J, Walker, J., and Welm, S. *Improved Performance Four Hours After Cocaine.* Psychopharmacology. 110. Pages 415-420 (1993); Farre, M., et al. *Alcohol and Cocaine Interactions in Humans.* J Pharmacol Exp Ther. 266. Pages 1364-1373 (1993); Higgins, S.T., et al. *Acute Behavioral and Cardiac Effects of Cocaine and Alcohol Combinations in Humans.* Psychopharmacology. 111. Pages 285-294 (1993)

It would appear that the affects of cocaine in the DUI setting are more concerning when the dosage is higher. According to research high doses of cocaine are most concerning and can cause impairment through fatigue, depression, and other physical consequences. Higgins, S.T., and Katz, J.L. *Cocaine Abuse: Behavior, Pharmacology and Clinical Applications.* Academic Press. (1998); Litcata, A.S., Taylor, S, Berman, M. and Cranston, J. Effects of Cocaine on Human Aggression. Pharmacol Biochem Behav. 45. Pages 569-552 (1993)

Another concern with cocaine is when it is consumed in conjunction with alcohol. When the two are mixed an active metabolite of "cocaethylene" is produced. This specific metabolite has a longer half-life than cocaine when the drug is taken by itself. Cani, J. et al. *Cocaine metabolism in humans after use of alcohol: Clinical and Research Implications.* Recent Developments in Alcohol.

No. 14, Pages 437-455 (1998)

Moskowitz and Burns conducted a study looking at the effects of cocaine consumption and driving performance and concluded that there was no impairment of driving-related laboratory tasks by cocaine (cocaine consumption was intranasally, 96 mg). Moskowitz, H. and Burns, M. *The Effects of a Single, Acute Dose of Cocaine Upon Driving-Related Skills Performance*. T89, 11th International Conference on Alcohol, Drugs and Traffic Safety. (1989)

Marijuana

Cannabis, also known as marijuana, is a psychoactive drug extracted from the plant "Cannabis sativa." The herbal form of the drug consists of dried mature flowers and subtending leaves of pistillate (female) plants and the major biologically active chemical compound in cannabis is Δ^9-tetrahydrocannabinol (delta-9-tetrahydrocannabinol), commonly referred to as THC.

People have been consuming cannabis for thousands of years although the last one hundred years has seen an increase in its use for recreational, religious or spiritual, and medicinal purposes. Rudgley, Richard. *Lost Civilisations of the Stone Age*. (1998). The possession, use, or sale of psychoactive cannabis products became illegal in most parts of the world in the early 20th century.

The use of cannabis, at least as fiber, has been shown to go back at least 10,000 years in Taiwan. Stafford, Peter. *Psychedelics Encyclopedia*. Ronin Publishing (1993) Evidence of cannabis being smoked can be traced as far back as the 3rd millennium BC as indicated by charred cannabis seeds found in a ritual brazier at an ancient burial site in present day Romania. Rudgley, Richard. *Lost Civilisations of the Stone Age*. Arrow Books, Ltd. (1999) The most famous users of cannabis were the ancient Hindus of India and Nepal. The herb was called "ganjika" in Sanskrit ("ganja" in modern Indic languages). Rudgley, Richard. *The Encyclopedia of Psychoactive Substances*. Little, Brown and Company. ed. (1998)

Cannabis was also known to the ancient Assyrians who

discovered its psychoactive properties through the Aryans. Franck, Mel. *Marijuana Grower's Guide*. Red Eye Press. Page 3 (1997) Members of the cult of Dionysus are also thought to have smoked cannabis.

Today recreational use in the western world drives a sizable demand for the drug. Cannabis is the largest cash crop in the United States generating an estimated $36 billion market. *"Marijuana Called Top U.S. Cash Crop"*. ABCNews Internet Ventures. (2008)

The effects caused by the use of marijuana include relaxation, euphoria, relaxed inhibitions, sense of well-being, disorientation, altered time and space perception, lack of concentration, impaired learning and memory, alterations in thought formation and expression, drowsiness, sedation, mood changes such as panic reactions and paranoia, and a more vivid sense of taste, sight, smell, and hearing. Couper, Fiona J., and Logan, Barry K. *Drugs and Human Performance Fact Sheets*. NHTSA. Page 7 (March 2004) Additionally, when taken concurrently with alcohol, marijuana is more likely to be a traffic safety risk factor than when consumed alone. *Id.*

In the DUI context relating to field sobriety testing, horizontal gaze nystagmus and vertical gaze nystagmus are not present although lack of convergence is present. Pupil size is normal to dilated and the reaction to light is normal to slow. Pulse rate and blood pressure are elevated and body temperature is normal to elevated.

Naturally, there are those who suggest that the combination of marijuana consumption and driving is not nearly as dangerous as alcohol consumption and driving; and some research suggests this may be correct. Certain driving studies actually suggest that marijuana users are more cautious, slow down, drive more safely and take fewer risks compared to alcohol users. Kruger, H.P. and Berghaus, G. *Behavioral Effects of Alcohol and Cannabis: Can Equipontoncies by Established?* Center for Traffic Sciences, University of Wurzburg, Rontgenring. 11, D-97070. Wurzburg, Germany; Robbe, H. *Marijuana's Effects on Actual Driving*

Performance. In: Kloeden, C. and McLean, A (Eds). *Alcohol, Drugs and Traffic Safety T-95.* Adelaide, Australia: HHMRC Road Research Unit, University of Adelaide. Pages 11-20 (1995) Further, a study found that cannabis intoxication leads to only slight impairment of psychomotor function: "The impairment in driving skills does not appear to be severe, even immediately after taking cannabis, when subjects are tested in a driving simulator." *UK House of Lords Select Committee on Science and Technology.* Ninth Report. Ch. 4: Sec. 4.7. London, United Kingdom. (1998)

Another study compares a driver's performance after consumption of both marijuana and alcohol and finds that both do impair performance but that cannabis users are more cautious than alcohol users and therefore the impact on driving performance is not as severe with the cannabis users. Smiley, A. *Marijuana: On-Road and Driving-Simulator Studies.* In: Kalant, H. et al (Eds). *The Health Effects of Cannabis.* Toronto: Center for Addiction and Mental Health. Pages 173-191 (1999) Along the same lines, another review of marijuana use and driving impairment concluded that "[t]here is no evidence that consumption of cannabis alone increases the risk of culpability for traffic crash fatalities or injuries for which hospitalization occurs, and may reduce those risks." Bates, M. and Blakely, T. *Roles of cannabis in motor vehicle crashes.* Epidemiologic Reviews. 21:222-232 (1999)

Finally, a NHTSA study concluded the following: "THC's adverse effects on driving performance appear relatively small." Hindrik, W, Robbe, J., O'Hanlon, J. *Marijuana and Actual Driving Performance.* Washington, D.C. U.S. Department of Transportation, National Highway Traffic Safety Administration. Report No. DOT HS 88 078 (1973)

Methanmpehtamine

Methamphetamine, or simply "Meth," is a psychostimulant and sympathomimetic drug. It is a member of the family of phenylethylamines and is used for weight loss and to maintain alertness, focus, motivation, and mental clarity for extended periods of time, and also for recreational purposes.

The drug was first synthesized from ephedrine in Japan in 1894 by chemist Nagayoshi Nagai. Nagai, N. *"Kanyaku maou seibun kenkyuu seiseki (zoku)"*. Yakugaku Zashi 13: 901. (1893) In 1919, crystallized methamphetamine was synthesized by Akira Ogata via reduction of ephedrine using red phosphorus and iodine. One of the earliest uses of methamphetamine was during World War II when the German military widely distributed the drug in chocolates dosed with methamphetamine. These chocolates were known as "fliegerschokolade" ("flyer's chocolate") when given to pilots, or "panzerschokolade" ("tanker's chocolate") when given to tank crews. It has been long rumored that from 1942 until his death in 1945, Adolf Hitler may have been injected with methamphetamine by his personal physician Theodor Morell as a treatment for depression and fatigue. Doyle, D. *Hitler's Medical Care*. Journal of the Royal College of Physicians of Edinburgh. 35: 75–82. (2005)

After World War II, a large supply of amphetamine, formerly stockpiled by the Japanese military, became available in Japan under the street name "shabu." The Japanese Ministry of Health banned it in 1951.

In the 1950s the American public became accustomed to the drug with a rise in legal prescriptions. According to the 1951 edition of *Pharmacology and Therapeutics* by Arthur Grollman, it was to be prescribed for "narcolepsy, post-encephalitic Parkinsonism, alcoholism, ... in certain depressive states... and in the treatment of obesity." The recreational use of methamphetamine peaked in the 1980s and since then tougher laws have been passed in the United States prohibiting possession of precursors and equipment for methamphetamine production.

The effects of methamphetamine include euphoria, excitation, exhilaration, rapid flight of ideas, increased libido, rapid speech, motor restlessness, hallucinations, delusions, psychosis, insomnia, reduced fatigue or drowsiness, increased alertness, heightened sense of well being, stereotypes behavior, feelings of increased physical strength, and poor impulse control. Couper, Fiona J., and Logan, Barry K. *Drugs and Human Performance Fact Sheets*. NHTSA. Page 63 (March 2004) However, during the late phase of consumption of this drug the effects change and include fatigue, sleepiness with sudden starts, itching/picking/scratching, normal heart rate, and normal to small pupils which are reactive to light.

In the DUI context as it relates to field sobriety testing, horizontal gaze nystagmus, vertical gaze nystagmus, and lack of convergence are not present. Pupil size is dilated and there is a slow reaction to light. Pulse rate and blood pressure is elevated and body temperature is normal to lower.

Generally it is conceded that methamphetamine is not usually a major cause of impairment in DUI situations. This is so because it is a stimulant and the time where the drug is active does not seem to cause great concern with researchers. However, the "hangover" effects are of more concern. Logan, B.K. *Methamphetamine and Driving Impairment*. J. Forensic Sci. 41:457-464 (1996) This study reported that methamphetamine users exhibited improved reaction time, relief from fatigue, and euphoria. *Id.* Further, an earlier study also concluded that therapeutic doses of amphetamine are no threat to traffic safety and may actually improve performance. Hurst, P.M. *Amphetamines and driving*. Alcohol, Drugs and Driving. 3:13-17 (1987) To confuse matters even more, an earlier study yet found there to be a high rate of traffic accidents among amphetamine abusers. Smart, R. G., Schmidt, W. and Bateman, K. *Psychoactive drugs and traffic accidents*. J. Safety Res. 1, 67-73 (1969)

In summary the effects of this drug seem to depend on the dose. At lower doses amphetamines have few effects on cognitive functioning but at higher doses risk-taking increases. Sherwood, N. *A critical review of the effects of drugs other than alcohol on driving*. Automobile Association (UK) Report. (Unpublished) (1998)

MDMA (Ecstasy)

MDMA (3,4-methylenedioxy-N-methamphetamine), or commonly known as "ecstasy" (or abbreviated E, X, or XTC), is a semisynthetic member of the amphetamine class of psychoactive drugs, a subclass of the phenethylamines.

Ecstacy's euphoric tendency produces a sense of intimacy with others and diminished feelings of fear and anxiety. Ecstacy is criminalized in all countries in the world under a UN agreement, but despite this it is one of the most widely used illicit drugs in the world. It is commonly associated with the rave culture and its related genres of music.

The effects after consuming Ecstacy include mild intoxication, relaxation, euphoria, an excited calm or peace, feelings of well-being, increase in physical and emotional energy, increased sociability and closeness, heightened sensitivity, increased responsiveness to touch, changes in perception, and empathy. At higher doses, agitation, panic attacks, and illusory or hallucinatory experiences may occur. Couper, Fiona J., and Logan, Barry K. *Drugs and Human Performance Fact Sheets.* NHTSA. Page 68 (March 2004)

In the DUI context as it relates to field sobriety testing, horizontal gaze nystagmus, vertical gaze nystagmus, and lack of convergence are not present. Pupil size is dilated and there is a slow reaction to light. Pulse rate is elevated while blood pressure and body temperature are normal to elevated.

To date, no studies have directly examined Ecstacy's effects on driving performance, although there are a few which have looked at cognitive and perceptual effects, which may have relevance to driving. One such study described the case of a young female who developed panic disorder after multiple ingestion of Ecstacy. Windhaber, J., Maierhofer, D., and Dantendorfer. *Panic order induced by large doses of 3,4-methylenedioxymethamphetamine resolved by paroxetine.* J. Clin. Psychopharmacol. 18(1), 95-6. (1998) And it is this type of unpredictable side-effect which makes ecstasy a potential danger amongst drivers.

Lysergic Acid Diethyladmide (LSD)

Lysergic acid diethylamide, otherwise known as LSD, LSD-25, or simply acid, is a semisynthetic psychedelic drug of the ergoline family. Its unusual psychological effects which include visuals of colored patterns behind the eyes in the mind, a sense of time distorting, and crawling geometric patterns have made it one of the most widely known psychedelic drugs. It has been used mainly as a recreational drug, and as a tool to supplement various practices for transcendence, meditation, psychonautics, art projects, and illicit (formerly legal) psychedelic therapy.

LSD is synthesized from lysergic acid derived from ergot, a grain fungus that typically grows on rye, and was first synthesized on November 16, 1938 by Swiss chemist Albert Hofmann at the Sandoz Laboratories in Switzerland. Its psychedelic properties were unknown until five years later, when Hofmann, acting on what he has called a "peculiar presentiment," returned to work on the chemical. Nichols, David. *Hypothesis on Albert Hofmann's Famous 1943 "Bicycle Day"*. Hofmann Foundation. (2003)

While conducting a further study on April 16, 1943, Hofmann became dizzy and was forced to stop work. Hofmann later wrote that after becoming dizzy he proceeded home and was affected by a "remarkable restlessness, combined with a slight dizziness." Hofmann stated that as he lay in his bed he sank into a not-unpleasant "intoxicated like condition" which was characterized by an extremely stimulated imagination. He stated that he was in a dreamlike state, and with his eyes closed he could see uninterrupted streams of "fantastic pictures, extraordinary shapes with intense, kaleidoscopic play of colors." The condition lasted for about two hours and then faded away. Hofmann, Albert. *"LSD: My Problem Child: Reflections on Sacred Drugs, Mysticism, and Science."* Council on Spiritual Practices. (2003) So, LSD was born.

Prior to October 6, 1966, LSD was available legally in the United States as an experimental psychiatric drug. There were a few believers who introduced many people to the drug while it was still, technically legal. Al Hubbard, who had no medical training, actively promoted LSD during the 1950, 1960s, and 1970s, and allegedly introduced as many as 6,000 people to it. Another disciple of LSD was Aldous Huxley who was an English writer and one of the most prominent members of the famous Huxley family. He spent the later part of his life in the United States living in Los Angeles from 1937 until his death in 1963 (he died the same day as C. S Lewis and John F. Kennedy). Huxley wrote extensively about the drug and his works allegedly influence the rock band "The Doors," and he appeared on the sleeve of The Beatles' album "Sgt. Pepper's Lonely Hearts Club Band."

Another promoter of LSD was Augustus Owsley Stanley III, usually known simply as Owsley. The former chemistry student constructed a private LSD lab in the mid-Sixties in San Francisco and supplied LSD to the central California area and to well known musicians of the area, including the Grateful Dead, Jefferson Airplane, Big Brother and The Holding Company. He was famously arrested in 1967 and later moved to Northern Australia and became an Australian citizen in 1996. The last of the most influence popularist advocates of LSD was Timothy Leary, an American writer, psychologist, futurist, and advocate of psychedelic drug research who coined and popularized the catch phrase, "[t]urn on, tune in, drop out."

The effects after consuming LSD are unpredictable and will depend on the dose ingested, the user's personality and mood, expectations and the surroundings. Couper, Fiona J., and Logan, Barry K. *Drugs and Human Performance Fact Sheets*. NHTSA. Page 52 (March 2004)

However, the effects typically include hallucinations, increased color perception, altered mental state, thought disorders, temporary psychosis, delusions, body image changes, and impaired depth, time and space perceptions. Users may feel several emotions at once or swing rapidly from one emotion to another. "Bad trips" may consist of severe, terrifying thoughts and feelings, fear of losing control, and despair.

In the DUI context as it relates to field sobriety testing, horizontal gaze nystagmus, vertical gaze nystagmus, and lack of convergence are not present. Pupil size is dilated and the reaction to light is normal. Pulse rate, blood pressure, and body temperature are elevated.

Gamma-Hydroxybutyrate (GHB)

Hydroxybutyric acid, 4-hydroxybutanoic acid, GHB, but commonly known as "the date rape drug," is a naturally-occurring substance found in the central nervous system, wine, beef, small citrus fruits, and almost all animals in small amounts. Weil, Andrew; Winifred Rosen. "Depressants". From Chocolate to Morphine. (2nd edition ed.). Boston/New York: Houghton Mifflin Company. Page. 77 (1993) GHB was first synthesized in 1960 as an experimental GABA analog, and was classified as a food and dietary supplement and sold in health food stores in early 1990. GHB is illegal in many countries and is currently regulated in the US and is used to treat cataplexy and excessive daytime sleepiness in patients with narcolepsy.

Historically, GHB has been used in a medical setting as a general anesthetic, to treat conditions such as insomnia, clinical depression, narcolepsy, and alcoholism, and to improve athletic performance. Synthesis of the chemical GHB was first reported in 1874 by Alexander Zaytsev, but the first major research into its use in humans was conducted in the early 1960s by Dr. Henri Laborit to use in studying the neurotransmitter GABA. Saytzeff, Alexander. "Über die Reduction des Succinylchlorids". Liebigs Annalen der Chemie 171: 258–290 (1874); Laborit, H., Jouany, J.M., Gerald, J., Fabiani, F. "Generalities concernant l'etude experimentale de l'emploi clinique du gamma hydroxybutyrate de Na". Aggressologie 1: 407 (1960)

GHB is a CNS depressant used as an intoxicant. At recreational doses, GHB can cause a state of euphoria, increased enjoyment of movement and music, increased libido, increased sociability and intoxication. At higher doses GHB may induce nausea, dizziness, drowsiness, agitation, visual disturbances, depressed breathing, amnesia, unconsciousness, and death.

The effects observed after having consumed GHB are similar to those effects observed with alcohol consumption. Couper, Fiona J., and Logan, Barry K. *Drugs and Human Performance Fact Sheets.* NHTSA. Page 42 (March 2004) These include relaxation, reduced inhibitions, euphoria, confusion, dizziness, drowsiness, sedation, inebriation, agitation, combativeness, and hallucinations.

In the DUI context as it relates to field sobriety testing, horizontal gaze nystagmus, vertical gaze nystagmus (in high doses), and lack of convergence are present. Pupil size is generally dilated and reaction to light is slow. Pulse rate and blood pressure are normal and body temperature is generally down.

Sedatives/Sleeping Pills

Sedatives are substances that induce sedation by reducing "irritability or excitement." At higher doses the user may experience slurred speech, staggering gait, poor judgment, and slow, uncertain reflexes.

All Sedatives can cause physiological and psychological dependence when taken regularly over a period of time, even at therapeutic doses. Barondes, Samuel H. *Better Than Prozac.* New York: Oxford University Press. Pages 47–59 (2003).; Mant, A, Whicker, SD, McManus, P, Birkett, DJ, Edmonds D, Dumbrell D. *"Benzodiazepine utilisation in Australia: report from a new pharmacoepidemiological database."* Aust J Public Health. 17 (4): 345–9 (December 1993)

Sedatives are divided into barbiturates, benzodiazepines (clonazepam (Klonopin)), diazepam (Valium), and alprazolam (Xanax) are a few examples), herbal sedatives (ie. kava, cannabis), solvent sedatives (ie.diethyl ether (Ether), ethyl alcohol (alcoholic beverage), methyl trichloride (Chloroform), nonbenzodiazepine sedatives (eszopiclone (Lunesta), zaleplon (Sonata), zolpidem (Ambien), and uncategorized sedatives (ie. gamma-hydroxybutyrate (GHB), diphenhydramine (Benadryl), methaqualone (Quaalude).

Diazepam (Valium)

Diazepam, a benzodiazepine, was approved for use in 1960 and in 1963 its improved version, valium, was released and became very popular helping its manufacturer, Roche, become a pharmaceutical industry giant. Valium is two and a half times more potent than its predecessor, chlordiazepoxide, which it quickly surpassed in terms of sales. After this initial success, other pharmaceutical companies began to introduce other benzodiazepine derivatives.

The benzodiazepine family gained popularity among medical professionals as an improvement upon barbiturates because they are far more sedating at therapeutic doses and importantly, are also far less dangerous. Valium is commonly used for treating anxiety, insomnia, seizures, muscle spasms, alcohol withdrawal and benzodiazepine withdrawal. It may also be used before certain medical procedures (such as endoscopies) to reduce tension and anxiety, and in some surgical procedures to induce amnesia. *Diazepam.* Medical Subject Headings (Mesh) National Institute of Health: National Library of Medicine (2006). In the driving under the influence context valium can cause impaired motor function, including but not limited to impaired coordination and balance.

Diazepam was the top-selling pharmaceutical in the United States from 1969 to 1982, with peak sales in 1978 of 2.3 billion tablets. Sample, Ian. *Leo Steinbach's Obituary.* The Guardian (Guardian Unlimited) (October 3, 2005)

The effects observed after consumption of valium at low doses include sleepiness, drowsiness, confusion, and some loss of intergraded memory. Couper, Fiona J., and Logan, Barry K. *Drugs and Human Performance Fact Sheets.* NHTSA. Page 31 (March 2004) Diazepam can produce a state of intoxication similar to that of alcohol, including slurred speech, disorientation, and drunken behavior. *Id.*

In the DUI context as it relates to field sobriety testing, horizontal gaze nystagmus, vertical gaze nystagmus (in high doses), and lack of convergence are present. Pupil size is normal and reaction to light is slow. Pulse rate and blood pressure are down and body temperature is normal. *Id.*

Alprazolam (Xanax)

Alprazolam, also known under the trade name Xanax, is a short-acting drug of the benzodiazepine class used to treat anxiety disorders, panic attacks, and anxiety associated with moderate depression.

Alprazolam was first synthesized by Upjohn (now a part of Pfizer) in 1969 and was first produced for use in 1976. Dangers in the context of DUI would be side effects that include drowsiness (common), dizziness (common), lightheadedness (common), fatigue, unsteadiness and impaired coordination, vertigo, slurred speech, and short-term memory loss and impairment of memory functions. Rawson, N.S., Rawson, M.J. *Acute adverse event signalling scheme using the Saskatchewan Administrative health care utilization datafiles: results for two benzodiazepines*. Can J Clin Pharmacol 6 (3): 159–66 (1999)

Eszopiclone (Lunesta)

Eszopiclone, best known as Lunesta, is a nonbenzodiazepine hypnotic agent (sedative) used as a treatment for insomnia. Lunesta, along with other related drugs, including Ambien and Sonata are the most commonly prescribed sedative hypnotics in the United States. There were 43 million prescriptions issued for insomnia medications during 2005 in the USA which generated a total of $2.7 billion for pharmaceutical companies. McKenzie, W.S. and Rosenberg M. *What every dentist should know about the z-sedatives*. J Mass Dent Soc 56 (53): 44–5 (2007)

It has been reported that people who have taken this prescription have engaged in activity such as driving, eating, or making phone calls and later having no memory of the activity. Lunesta can also cause side effects that impair thinking or reaction times.

Zaleplon (Sonata)

Zaleplon (marketed under the brand name Sonata) is a sedative/hypnotic mainly used for insomnia. It is a nonbenzodiazepine hypnotic from the pyrazolopyrimidine class. Elie, R., Rüther, E., Farr, I., Emilien, G., and Salinas, E. *Sleep latency is shortened during 4 weeks of treatment with zaleplon, a novel nonbenzodiazepine hypnotic. Zaleplon Clinical Study Group.* J Clin Psychiatry: 536–44 (Aug 1999) Zaleplon is one of few sleep medications which have been found to not cause an increase in road traffic accidents, thus demonstrating a much higher safety profile than many other hypnotics currently on the market. Menzin, J., Lang, K.M., Levy, P., and Levy, E. *A general model of the effects of sleep medications on the risk and cost of motor vehicle accidents and its application to France.* Pharmacoeconomics 19 (1): 69–78 (January 2001); Vermeeren, A., Riedel, W.J., van Boxtel, M.P., Darwish, M., Paty, I., and Patat, A. *Differential residual effects of zaleplon and zopiclone on actual driving: a comparison with a low dose of alcohol.* Sleep Med. 25 (2): 224–31 (March 2002)

The side effects of Sonata are similar to the side effects of benzodiazepines, and its use may cause hallucinations, abnormal behavior, severe confusion, day-time drowsiness, dizziness or lightheadedness, unsteadiness and/or falls, double vision or other vision problems, agitation, headache, nausea, vomiting, diarrhea or abdominal pain, depression, muscle weakness, tremor, vivid or abnormal dreams and memory difficulties or amnesia. Sonata is habit-forming, meaning addiction or drug dependence may occur.

Zolpidem (Ambien)

Zolpidem, or known popularly as Ambien, is a prescription medication used for the short-term treatment of insomnia, as well as some brain disorders. Some users have reported unexplained sleepwalking while using Ambien, and a few have reported driving, binge eating, sleep talking, and performing other daily tasks while sleeping.

'hile under the drug's influence is generally considered
ngerous than the average impaired driver due to
ed motor controls and delusions that may affect the
ual 'hangover' effects such as sleepiness, impaired
or skills may persist into the next day which may impair
ty of users to drive safely. Vermeeren A. *Residual effects of
otics: epidemiology and clinical implications.* CNS drugs. 18
): 297–328 (2004)

Studies suggest that the use of Ambien may impair driving skills
with a resultant increased risk of road traffic accidents. Gustavsen, I.,
Bramness, J.G., Skurtveit, S., Engeland, A., Neutel, I., and Mørland,
J. *Road traffic accident risk related to prescriptions of the hypnotics
zopiclone, zolpidem, flunitrazepam and nitrazepam.* Sleep Med. 9
(8): 818–22 (December 2008)

The effects observed after having consumed Ambien are
sleep induction, drowsiness, dizziness, lightheadedness, amnesia,
confusion, concentration difficulties, and memory impairment.
Couper, Fiona J., and Logan, Barry K. *Drugs and Human Performance
Fact Sheets.* NHTSA. Page 93 (March 2004)

In the DUI context as it relates to field sobriety testing, horizontal
gaze nystagmus, vertical gaze nystagmus (for high doses) and lack
of convergence are present. Pupil size is normal and reaction to
light is slow. *Id.* Pulse rate and blood pressure are down while body
temperature is normal. Other characteristic indicators may include
slow and slurred speech, and generally poor performance on field
sobriety tests.

Carisoprodol (Meprobamate)

Carisoprodol is a centrally-acting skeletal muscle relaxant
whose active metabolite is meprobamate. Carisoprodol is marketed
in the United States under the brand name Soma, and in the United
Kingdom and other countries under the brand names Sanoma and
Carisoma. The brand name Soma is shared with the Soma/Haoma
of ancient India, a drug mentioned in ancient Sanskrit writings and

is also the name of the fictional drug featured in Aldous H\
Brave New World. *Brave New Soma*. Time Magazine. (June
1959) Soma is also the Greek word for "body."

On June 1, 1959 several American pharmacologists conver.
at Wayne State University in Detroit, Michigan to discuss a ne
drug. The drug, originally thought to have antiseptic properties,
was found to have central muscle relaxing properties. Miller, J.G.
The pharmacology and clinical usefulness of carisoprodol. Detroit:
Wayne State University. (1959) The drug had been developed by
Dr. Frank M. Berger at Wallace laboratories and had been named
carisoprodol (trade name Soma). Carisoprodol was developed with
the hope that it would have better muscle relaxing properties, less
potential for abuse, and less risk of overdose than meprobamate.
Berger, F., Kletzkin, M., Ludwig, B., and Margolin, S. *The history,
chemistry, and pharmacology of carisoprodol*. Annals of the New
York Academy of Sciences. 86:90-107 (1959)

As of November 2007 carisoprodol (Somadril, Somadril
comp.) was taken off the market in Sweden due to problems
with dependence, abuse and side effects. The agency overseeing
pharmaceuticals has considered other drugs used with the same
indications as carisoprodol to have the same or better effects
without the risks of the drug. *Marknadsföringen av Somadril och
Somadril comp rekommenderas upphöra tillfälligt*. Lakemedelsverket
Medical Products Agency. (November 16, 2007) In the EU, the
European Medicines Agency issued a release recommending that
member states suspend marketing authorization for this product.
*European Medicines Agency recommends suspension of marketing
authorisations for carisoprodol-containing medicinal products*.
European Medicines Agency Press office. (November 16, 2007)

The effects observed after consuming carisoprodol include
dizziness, drowsiness, sedation, confusion, disorientation, slowed
thinking, lack of comprehension, drunken behavior, obtunded
(reduction in alertness), and alarmingly, coma. Couper, Fiona J.,
and Logan, Barry K. *Drugs and Human Performance Fact Sheets*.
NHTSA. Page 15 (March 2004)

In the DUI context relating to field sobriety testing, horizontal gaze nystagmus, vertical gaze nystagmus (in high doses) and lack of convergence are present. Pupil size is normal to dilated and reaction to light is slow. Pulse rate, blood pressure, and body temperature are normal to lower. Other characteristic indicators may include slurred speech, drowsiness, disorientation, drunken behavior without the odor of alcohol, and generally poor performance on field sobriety tests.

Dextromethorphan (DXM or DM)

Dextromethorphan (DXM or DM) is an antitussive drug and is one of the active ingredients used to prevent coughs in many over-the-counter cold and cough medicines. Dextromethorphan has also found other uses in medicine, ranging from pain relief to psychological applications. It is sold in syrup, tablet, and lozenge forms manufactured under several different brand names and generic labels. In its pure form, dextromethorphan occurs as a white powder.

The FDA approved DXM in 1958 after research supported its legitimacy and effectiveness as a cough suppressant. After its approval, it was introduced as an OTC medication under the name Romilar. As early as 1975, the popularity and extensive abuse of DXM was recognized, and Romilar was removed from the OTC market. Shulgin, A.T. *Drugs of Abuse in the Future*. Clinical Toxicology 8: 405-56 (1975) However, DXM was specifically excluded from the Controlled Substances Act (CSA) of 1970, therefore it was still legal to produce and use. A few years after its removal from OTC, companies began introducing refined DXM products (e.g., Robitussin, Vicks-44, Dextrotussion) that were designed to limit recreational use by creating an unpleasant taste if consumed in large quantities.

During the 1960s and 1970s, dextromethorphan became available in an over-the-counter tablet form by the brand name Romilar. In 1973, Romilar was taken off the shelves after a burst in sales due to frequent abuse, and was replaced by cough syrup in an attempt to cut down on abuse. More recently (the early 1990s), gel capsule forms began reappearing in the form of Drixoral Cough Liquid Caps and later Robitussin CoughGels as well as several generic forms of that preparation.

The observed effects after consumption of DXM at recommended doses is minimal, although at higher recreational doses effects may include acute euphoria, elevated mood, dissociation of mind from body, creative dream-like experiences, and increased perceptual awareness. Other effects include disorientation, confusion, pupil dilation, and altered time perception, visual and auditory hallucinations, and decreased sexual functioning. Couper, Fiona J., and Logan, Barry K. *Drugs and Human Performance Fact Sheets.* NHTSA. Page 35 (March 2004)

In the DUI context relating to field sobriety testing, horizontal gaze nystagmus, vertical gaze nystagmus (at high doses), and lack of convergence are present. Pupil size is normal to dilated and reaction to light is slow. Pulse rate and blood pressure are down and body temperature is normal.

Diphenhydramine (Benadryl)

Diphenhydramine hydrochloride is a chemical mainly used as an antihistamine, antiemetic, sedative, and hypnotic. It is produced and marketed under the trade name Benadryl by McNeil-PPC (a division of Johnson & Johnson) in the U.S. & Canada, and Dimedrol in other countries. It is also found in the name-brand products Nytol and Unisom, though some Unisom products contain doxylamine instead.

Diphenhydramine was one of the first known antihistamines and was invented in 1943 by Dr. George Rieveschl, a former professor at the University of Cincinnati. Hevesi, D. *George Rieveschl, 91, Allergy Reliever, Dies.* New York Times. (September 29, 2007) It became the first FDA-approved prescription antihistamine in 1946. Ritchie, J. *UC prof, Benadryl inventor dies.* Business Courier of Cincinnati. (September 24, 2007)

The observed effects of having consumed diphenhydramine may result in marked sedation, including drowsiness, reduced wakefulness, altered mood, impaired cognitive and psychomotor performance. Couper, Fiona J., and Logan, Barry K. *Drugs and Human Performance Fact Sheets*. NHTSA. Page 35 (March 2004)

In the DUI context relating to field sobriety testing, horizontal gaze nystagmus, vertical gaze nystagmus (at high doses), and lack of convergence are present. Pupil size is normal, dilatation may occur and reaction to light is slow. Pulse rate, blood pressure, and body temperature are normal. *Id.*

When this drug is mixed with alcohol the effects become more intense and therefore will likely cause increased impairment. Seppala, T., Linnoila, M, and Mattila, M.J. *Drugs, Alcohol and Driving*. Drugs. 17:389-408 (1979)

Ketamine

Ketamine is a drug used in human and veterinary medicine and was developed by Dr. Craig Newlands of Wayne State University. It was then further developed by Parke-Davis (today a part of Pfizer) in 1962 as part of an effort to find a safer anesthetic alternative to phencyclidine (PCP), which was more likely to cause hallucinations, neurotoxicity and seizures. The drug was first given to American soldiers during the Vietnam War.

The drug was used in psychiatric and other academic research through the 1970s, culminating in 1978 with the publishing of John Lilly's *The Scientist and Marcia Moore* and Howard Alltounian's *Journeys into the Bright World*, which documented the unusual phenomenology of ketamine intoxication. Moore, Marica and Alltonnian, Howard M.D. *Journeys into the Bright World*. Para Research, Inc. (1978) The incidence of recreational ketamine use increased through the end of the 20th century, especially in the context of raves and other parties.

The observed effects after having consumed ketamine includes decreased awareness of general environment, sedation, dream-like state, vivid dreams, feelings of invulnerability, increased distractibility, disorientation, and subjects are generally uncommunicative. Delirium and hallucinations can be experienced after awakening from anesthesia. Couper, Fiona J., and Logan, Barry K. *Drugs and Human Performance Fact Sheets*. NHTSA. Page 45 (March 2004)

In the DUI context relating to field sobriety testing, horizontal gaze nystagmus, vertical gaze nystagmus, and lack of convergence are present. Pupil size and reaction to light are normal while pulse rate, blood pressure, and body temperature are elevated. *Id.*

Phencyclidine (PCP)

Phencyclidine (full name is phenylcyclohexylpiperidine but is commonly initialized as PCP), also known as angel dust and other street names, is a dissociative drug formerly used as an anesthetic agent. Maisto, Stephen A., Galizio, Mark and Connors, Gerard Joseph. *Drug Use and Abuse*. Thompson Wadsworth. (2004)

PCP was first synthesized in 1926 and later tested after World War II as a surgical anesthetic. Because of its adverse side-effects such as hallucinations, mania, delirium, and disorientation, it was not used again until the 1950s. In 1963, it was patented by Parke-Davis and named Sernyl (referring to serenity), but was withdrawn from the market two years later because of side-effects. It was renamed Sernylan in 1967, and marketed as a veterinary anesthetic, but again it was discontinued. Its side-effects and long half-life in the human body made it unsuitable for medical applications.

The observed effects after consuming PCP include euphoria, calmness, feelings of strength and invulnerability, lethargy, disorientation, loss of coordination, distinct changes in body awareness, distorted sensory perceptions, impaired concentration, disordered thinking, illusions and hallucinations, agitation, combativeness or violence, memory loss, bizarre behavior, sedation, and stupor. Couper, Fiona J., and Logan, Barry K. *Drugs and Human Performance Fact Sheets*. NHTSA. Page 79 (March 2004)

In the DUI context relating to field sobriety testing, horizontal gaze nystagmus, vertical gaze nystagmus, and lack of convergence are present. Pupil size and reaction to light are normal, which pulse rate, blood pressure, and body temperature are elevated. *Id.*

Toluene

Toluene, also known as methylbenzene, phenylmethane, and Toluol, is a clear water-insoluble liquid with the typical smell of paint thinners, redolent of the sweet smell of the related compound benzene. Toluene is a common solvent, able to dissolve paints, paint thinners, silicone sealants, many chemical reactants, rubber, printing ink, adhesives (glues), lacquers, leather tanners, and disinfectants.

Like other solvents toluene is also used as an inhalant drug for its intoxicating properties; however this causes severe neurological harm. Streicher HZ, Gabow PA, Moss AH, Kono D, Kaehny W.D. *Syndromes of toluene sniffing in adults.* Ann. Intern. Med. 94 (6): 758–62 (1981); Devathasan G., Low D., Teoh P.C., Wan S.H., Wong P.K. *Complications of chronic glue (toluene) abuse in adolescents.* Aust N Z J Med 14 (1): 39–43 (1984)

The name toluene was derived from the older name toluol, which refers to tolu balsam, an aromatic extract from the tropical Colombian tree Myroxylon balsamum, from which it was first isolated. It was originally named by Jöns Jakob Berzelius.

The observed effects after consuming toluene include dizziness, euphoria, grandiosity, floating sensation, drowsiness, reduced ability to concentrate, slowed reaction time, distorted perception of time and distance, confusion, weakness, fatigue, memory loss, delusions, and hallucinations. Couper, Fiona J., and Logan, Barry K. *Drugs and Human Performance Fact Sheets.* NHTSA. Page 85 (March 2004)

In the DUI context relating to field sobriety testing, horizontal gaze nystagmus (in high doses), vertical gaze nystagmus (in high doses), and lack of convergence are present. Pupil size is normal and reaction to light is slow. Pulse rate and blood pressure are elevated while body temperature is normal. *Id.*

CHAPTER 4

The History of Law Enforcement

History is a race between education and catastrophe.
—H. G. Wells

Law enforcement in one form or another has been present in human society for thousands of years. The first policing organization can be traced back 4000 years to ancient Egypt. The ancient Egyptian empire was divided into 42 administrative jurisdictions and for each jurisdiction the Pharaoh appointed an official who was responsible for justice and security. He was assisted by a "chief of police," who bore the title "sab heri seker," or "chief of the hitters" (a body of men responsible for tax collecting, among other duties).

It has been argued that the first police force comparable to present-day police was established in 1667 under King Louis XIV in France. Alternatively many more have argued that modern police can trace their origins to the 1800s with the establishment of the Marine Police in London, the Glasgow Police in Scotland, and the Napoleonic Police of Paris. Dinsmor, Alastair. *Glasgow Police Pioneers.* The Scotia News (Winter 2003); *La Lieutenance Générale de Police. La Préfecture de Police fête ses 200 ans.* Juillet 1800 - Juillet (2000) The London Metropolitan Police was established in 1829 and promoted the preventive role of police as a deterrent to urban crime and disorder. Brodeur, Jean-Paul; Eds., Kevin R. E. McCormick and Livy A. Visano. *High Policing and Low Policing: Remarks about the Policing of Political Activities. Understanding*

Policing. Canadian Scholars' Press. Pages 284–285, 295 (1992)

The word 'police' stems from the Greek word 'politeia' (or "polis," meaning "city") meaning, state, administration, and government. In Chaucer's *Canterbury Tales* the word 'policie' was used to mean organized government and civil administration. Later, in approximately 1589 the French word 'policer' appears and means "to keep order." Prior to the 19th century, the only official use of the word "police" used in the English language was in 1714 and was regarding the appointment of Commissioners of Police for Scotland and also referred to the creation of the Marine Police in 1798 (set up to protect merchandise at the Port of London). Even today, many British police forces are suffixed with "Constabulary" rather than "Police".

Pre-modern Europe

In the city-states of ancient Greece, policing duties were assigned to magistrates. In order to perform their duties the magistrates depended in part on the military, which viewed itself as primarily responsible for the external security of the state. Hunter, Virginia J. *Policing Athens: Social Control in the Attic Lawsuits, 420-320 B.C.*. Princeton, NJ: Princeton University Press. Page 3 (1994) In Athens Scythian slaves (Ancient Iranian people who were horse-riding nomadic pastoralists) were used to guard public meetings to keep order and for crowd control, and also assisted with dealing with criminals, handling prisoners, and making arrests. Other duties associated with modern policing, such as investigating crimes, were left to the citizens themselves. *Id.*

The Roman Empire was known to have had a relatively effective law enforcement system and many believe that the first organized "police force" was actually formed during this time. Under the reign of Augustus the capital had grown to almost one million inhabitants. The Emperor created a police and firefighter system called "Vigiles Urbani," ("watchmen of the City") to protect the growing city. Wells, Colin. *The Roman Empire*. 2nd Ed. Harvard University Press (1995)

Emperor Augustus levied a 4% tax on the sale of slaves in 6 AD in order to pay for this new firefighter and police force system. *Id.* In addition to extinguishing fires, the Vigiles were the night watchmen of Rome and their duties included apprehending thieves and robbers and capturing runaway slaves. The Vigiles dealt primarily with petty crimes and looked for disturbances of the peace while they patrolled the streets.

After the collapse of the Roman Empire in the 5th century AD, the Eastern, or Byzantine, Empire retained some of the older Roman policing institutions including a "koiaistor" (a Hellenized equivalent of the Roman quaestor) which was the main policing authority assigned with the specific responsibility of overseeing the large population of foreigners that resided in the capital. Outside the Byzantine Empire, however, the urban basis for the existence of policing organizations had almost disappeared. What order that existed was enforced either by the military, often consisting of little more than armed bands, or by the community itself.

Outside of Europe, "prefects" were used in ancient China as its law enforcement personnel. The practice of a "prefect" has been in use as law enforcement in China for thousands of years. Prefects were government officials who were appointed by local magistrates who in turn were appointed by the head of state, usually the emperor of the dynasty. The prefects oversaw the civil administration of their "prefecture," or jurisdiction. These prefects usually reported directly to the local magistrate. The "prefecture system" eventually spread to neighboring cultures, including Korea and Japan.

European development

Modern police in Europe has a precedent in the "Hermandad." "Hermandad" is literally translated into "brotherhood" and was a peacekeeping association of armed individuals in medieval Spain. Because medieval Spanish kings were often unable to offer adequate protection for its people, protective municipal leagues began to emerge in the 12th century and fought back against bandits and other rural criminals. Burke, Ulick Ralph. *A History of Spain: From the Earliest Times to the Death of Ferndinand the Catholic.* London: Longman's, Green, & Co. Vol. II. Page 79 (1895)

This type of policing system was common in the Middle Ages and such alliances were frequently formed by a number of towns in order to protect the roads connecting them. The original hermandades continued to serve as modest local police units until their final suppression in 1835. *Id.*

The contemporary concept of a paid centralized and governmentally controlled police force was developed by French legal scholars and practitioners in the 17th and early 18th centuries. Notable is the treatise *Traité de la Police* ("Treatise on the Police"), written by Nicolas Delamare and first published in 1705. The German *Polizeiwissenschaft* ("Science of Police") was also an important theoretical formulation of police in western culture.

As previously mentioned, there are many who argue that the first "modern" police force was created by the government of King Louis XIV in 1667 to serve and protect the city of Paris, then the largest city in Europe. On March 15, 1667, the government created the office of "lieutenant général de police" ("lieutenant general of police") who was to be the head of the new Paris police force. This governmental edict defined the task of the police as "ensuring the peace and quiet of the public and of private individuals, purging the city of what may cause disturbances, procuring abundance, and having each and everyone live according to their station and their duties". *La Lieutenance Générale de Police. La Préfecture de Police fête ses 200 ans Juillet 1800 - Juillet* (2000) The scheme of the Paris police force was extended to the rest of France by Royal edict in October 1699 and resulted in the creation of a "lieutenant general of police" in all large French cities and towns.

The French system for policing was changed once again, this time at the conclusion of the French Revolution. On February 17, 1800, Napoléon I reorganized the police in Paris and all cities in France with populations of more than 5,000 inhabitants, as the Prefecture of Police. Then, on March 12, 1829, a government decree created the first uniformed police in France, known as "sergents de ville" ("city sergeants"). The organization claims that the "sergents de ville" were the first uniformed policemen in the world. *Id.*

In the United Kingdom, the development of police forces was seemingly much slower than in the rest of Western Europe. The British police function was historically performed by private "watchmen" and "thief takers" (a private individual hired to capture criminals – an 18th Century Bounty Hunter of sorts). Watchmen were usually funded by private individuals and organizations and thief takers were privately-funded (usually by victims of crime) and paid after they had caught the criminals.

King George II began paying some London and Middlesex watchmen in 1737 with tax money and this began the shift from private to government policing. In 1750, English novelist and dramatist Henry Fielding began organizing a force of quasi-professional constables. Because this system of policing was largely unorganised and lacked a criminal investigation capability, Fielding (who had been appointed a Magistrate in 1748) introduced the first detective force, known as the Bow Street Runners, in 1753.

In 1754 the "Macdaniel affair" added further fuel to fire for implementing a governmentally controlled police force. The "Macdaniel affair" involved a gang, led by Stephen MacDaniel, who had been prosecuting innocent men to their deaths in order to collect reward money. Mireille, Delmas-Marty and Spencer, J.R. *European Criminal Procedures.* Presses Universitaire de France / Cambridge University Press (first published in French 1995, English translation 2002) This horrid activity was undoubtedly an unintended consequence of the British government reward system for the capture of criminals. The Macdaniel affair did, however, aid in the public's outcry for the formation of a salaried public police, one that did not depend on rewards. Benson, Bruce. *To Serve and Protect: Privatization and Community in Criminal Justice.* NYU Press. (1998); Rawlings, Philip; Tim Newburn, Les Johnston, Frank Leishman. *Policing: A Short History.* Willan Publishing (2002); McLynn, Frank. *Crime and punishment in eighteenth-century England.* Routledge

(1989); Langbein, John H. *The Origins of Adversary Criminal Trial.* Oxford University Press (2003)

By 1798, salaried constables in England were being paid by local magistrates but there was still no centralized and organized police force. It was not until 1798 that this void was filled. The Marine Police Force, sometimes known as the Thames River Police is considered to be England's first Police force. The Marine Police Force was formed by magistrate Patrick Colquhoun and a Master Mariner, John Harriott in an attempt to combat theft and looting from ships anchored in the Pool of London and along the River Thames. The Marine Police was initially made up of 220 Constables assisted by 1,000 registered dock workers, and was responsible for preventing the theft of cargo. In its first year of operation 2,000 offenders were found guilty of theft from the docks. Critchley, T. A. *A History of Police in England and Wales.* 2nd edition. Montclair, NJ: Patterson Smith. Pages 38-39. (1978)

Scotland, which had used the word "police" before any other English speaking county, established a professional police force on June 30, 1800. On this date the authorities of Glasgow, Scotland successfully petitioned the government to pass the Glasgow Police Act which established the City of Glasgow Police. Many consider this to be the first professional police service in modern history as it differed from previous law enforcement in that it was a preventive police force. Other Scottish towns soon followed and established their own police forces through acts of parliament. http://www.policemuseum.org.uk/

Across the pond in Ireland their first organized police force was established through the Peace Preservation Act of 1814, although the Irish Constabulary Act of 1822 marked the true beginning of the Royal Irish Constabulary. Among its first duties after organization was the forcible seizure of tithes during the "Tithe War" in Ireland. The Tithe War involved a series of violent incidents in Ireland between 1831 and 1836 and was in reaction to the seizure of goods and chattels ("Tithes," or taxes) by the Irish Constabulary for the upkeep of the Anglican protestant Church of Ireland irrespective of an individual's religion. By 1841 this force numbered over 8,600 men.

Back in England, the early forms of law enforcement which was known for their lack of organization and efficiency, was often a source of public controversy. Because of this, a parliamentary committee was appointed to investigate the current system of policing. Sir Robert Peel, after he had been appointed Home Secretary in 1822, established a second and more effective committee, and acted upon its findings. Peel believed that in order to change the problems with organization and efficiency law enforcement must be made an official and paid profession and therefore answerable to the public. Parliament approved Peel's presentation and the Metropolitan Police Act of 1829 was born. http://www.met.police.uk/history

The City of London grew exponentially during the Industrial Revolution of the early 19th century. During this time it was clear that the locally maintained system of volunteer constables and "watchmen" was ineffective in both detecting and preventing crime. Because of this the Metropolitan Police Act was given Royal Assent on June 19, 1829 which placed policing for London directly under the control of Sir Robert Peel. Neocleous, Mark. *Fabricating Social Order: A Critical History of Police Power.* Pluto Press. Pages 93–94 (2004)

Peel organized the police force to appear more neutral rather than paramilitary. To that end the uniform was deliberately manufactured in blue, rather than red which was a military color, along with the officers being armed only with a wooden baton and a rattle to signal the need for assistance. Along with an independent color scheme, the police ranks did not include military titles, with the exception of Sergeant. Siegel, Larry J. *Criminolgy.* Thomson Wadsworth. Pages 515-516 (2005)

The original headquarters of the then newly formed Metropolitan Police was located at 4 Whitehall Place with a back entrance onto Scotland Yard – Scotland Yard later because a name for the force itself. The force became the third official non-paramilitary city police force in the world, after the City of Glasgow Police and the Paris

Police. The London Metropolitan Police officers are often referred to as 'Bobbies' or 'Peelers' after Sir Robert (Bobby) Peel. They became a model for the police forces in most countries, such as the United States, and most of the British Empire.

In the "New World," Canada was the first country to organize municipal police departments. Using England's Metropolitan Police Act as a model the Toronto Police became the very first municipal police department in North America in 1834. Quebec City and Montreal quickly followed suit in 1838 and 1840 respectively and in 1867, to official birth of Canada as an independent nation, the provincial police forces were established for the vast rural areas in eastern Canada.

The famous Royal Canadian Mounted Police (RCMP), better known internationally as the "Mounties," began in 1873 as the North-West Mounted Police. The RCMP represented a significant departure from Anglo-Saxon policing traditions as it was similar in organization, style, and method to the models of France and Ireland because they operated more like a military organization than a traditional police force. http://www.mountieshop.com/history.asp The RCMP were formed by the Canadian Government to ensure peace and order in the Canadian wilderness but their primary responsibility was to suppress the practice of the European settlers using alcohol as currency for buffalo hides. *Id.* The famous red-coats were introduced in July, 1874. *Id.*

Like English speaking Canada the United States inherited England's Anglo-Saxon common law and its system of social obligation, sheriffs, constables, watchmen, and stipendiary justice. As America became more urban and industrialized, crime and public disturbances became more common and therefore concerning for larger cities. Among the first public police forces established in colonial North America were the watchmen organized in Boston in 1631 and in New Amsterdam (New York City) in 1647. Similar to the watchmen in England most officers in colonial America did not receive a salary but were paid by private citizens.

In the southern hemisphere Australia, which was settled as a penal colony in 1788, used the constabulary and watch-and-ward systems. One of the many problems with this system in Australia was that recruits often came from the ranks of convicts. Modeled after England's Metropolitan Police Act, the Sydney Police Act of 1833 led to the establishment of urban police forces. Police coverage was extended to rural areas in 1838, when each of the country's six states created its own police agency. In 1862 the New South Wales Police Force was established with the passing of the Police Regulation Act.

The first "modern" police department in the United States was established in New York City in 1844 (it was officially organized in 1845). Other cities soon followed suit, including: New Orleans in 1852; Boston and Philadelphia in 1854; and Chicago in 1855. Like the Toronto Police Department the American cities initiated their police departments using the London Metropolitan Police as a model. Therefore, their main task was the prevention of crime and disorder while providing a number of other public services.

In addition to the creation of local police departments that policed the urban centers, other forms of law enforcement were being created in the United States, such as the United States Secret Service which was created in 1865 to prevent counterfeiting. During the 1890s the Secret Service occasionally was called upon to guard the president, a duty that did not become permanent until 1901.

The Bureau of Investigation, which later developed into the Federal Bureau of Investigation (FBI), was created in 1908. Despite some initial reluctance from certain politicians, namely some members of Congress, President Theodore Roosevelt pushed through the creation of the Bureau of Investigation. The Bureau began with a modest mandate to investigate antitrust cases, several types of fraud, and certain crimes committed on government property or by government officials.

In 1920 the Department of the Treasury created the first sizable federal police agency. Charged with enforcing Prohibition, the "T-Men," as they came to be known, grew to a force of approximately 4,000 officers during the peak of the crusade against alcohol.

During the early 20th century states began to create their own police forces on a larger scale than had previously been done. In 1905 Pennsylvania established what is considered to be the first modern state police department. Pennsylvania's state police force was soon followed by other states, including New York (1917), Michigan, Colorado, and West Virginia (1919), and Massachusetts (1920).

During the early 20th century pressures to reform police departments were beginning to surface nationwide and were initiated from within the police system itself. One of the many motivating factors for police reform in the United States in the 1920s and early '30s was Prohibition. The nationwide ban on the manufacture, sale, and transportation of alcohol led to a vast black market in the major cities and to the rise of powerful criminal gangs that corrupted and intimidated political leaders and police.

The founder of the professional policing reform movement in the United States was August Vollmer. Vollmer and his professional colleagues were concerned about the broad social issues of policing and saw changes in morals, increasing crime and corruption, and later the Great Depression as symptoms of the erosion of such basic social institutions as the family, churches, schools, and neighborhoods.

When J. Edgar Hoover became head of the Bureau of Investigation in 1924, he laid the groundwork for a strategy that would make the FBI one of the most prestigious police organizations in the world. By the 1930s the public's opinion of detectives was ready for change. Inspired by detective-heroes in the novels and short stories of Charles Dickens, Edgar Allan Poe, and Sir Arthur Conan Doyle, readers developed a new interest in real-life accounts of detectives' exploits. Hoover set out to make the fictional image of the detective into reality. He eliminated corruption by suspending bureau investigations requiring considerable undercover or investigative work (e.g., vice and, later, organized crime) and by creating a strong bureaucracy that emphasized accountability. He also established educational requirements for new agents and a formal training course in modern policing methods. In 1935, J. Edgar Hooever, who had become the head of the Bureau of Investigation by that time, created the FBI National Academy (originally the Police Training School), which trained local police managers. The Academy extended the influence of the FBI, and Hoover, over local police departments while at the same time contributing to the exchange of professional expertise.

The motorization of the American police steadily increased and was largely complete shortly after World War II, when the automobile became a more important part of American life. Vehicular police officers provided random and rapid movement of police cars through city streets that created a feeling of police presence that was designed to deter potential criminals and reassure citizens of their safety. Rapidly patrolling police also would be able to spot and intercept crimes in progress, such as drivers who are driving under the influence.

Modern Policing

Today, police forces are typically organized and funded by government. The level of government responsible for policing may be at the national, regional or local level and in some places there may be multiple police forces operating in the same region, with different ones having jurisdiction according to the type of crime or other circumstances. The United States has a highly decentralized and fragmented system of law enforcement. According to the United States Department of Justice, Bureau of Justice Statistics, there are over 17,000 state and local law enforcement agencies and more than 800,000 full-time sworn officers employed. United States Department of Justice, Bureau of Justice Statistics (2004)

In the United States policing is usually a combination of a state police force in conjunction with local municipal policing. In the United States there also exists national police agencies which have jurisdiction over serious crimes or those with an interstate component. In addition to the conventional urban or regional police forces there are other police forces with specialized functions or jurisdiction. For instance, the federal government has a number of police forces with their own specialized jurisdictions. Examples include the Federal Protective Service, which patrols and protects government buildings; the postal police, which protect postal buildings, vehicles and items; the Park Police, which protect national parks, or Amtrak Police which patrol Amtrak stations and trains; and the U.S. Coast Guard, which carries out many police functions for boaters in additional to other duties.

In significant cities, there may be a separate police agency for public transit systems, such as the New York City Port Authority Police, the Port of Los Angeles Port Police, the Port of Seattle Port Police, and so on.

In the United Kingdom policing is primarily the responsibility of a regional police force however specialist units do exist at the national level also. In Canada there is a federal police authority with the RCMP (the "Mounties") and also significant municipal police departments (Toronto, Montreal, Vancouver, and Calgary, to name a few).

Some countries, such as Sweden, Chile, Israel, the Philippines, France, Austria, New Zealand and South Africa, use a centralized system of policing. Das, Dilip K., Otwin Marenin. *Challenges of Policing Democracies: A World Perspective*. Routledge. Page 17 (2000). Other countries where jurisdiction of multiple police agencies overlap, include Guardia Civil and the Policía Nacional in Spain , the Polizia di Stato and Carabinieri in Italy and the Police Nationale and Gendarmerie Nationale in France. Bayley, David H. *Police Function, Structure, and Control in Western Europe and North America: Comparative and Historical Studies*. Crime & Justice 1: Pages 109–143 (1979)

Other countries have what is considered regional centralization under federal authority, such as Germany and The Netherlands. Germany has two federal police forces, the Federal Criminal Police Office (similar to that of the FBI in the United States), and the Federal Border Guard. However basic policing is controlled by the state or province police forces. In The Netherlands, the National Police

Agency operates under the authority of the Ministry of the Interior, but the regional police forces provide the backbone of the policing system.

Most countries are members of the International Criminal Police Organization (INTERPOL), which facilitates international police cooperation and is located in Lyon, France. (http://www.interpol. int/) INTERPOL was established as the International Criminal Police Commission in 1923 and adopted its telegraphic address as its common name in 1956. INTERPOL is the world's largest international police organization, with 187 member countries and is the second largest intergovernmental organization after the United Nations. *Id.*

Police Education

The idea of college-educated police officers has been a dream almost a century old and remains largely unrealized. Though advancements in educating police departments have been made over the decades a relatively high percentage of police officers are void of higher education. As demands on police departments and individual officers grow and as advancing technology is finding its place into the everyday world of the officer there must be further advancements in training and education.

Prior to World War I the study of criminal sociology, criminal anthropology, and criminology were offered for study but typically only available at law schools or institutes which drew upon the faculties of law, medicine, and the social sciences for instructional purposes. In June 1909 the first National Conference on Criminal Law and Criminology was convened in Chicago by the faculty of law at Northwestern University. This conference was significant for a number of reasons but perhaps the most important reason is that the Conference brought together selected educators and practitioners from every branch of the American criminal justice system.

At the 1909 Conference, three resolutions were passed which resulted in: 1) the establishment of the American Institute of Criminal

Law and Criminology; 2) the founding and publication in 1910 of the Journal of the American Institute of Criminal Law and Criminology; and, 3) the translation into English of some of the most important and significant books on criminology written by foreign scholars. As a result of this third resolution, nine books were published by the Institute and some of these books were used as references and texts in the early development of police courses at institutions of higher learning.

A few years prior to the conference a gentleman by the name of August Vollmer (mentioned earlier in this chapter) was elected Town Marshall of Berkeley, California and he was later appointed Chief of Police at Berkeley. Vollmer pursued the application of scientific methods to police work, the need for increased training for police officers, and the provision for pre-employment training comparable in quality to that provided for lawyers, doctors and the other professions. *Journal of Criminal Law, Crimonology and Police Science*, 44(1), Page 101 (May-June 1953) To that end, Vollmer established a police training school in the Berkeley Police Department, with most of the instruction provided by his friends on the University of California faculty. Vollmer's training school lasted from approximately 1916 until 1932, at which time the program was extended and similar courses were offered during the regular school year. Vollmer encouraged his police officers to attend these courses and the press referred to these officers as "college cops." *Id.*

In 1929, the University of Chicago entered the field of police education by offering a limited number of police courses and employed Vollmer as a Professor of Police Administration in the political science department. *Journal of Criminal Law, Criminology and Police Science*, 52(1), Page 103 (May-June 1961) Vollmer returned to Berkeley in 1930 and accepted a professorship in police administration at the University of California. Soon thereafter Vollmer and O.W. Wilson began the School of Criminology at the same school. Between 1929 and 1932, the University of Southern California offered police courses, both inservice and for credit, through its School of Citizenship and Public Administration. *Id.*

In 1930, San Jose State College got into the act and established its own two-year curriculum plan that eventually expanded into a four-year degree. The 1932-33 brochure from the San Jose College program contained the following announcement:

> If you have local applicants for any positions on your force in whom you are especially interested, you will find their value to you materially increased by a two year course at San Jose. Just tell the young man that the day is fast approaching when college training will be required of every policeman. The cost is negligible. San Jose is a public institution. Student fees amount to $9.00 a quarter, and the cost of books and supplies is small. It is cheaper to train young men here than in your own department.

Michigan State University created a five year curriculum plan in 1935 designed to prepare students for careers in the police service. A significant feature of the program was the requirement of 18 months of field experience with Federal, state, and local law enforcement agencies. The program's curriculum focused more on the laboratory sciences requiring at least two years of study in chemistry, physics, and mathematics. Additionally, students were paid $1 a day during the field experience and were permitted to reside in the State Police barracks. After graduating the program those students who joined the State Police were employed at the salary level of an officer beginning his third year of service – significant considering this program was introduced during the depression.

Other Universities became involved in providing courses in criminology between World Wars I and II. The University of Wisconsin developed a series of zone schools in 1927 that offered courses for police officers through its extension division. However, this program did not last long and was discontinued in 1931. Northwestern University in Chicago made a significant contribution through its Traffic Institute and also offered courses in connection with the work of its Scientific Crime Detection Laboratory. This program continues to present day. Even the Harvard University Law School got into the fray and offered seminars and courses dealing with police subjects, such as Homicide Investigations.

On June 15, 1935 the Indiana University Board of Trustees established the Institute of Criminal Law and Criminology. The Institute sought to coordinate, extend, and supplement the facilities and services of the University's departments and schools that were related to the administration of criminal law. During the 1930s and 1940s, the Institute's student enrollments grew rapidly and its research projects broadened to the point where following World War II the University transformed the Institute into the Department of Police Administration. The Department offered a four-year Bachelor of Arts degree with a certificate in Police Science.

After World War II the increase in advanced education recognizing the importance of educating the police continued to grow. In 1954, the City College of New York established a Police Science Program under the joint sponsorship of the Bernard Baruch School of Business and Public Administration and the New York City Police Department. The program was primarily a two-year program offering an Associate degree in Police Science. A graduate program leading to the Master of Public Administration with a major in Police Science was offered shortly after the undergraduate program was introduced.

The John Jay College of Criminal Justice developed out of the program at City College of New York. Although the college still serves the New York City Police Department primarily, the admission policy has been liberalized and a limited number of general students are admitted to the program. The school proudly states that it "is probably the largest and most comprehensive assemblage of criminal justice scholars and practicing professionals of any college in the world." http://www.jjay.cuny.edu/lawpolice/

Combining traditional policing and education formally began in 1967 with the *Report of the President's Commission on Law Enforcement and the Administration of Justice*. This report made the policing community confront their weaknesses and produce "better-educated police officers." Katzenbach, Nicholas deB. *United States President's Commission on Law Enforcement and Administration of Justice. Task Force on the Police.* Washington, D.C.: Govt Print Off. (1967) Specifically, the President's Commission recommended that "the ultimate aim of all police departments should be that all personnel with general enforcement powers have baccalaureate degrees," and "police departments should take immediate steps to establish a minimum requirement of a baccalaureate degree for all supervisory and executive positions."

Following this federal "encouragement" criminal justice education expanded rapidly with the availability of Law Enforcement Education Program (LEEP) funds from the Omnibus Crime Control and Safe Streets Act of 1968. Even still, there was much debate over the quality of initial education programs in the criminal justice field and there was also significant push-back from traditional law enforcement.

Later, in 1973, the National Advisory Commission on Criminal Justice Standards and Goals stated in Standard 15.1 that every police agency should no later than: 1975, require as a condition of initial employment the completion of at least 2 years of college education; 1978, require as a condition of initial employment the completion of at least 3 years of college education; and by 1982, require as a condition of initial employment the completion of at least 4 years of college education.

Since the 1970s the practice of law enforcement education and training has altered the basic framework of police departments. Legislative mandates have enforced improvements over the traditional police training curricula. As a result, despite initial concerns, many 4-year Degree programs now give academic credit for completing police academy training in some systems under transfer rules that carry 2-year students into the 4-year institutions (even though the actual number of credit hours tends to be limited).

By 1988 (in a survey of 531 law enforcement agencies with 100 or more sworn officers or serving a population of 50,000 or more) the average educational level of officers was 13.6 years. Carter,

David L. and Sapp, Allen D. *College Education and Policing: Coming of Age*. FBI Law Enforcement Bulletin (January 11, 1992) Although the minimum educational requirements for entry into the field are not increasing significantly, the competition for police employment, is.

A study published by the Police Executive Research Forum (PERF) in 1989 also reported on the state of education in the police field. Carter, David L., Sapp, Allen D., and Stephens, Darrel W. *The State of Police Education: Policy Direction for the 21st Century*. Washington, DC: Police Executive Research Forum (1989) It found that 55% of all police officers in the study had completed two years of college, as compared to 15% in 1970.

Since the 1960s the range of available law enforcement classes has grown exponentially. By the early 1960s, only about 60 educational programs existed for law enforcement in the United States. However, since the creation of the Law Enforcement Education Program (LEEP) as part of the Law Enforcement Assistance Administration of the late 1960s and early 1970s this number increased to over 750 programs available by 1977. Hoover, Larry T. *The Educational Criteria: Dilemmas and Debate in Swank, Calvin and James A. Conser. The Police Personnel System*. New York: John Wiley and Sons, Inc. (1983) Although exact data is not available it is estimated that there are about 1,000 criminal justice education programs in the United States today.

Recently, Tulsa, Oklahoma became the largest city in the nation and the only city in that state to require a baccalaureate degree for new recruits, effective January 1998. Chief Palmer states that officers with college degrees "come to you a little bit more mature, they're a little more aware of diversity issues, and they're more prone to use their minds to problem-solve than one that doesn't have that type of background... What I've seen here is that there's a world of difference between high school graduate and a college graduate in regard to skill levels and the handling of people." *Men & Women of Letters*. Law Enforcement News (November 30, 1997) Of Tulsa's 794 officers, 73% have baccalaureate degrees, and another

20% have 60 hours or more of college; 40 officers have master's degrees, three have law degrees, and one has a Ph.D. *Id.*

In 2000 the Law Enforcement Management and Administrative Statistics (LEMAS) completed a survey, their sixth, presenting information on law enforcement agencies in the United States. LEMAS found that in agencies of 100 or more sworn personnel about 25% of local agencies required some college; 10% required a degree, and only 2% required a baccalaureate degree. Reaves, Brian and Hickman, Matthew J. *Law Enforcement Management and Administrative Statistic, 2000: Data for Individual State and Local Agencies with 100 or More Officers.* Washington, DC: US Department of Justice (2004) Further, of the 49 state agencies, approximately one-third required some college; 12% required an associate degree, and 2% required a baccalaureate degree at the time of appointment. *Id.* Additionally, two states, Minnesota and Wisconsin, reported that law enforcement personnel were required by state standards to possess a minimum of an associate degree (however, in Wisconsin, an officer has up to 5 years to complete the associate degree after appointment).

One of the problems with marrying "education" and "training" is that the two have fundamentally different roles, even though they should complement each other. Education should be used as a foundation and prepare students to excel in any training regimen or philosophy or in any occupation, regardless of their academic major. The process of education is focused on obtaining the skills that are necessary to learn while training emphasizes the transfer of fact or philosophy.

While the benefits of education are obvious to many, not surprisingly there has been conflicting research on the matter. However, the general scholastic view is that on the whole an educated police force is better equipped and holds greater community respect. In his review of the literature, David Hayeslip argued that officers with higher education have superior motivation, are better able to utilize innovative techniques, display clearer thinking, have a better understanding of the world of policing, and the necessity of education in law enforcement given the role of police. Hayeslip, David W. Jr. *Higher Education and Police Performance Revisited: The Evidence Examined through Meta-Analysis.* American Journal of Police. 8(2): 49-63 (1989)

Police Training

Training at the Police Academy generally provides the recruits with more practical education than do the universities or colleges. Such training typically encompasses the basics of police work including weapons training, traffic accident reconstruction, commercial enforcement, emergency medical technician training, emergency vehicle operations, tactical riot and general law enforcement training. Generally a candidate must complete the academy before entering the police department full time as a fully accredited officer. A quick look at different law enforcement agencies reveal similar requirements of their recruits in academy training, namely that most state and municipal law enforcement agencies require approximately six months of training at their respective academies.

The New York City Police Department sends their cadets to its Academy for 26 weeks (approximately 600 hours) of classroom instruction and field instruction. This training is supplemented by another six months in the Community Patrol Officer Program under the close supervision of experienced officers.

The California Highway Patrol (CHP) Academy includes 27 weeks of training which amounts to 1,100 training hours. According to CHP the cadets are responsible for 42 "learning domains" mandated by the Commission on Peace Officer Standards and Training (POST), in addition to agency-specific policies and procedures. The CHP training information mentions that cadets must perform a 48-hour course in Emergency Medical Services, complete the Emergency Vehicle Operations Course (EVOC), and complete Weapons Training, traffic accident reconstruction, commercial enforcement, emergency medical technician, emergency vehicle operations, tactical riot and general law enforcement training.

The Washington State Patrol (WSP) has its own "Training Division" which administers all of the training programs for their employees. The "trooper cadets" attend a 26-week basic training course which is followed by eight weeks of practical instruction with experienced training officers.

In England, the Metropolitan Police Service uses the Hendon Police College as its principal training centre for recruits. The college is commonly referred to as the Peel Centre and between 2,000 and 2,500 recruits pass through the centre each year to undertake its 25-week basic training course. The training course consists of training in forensic and crime scene analysis, radio operations, driving skills, and investigations of serious crimes.

In Canada, the Royal Canadian Mounted Police (RCMP) Cadet Training Program consists of a 24-week basic training course, in both French and English. The Cadet Training Program consists of 785 hours which is divided into the following areas of study and practice: Applied Police Sciences (373 hours); Police Defensive Tactics (75 hours); Fitness and Lifestyle (45 hours); Firearms (64 hours); Police Driving (65 hours); Drill, Deportment and Tactics (48 hours) and Detachment Visits, Exams, etc (115 hours). Upon successful completion of the Cadet Training Program and employment with the RCMP, cadets must then complete a six-month Field Coaching Program under the supervision of a Field Coach.

In Australia, recruit training for the Victorian Police Department consists of 100 days of training at the Victoria Police Academy. The training is designed to provide recruits with the "knowledge, skills and confidence" to enable them to undertake on-the-job training while performing operational duties as probationary constables. The training is divided into academics and physical training. The academic subjects include law and policing procedures, communication skills, computers and keyboarding, and scenario training. The physical training includes drills, water safety, defensive tactics, firearms training, and physical education.

When it comes to DUI training for law enforcement, Lt. Scott Laird of Springettsbury Township Police and Sgt. Rod Varner of York Area

Regional Police believe the DUI training that most officer's receive is sufficient for officers to successfully detect, test and prosecute DUI cases. Hoover, Mike. *Official: Police need more DUI training.* The Evening Sun, Hanover, PA (December 3, 2008). This appears to be the party line in most police departments and organizations.

Alternatively, George Geisler, the director of law enforcement personnel at the Pennsylvania DUI Association in Harrisburg and with over 25 years in law enforcement, believes that police officers do not receive enough training. *Id.* In Geisler's jurisdiction municipal police officers get basic, standard field sobriety training but could do better with more training, according to Geisler. Municipal police officers get less than a day of DUI training at the academy while getting their certification according to Geisler and he believes that this should change. *Id.* And the debate goes on.

Standardized Field Sobriety Test Training

An imperative component of proper law enforcement training in the DUI arena is certification in standardized field sobriety testing. Typically this training is included in the police academy training. The NHTSA DUI detection and standardized field sobriety testing curriculum consists of 16 sessions that span approximately 22 hours of instruction. The training is fairly standardized but NHTSA recognizes there may be some need of flexibility in the curriculum, and as such they state that:

All of the training objectives are considered appropriate and essential for police officers who wish to become proficient at detecting evidence of DWI and at describing that evidence in written reports and verbal testimony. All of the subject matter is considered necessary to achieve those objectives. All of the learning activities are needed to ensure that the students master the subject matter. This course is "flexible" in that it can easily be expanded since it does not cover all dimensions of DWI enforcement.

SFST Instructor Manual (2006) at 7.

Further, despite the accepted flexibility in training NHTSA emphasizes that:

[V]alidation applies only when: the tests are administered in the prescribed, standardized manner; the standardized clues are used to assess the suspect's performance; and the standardized criteria are employed to interpret that performance. If any one of the standardized field sobriety test elements is changed, the validity is compromised.

SFST Student Manual (2006) at VIII-19.

After the officer is certified he/she must attend an 8 hour (16 hours for instructors) refresher course every two years. More information on the history of the standardized field sobriety testing program will be covered in Chapter 5.

Drug Recognition Expert (DRE) Training

A drug recognition expert or drug recognition evaluator (DRE) is a police officer who is trained to recognize impairment in drivers who are under the influence of drugs other than, or in addition to, alcohol. The International Association of Chiefs of Police (IACP) coordinates the International Drug Evaluation and Classification (DEC) Program with support from the National Highway Traffic Safety Administration (NHTSA) of the U.S. Department of Transportation. More information on the history of the DRE program will be covered in Chapter 5.

Training for a drug recognition expert can only be undertaken once the law enforcement officer has completed basic training and is certified in the NHTSA standardized field sobriety testing. Once these formalities are met the officer is permitted to begin the three-phase Drug Evaluation and Classification (DEC) Program, which includes three distinct phases.

Phase One: The 16-hour DRE Pre-school includes an overview of the DRE evaluation procedures, the seven drug categories, eye examinations and proficiency in conducting the SFSTs.

Phase Two: The 56-hour DRE School includes an overview of the drug evaluation procedures, expanded sessions on each drug category, drug combinations, examination of vital signs, case preparation, courtroom testimony, and Curriculum Vitae (C.V.) preparation. At the conclusion of the 7-days of training, the officer must successfully complete a written examination before moving to the third and final phase of training.

Phase Three: During this phase the candidate must complete a minimum of 12 drug evaluations under the supervision of a trained DRE instructor. Of those 12 evaluations, the officer must identify an individual under the influence of at least three of the seven drug categories and obtain a minimum 75% toxicological corroboration rate. The officer must then pass a final knowledge examination and be approved by two DRE instructors before being certified as a certified DRE.

Presently 45 states in the US, plus the District of Columbia, are participating in the program. These states are: Alaska, Arizona, Arkansas, California, Colorado, Delaware, Florida, Georgia, Hawaii, Idaho, Illinois, Indiana, Iowa, Kansas, Kentucky, Louisiana, Maine, Maryland, Massachusetts, Minnesota, Mississippi, Missouri, Montana, Nebraska, Nevada, New Hampshire, New Jersey, New Mexico, New York, North Carolina, North Dakota, South Dakota, Oklahoma, Oregon, Pennsylvania, Rhode Island, South Carolina, Tennessee, Texas, Utah, Vermont, Virginia, Washington, Wisconsin, and Wyoming.

The Advanced Roadside Impaired Driving Enforcement (ARIDE)

NHTSA has developed another training program that is designed to "bridge the gap" between the SFST training and certification and the DRE training and certification. The Advanced Roadside Impaired

Driving Enforcement (ARIDE) program was developed by NHTSA with input from the International Association of Chiefs of Police (IACP), Technical Advisory Panel (TAP), and the Virginia Association of Chiefs of Police. ARIDE was created to address the gap in training between the SFST and the Drug Evaluation and Classification (DRE/DEC) Program.

The idea behind ARIDE is that it is intended to bridge the gap between these two programs by providing officers with general knowledge related to drug impairment and by promoting the use of DREs in states that have the DEC Program. The ARIDE program focuses attention on its review and required student demonstration of the SFST proficiency requirements. Critics would argue that the SFST training program should cover this arena sufficiently enough and that this new program is potentially exposing the SFST for its lack of coverage. Additionally, the ARIDE program also stresses the importance of obtaining the most appropriate biological sample in order to identify substances likely causing impairment.

The ARIDE program involves a 16-hour training course and may be taught by DREs, DRE instructors or SFST instructors who are also DREs. The training is conducted under the control and approval of the DEC Program state coordinator. The ARIDE program was piloted in Connecticut, Kentucky, Washington and West Virginia.

CHAPTER 5

The History of DUI Investigations

*"History" is a Greek word which means, literally,
just "investigation."*
—Arnold Toynbee

The first indicator that a driver may be under the influence usually comes from an officer's observation of the individual's driving. Moreover, with limited exceptions an officer must observe driving that creates reasonable suspicion of criminal activity or otherwise violates the traffic code before making any contact with the driver. Specifically, the Supreme Court in the seminal case *Terry v. Ohio*, 392 US 1 (1968) stated that a Fourth Amendment prohibition on unreasonable searches and seizures is not violated when a police officer stops a suspect and has a reasonable suspicion that the person has committed, is committing, or is about to commit a crime. Moreover, this reasonable suspicion must be based on "specific and articulable facts" and not merely upon an officer's hunch. To that end, and again, with limited exceptions, officer's must observe specific facts that they can articulate in order to validate the stop of a person's vehicle and therefore contact with the driver.

The National Highway Traffic Safety Administration (NHTSA) has produced a pocket-size booklet intended primarily for law enforcement entitled Guide for Detecting Drunk Drivers at Night which contains a "DUI Detection Guide" that identifies, according to NHTSA, the nineteen most common and reliable initial indicators of drunk driving. http://www.nhtsa.dot.gov The booklet also indicates the probability that the driver exhibiting the symptoms is, in fact, under the influence.

The following is a list of the symptoms and their related indicia of intoxication. The corresponding number is the percentage that the driver has a blood-alcohol concentration of 0.10 percent or higher.

Turning with Wide Radius	65
Straddling Center or Lane Marker	65
Appearing to be Drunk	60
Almost Striking Object or Vehicle	60
Weaving	60
Driving on Other Than Designated Roadway	55
Swerving	55
Slow Speed (more than 10 miles per hour below limit)	50
Stopping (without cause) in Traffic Lane	50
Drifting	50
Following too closely	45
Tires on Center or Lane Marker	45
Braking Erratically	45
Driving Into Opposing or Crossing Traffic	45
Signaling Inconsistent with Driving Actions	40
Stopping Inappropriately (other than in lane)	35
Turning Abruptly or Illegally	35
Accelerating or Decelerating Rapidly	30
Headlights Off	30

Once an officer has made a lawful stop of the suspected impaired driver, or otherwise has reason to contact the driver, he then will be looking for signs of possible impairment. The initial observations of a DUI driver by an officer typically refer to the driver showing signs of suspected intoxication. These observations include odor of alcohol, slurred speech, red/watery eyes, flushed face and so on. From the beginning researchers have attempted to find a connection between the initial observations and the possible DUI driver. Bogen, Emil M.D. *The Diagnosis of Drunkenness – A Quantitative Study of Acute Alcoholic Intoxication.* California and Western Medicine: Vol. XXVI, No. 6. Los Angeles (June 1927)

In DUI cases involving alcohol, which are still the great majority, the odor of alcohol on a driver's breath is one of the first clues an officer relies upon to initially determine that a driver has been drinking. Many studies have been conducted to determine how accurate this particular observation is and no study known to this author has proven the value of alcohol detection by odor in relation to intoxication. In a 1999 study on the ability to detect alcohol use by odor, 20 officers with significant DUI experience were requeseted to detect an alcohol odor from 14 different individuals with a BAC level of between 0 and 0.13%. The individuals were hidden behind a screen and blew through a 6-inch tube while the officers attempted to detect the beverage type while they were on the other side of the screen and noses against the end of the 6 inch tube. The end result was that the officers were not able to identify what beverage type (e.g. beer, wine, bourbon or vodka) was on the subject's breath. The study also determined that the odor strength detected by the officers were unrelated to the subjects BAC levels. Moskowitz, H, Burns, M, Ferguson S. *Police Officers' Detection of Breath Odors From Alcohol Ingestion.* Accid Anal Prev. 31(3):175-180, Page 175 (May 1999)

Another common observation by police officers in DUI arrests is the observation of the driver having slurred speech. A study conducted in 2000 researched the ability for an officer to determine the degree of alcohol impairment (light, moderate and heavy drinkers) of individuals who were asked to speak during a learning phase, when sober, and at four BAC levels (3 ascending curve and one descending). The participants in the study displayed considerable changes in speech as the level of alcohol impairment increased. Importantly the study warned that these speech patterns "cannot be viewed as universal since a few subjects (about 20%) exhibited no (or negative) changes." Hollien, H., DeJong, G., Martin, C.A., Schwartz, R., Liljegre, N. K. *Effects of Ethanol Intoxication on Speech*

Suprasegmentals. J Acoust Soc Am.; 110(6):3198-3206, Page 3198. (December 2001)

Not all researchers have agreed that slurred speech or changes in speech is evidence of intoxication. While there are numerous studies that have found that impairment can be determined by slurred speech it is equally true that there are several other studies that have found the opposite. Hollien, H., Liljegren, K., Martin, C.A., DeJong G. *Production of Intoxication States by Actors—Acoustic and Temporal Characteristics.* J Forensic Sci. Jan;46(1):68-73. (January 2001); Pisoni, DB, Martin, CS. *Effects of alcohol on the acoustic-phonetic properties of speech: perceptual and acoustic analyses.* Alcohol Clin Exp Res. 13(4):577-87. (August 1989); Klingholz, F., Penning, R., Liebhardt, E., *Recognition of Low-Level Alcohol Intoxication From Speech Signal.* J Acoust Soc Am. 84(3):929-35. (September 1988)

Another observation that is typically made in an average DUI stop and arrest is that the driver's eyes are red, watery, and glassy. While this physical observation is consistently made there are no studies showing a direct correlation between red and watery eyes and intoxication.

Sobriety Checkpoints/Check Stops

One of the limited exceptions to the requirements of probable cause to stop a vehicle (the *Terry* stop) is the sobriety checkpoint. If a driver is stopped at a sobriety checkpoint in a State that permits them, no probable cause to validate such an intrusion is required.

Sobriety checkpoints, roadblocks, check stops, as they are collectively called depending on jurisdiction, involve law enforcement officials positioning themselves on a road way and stopping every vehicle, or random vehicles and investigating the possibility that the driver is under the influence of alcohol or drugs. Such check points are established late at night or in the very early morning hours, typically on weekends which is when a higher percentage of impaired drivers tend to be on the road.

The officer's task after contact with the driver is to determine whether the driver has consumed alcohol or drugs and if so whether there is suspicion of being under the influence of these substances. If the officer suspects the driver is possibly under the influence the driver will be asked to exit the vehicle and take voluntary field sobriety tests. If the driver's performance on these tests is poor he will then be required to take an alcohol breath test.

The legality of such checkpoints has been in question in the United States for some time. In these scenarios drivers are stopped and contacted without reasonable suspicion and may be tested summarily and without probable cause.

The Fourth Amendment to the United States Constitution states that:

The right of the people to be secure in their persons, houses, papers, and effects, against unreasonable searches and seizures, shall not be violated, and no Warrants shall issue, but upon probable cause, supported by Oath or affirmation, and particularly describing the place to be searched, and the persons or things to be seized.

On its face the United States Constitution appears to prohibit drivers from being stopped without a search warrant or probable cause that they have committed a criminal offense (or violated the law). The United States Supreme Court was asked to rule on this very issue in 1990 with the case *Michigan Dept. of State Police v. Sitz*, 496 U.S. 444 (1990).

The United States Supreme Court found that properly conducted sobriety checkpoints were constitutional while also concluding that such checkpoints did in fact infringe on a constitutional right. Former Chief Justice Rehnquist argued that the state interest in reducing drunk driving outweighed this infringement. *Id*. He further stated that sobriety roadblocks were effective and necessary. *Id*.

Dissenting justices argued that the Constitution doesn't provide exceptions. Justice Brennan dissented and stated "[t]hat stopping every car might make it easier to prevent drunken driving...is an insufficient justification for abandoning the requirement of individualized suspicion." *Id.* Justice Stevens also dissented stating that "the findings of the trial court, based on an extensive record and affirmed by the Michigan Court of Appeals, indicate that the net effect of sobriety checkpoints on traffic safety is infinitesimal and possibly negative." *Id.*

Despite the Unites States Supreme Court ruling not all states have agreed that sobriety checkpoints are constitutionally valid. In fact ten states have found that sobriety roadblocks violate their own state constitutions or have outlawed them (Idaho, Iowa, Michigan, Minnesota, Oregon, Rhode Island, Texas, Washington, Wisconsin, and Wyoming).

In an effort to provide standards for use by states with sobriety roadblocks NHTSA issued a report that reviewed the recommended checkpoint procedures in keeping with federal and state legal decisions. *The Use of Sobriety Checkpoints for Impaired Driving Enforcement.* DOT HS-807-656 (November 1990); National Highway Traffic Safety Administration. *Saturation Patrols and Sobriety Checkpoints Guide: A How-To Guide for Planning and Publicizing Impaired Driving Mobilizations.* Washington, DC: National Highway Traffic Safety Administration. (October 2002)

Advocates for sobriety checkpoints, most notably MADD, point to reports that have concluded that such sobriety checkpoints have value and discourage drinking and driving. For example, the Centers for Disease Control in a 2002 Traffic Injury Prevention report, found that in general the number of alcohol related crashes was reduced by 20% in states that implement sobriety checkpoints compared to those that do not. CDC Community Guide. *Effectiveness of Sobriety Checkpoints for Preventing Alcohol-Involved Crashes.* (2001); Elder, Randy, et al. *Effectiveness of Sobriety Checkpoints for Reducing Alcohol-Involved Crashes.* Traffic Injury Prevention (2002); Lacey, John, Jones, Ralph, and Smith, Randall. *Evaluation of Checkpoint Tennessee: Tennessee's Statewide Sobriety Checkpoint Program.* DOT HS 808 641. Washington, DC: National Highway Traffic Safety Administration (1999); Miller, Ted, Galbraith, M.S., and Lawrence,

B.A. *Costs and Benefits of a Community Sobriety Checkpoint Program.* Journal of Studies on Alcohol 59 (1998); Shults, Ruth, et al. *Reviews of Evidence Regarding Interventions to Reduce Alcohol-Impaired Driving.* American Journal of Preventive Medicine 21(4S) (2001); Stuster, Jack and Blowers, Paul. *Experimental Evaluation of Sobriety Checkpoint Programs.* DOT HS 808 287. Washington, DC: U.S. Department of Transportation, National Highway Safety Traffic Administration (1995)

Another report reviewed research in the area of sobriety checkpoints and concluded that reliable studies consistently demonstrate the deterrent effect of sobriety checkpoints programs. Elder, R.W., Schults, R.A., Sleet, D.A., Nichols, J.L.; Zaza, S., and Thompson, R.A.. *Effectiveness of sobriety checkpoints for reducing alcohol-involved crashes.* Traffic Injury Prevention. 3:266-74 (2002)

There have been studies that have compared the value of sobriety checkpoints and saturation patrols and have concluded that even though checkpoints may not be as efficient as saturation patrols they are still good value. A Swiss study has shown that random breath testing is cost-effective with a cost-benefit ratio estimated at 1:19. Eckardt, A, Seitz, E. *Wirtschaftliche Bewertung von Sicherheitsmassnehmen [Economic elaboration of safety measures].* Berne, Swiss Council for Accident Prevention. Report No. 35 (1998). In New South Wales, Australia, the estimated cost-benefit ratio of random breath testing ranged from 1:1 to 1:56 Arthurson, R.M. *Evaluation of random breath testing.* Sydney, New South Wales Traffic Authority. Report RN 10/85 (1985); Camkin, H.L., Webster, K.A. *Cost-effectiveness and priority ranking of road safety measures.* Roseberry, New South Wales Traffic Authority. Report RN 1/88 (1988) Similarly, economic analyses on the sobriety checkpoint programs in the US estimated benefits totaling between 6 and 23 times their original costs (153, 154) Miller, T.R., Galbraith, M.S., Lawrence, B.A. *Costs and benefits of a community sobriety checkpoint program.* Journal of Studies on Alcohol. 59:462-468 (1998)

To confuse matters there are reports that suggest that saturation patrols are preferred over sobriety checkpoints because they are more cost effective and just as efficient. An investigation in Arizona of Pima County sobriety checkpoints found that for a two year period the checkpoints in the region resulted in 46,000 drivers being stopped and checked. Gillum, Jack. *DUI checkpoints costly, catch few*. Arizona Daily Star. Tucson, AZ (August 26, 2007) Despite this great number of contacts only 0.06 % (282 people) of those stopped were arrested and only a total of 75 individuals were convicted. *Id*. According to the report the Sheriff's Department had spent $142,000, mostly in federal and state money, on 63 staffed checkpoints. *Id*.

In Kansas City a similar investigation occurred regarding the success of their checkpoint program and how well funds were allocated to this program. In 2007, 18,747 vehicles were stopped by Kansas City police at various checkpoints. Bennett, Frank, and Williams, Benita Y. *Unconstitutional? Effectiveness of sobriety checkpoints questioned*. The Kansas City Star (July 7th, 2008) The investigation revealed that only 1.6 percent of those drivers were arrested. *Id*.

The Kansas City investigation also compared the cost of checkpoints versus saturation patrols, where police drive city streets deliberately searching for vehicles that exhibit signs of possibly being driven by a DUI driver (ie. the vehicle swerving, etc). The investigation revealed that it was far more cost effective to spend tax payer money of saturation (also known as "emphasis") patrols. According to this report the saturation patrols cost $31.68 per arrest while the checkpoints cost $184.84 per arrest. *Id*.

There are even those in law enforcement who agree that saturation patrols are more effective than checkpoints. One of many examples is the sheriff's department in Ohio County, West Virginia, which have stopped doing checkpoints in favor of more saturation patrols. "I'm no big fan of them," Chief Deputy Pat Butler said about checkpoints. "They're okay for informational purposes, but I think DUI saturation patrols are much more effective." *Id*.

Eugene O'Donnell, a former prosecutor and New York City

police officer who now teaches police studies at New York's John Jay College of Criminal Justice, has been critical stating: "You could say if you catch one drunk driver out of a thousand it sends a message," O'Donnell said. "But is that (a checkpoint) really a good use of resources? ... Law enforcement is loath to acknowledge whether anything is ineffective." Id.

Even NHTSA has recognized there is room for improvement with the DUI checkpoints. In one of their studies it was found that there was a false positive rate of as high as 54% for alcohol-free drivers at sobriety checkpoints. Compton, R. *Pilot Test for Selected DWI Detection Procedures for use at Sobriety Checkpoints*. NHTSA. Final Report. DOT-HS-806-724 (1985).

DUI checkpoints will undoubtedly remain a hotly contested issue in the DUI realm. This is particularly interesting considering the fact that law enforcement generally favors them, the US Supreme Court has ruled them constitutional, and MADD aggressively advocates for their inclusion in every state. The bigger debate however, may be whether they are a good use of taxpayers dollars and how ultimately successful they really are.

Field Sobriety Tests

Once the driver has been detained and there is suspicion of DUI, the officer must then utilize tools to further detect indicators of impairment. Field sobriety tests have been used throughout the past century by police officers to help them assess whether an individual is too impaired to drive an automobile. Initially these tests were not very sophisticated and included the smell of alcohol on the breath, the ability of a person to walk a chalk line, and various behavioral signs and symptoms of inebriation. Prior to NHTSA standardizing field sobriety tests in the 1980s, such tests in the United States had little consistency, no standardization, and as a result questionable reliability: "[b]ecause of the inconsistencies in the experimental procedures and approaches used by investigators, few generalizations regarding the influence of alcohol on performance can be advanced." *The Effect of Alcohol on Human Performance: A Classification and Integration of Research Findings.* American Institutes for Research. Page iv. (May 1973) Moreover, until the late 1970s very few studies had been undertaken by American researchers in this area. However, there were studies completed in other countries that evaluated the value and reliability of certain field sobriety testing and detecting alcohol intoxication.

In Denmark the Danish Medico-Legal Council outlined the 15 sobriety tests that were required for DUI processing, including pulse, gait, steadiness of the hands, appearance of the eyes, pupils (size, response to light), smell of spirits from mouth, appearance (dull, sleepy, heavy eyelids), speech, manners, orientation as regards to place, year, date and hour, ability of remembering, counting backwards with at least 30 numbers, descriptive power and memory, the opinion of examined person himself as to his condition and its connection with consumption of spirits, and handwriting. Andresen, P.H. *Traffic and Alcohol.* Medico-Legal Journal. 18:98 (1950)

In the 1950s a number of studies were performed that examined driving performance after consumption of alcohol. A study in 1958 examined the effect of alcohol on the ability of experienced bus drivers to drive between posts. Cohen, J., Dearnalcy, B.J. and Hantsel, C.M.M. *The risk taken in driving under the influence of alcohol.* Brit. Med. J. (1958). The researchers found that performance was affected by very small amounts of alcohol and that performance deteriorated as the amount of alcohol taken was increased. Similar studies and results were achieved by Bjerver and Goldberg in 1951, Gelia and Wretmark in 1951, and Coldwell et al in 1958. Bjerver, K. and Goldberg, L. *Effect of alcohol ingestion on driving ability.* Quarterly Journal of Studies on Alcohol. (1951); Gelia, L.E. and Wretmark, S. R. and Fisher, R. S. *Alcohol and highway fatalities.* J. Forensic Sci. 3, 65 (1957); Coldwell, B. B., Penner, D.W., Smith, H.W., Lucas, G.H.W., Rodgers, R. F., and Darroch, F. *Effect of ingestion of distilled spirits on automobile driving skills.* Quarterly Journal of Studies on Alcohol. 19(4). 590-617 (1958) These studies collectively concluded that drivers with BACs as low as 0.02 to 0.03

may make more mistakes and their driving performance may be adversely affected.

The initial NHTSA study in 1977 referenced a previous and related study in Finland and commented on its importance and value. The Finnish study was thought to be the most comprehensive and rigorous investigation at that time, largely due to the fact that sobriety testing was critical in Finland because there was no statutory blood alcohol limit. Like the NHTSA studies that followed, the earlier Finnish study was heavily scrutinized. Pentillä, A., Tenhu, M., and Kataja, M. *Clinical Examination for Intoxication in Cases of Suspected Drunken Driving, An Evaluation of the Finnish System on the Basis of 6,839 Cases.* Statistical & Research Bureau of Talja. Finland (June 15, 1971)

In the Finnish study the researchers analyzed records from 6,839 clinical examinations for intoxication which were executed at the Department of Forensic Medicine, University of Helsinki from 1965-1969. The testing of these subjects included the following: walking tests, gait in turning, Romberg tests, finger to finger test, match test, speech and behavior, counting backwards, and orientation to time and place. According to the Finnish researchers they found connections for all tests with blood alcohol levels however they also found that there was significant overdiagnosis of intoxication due to unreliable performance of the tests at low blood alcohol content (BAC). The researchers concluded that improvement in the reliability could be achieved by "...carefully defining what constitutes a state of intoxication on the basis of all the clinical tests and observations." *Id.* at 40

Following the initial study the same Finnish investigators embarked on a second project in 1974 that used data compiled from 495 clinical examinations in an effort to configure an optimal set of field sobriety tests. Penttilä, A, Tenhu and M, Kataja, M. *Reports from Liikenneturva, Central Organization for Traffic Safety in Finland.* (1974)

Although the tests in the second study were largely the same there was one important change, that being the inclusion of three measures of nystagmus. According to the researchers of this second Finnish study the additional nystagmus measures added to this study were determined to be the most valuable indicators of intoxication. *Id.* Following the nystagmus findings the other tests determined to be of value were, in decreasing order of value: walking along a line, walking test with eyes closed, Romberg's test with eyes open, collecting small objects test, counting backwards test, orientations as to time, finger-finger test, and gait in turning. The study concluded that tests which were based exclusively on a doctors' estimation of intoxication were of no value. *Id.*

In addition to the sobriety tests that were studied in Finland in the early 1970s, there was another study ongoing in New Zealand. At that time any driver in New Zealand who was suspected of driving under the influence was given a medical examination. To assist in this process, researchers developed a clinical examination that consisted entirely of eye signs of alcohol intoxication. Simpson-Crawford, T., and Slater, S.W. *Eye signs in suspected drinking drivers: clinical examination and relation to blood alcohol.* N Z Med J. (1971) The six point "oculiser scale" included: (1) conjuctivae are suffused (i.e., "bloodshot" eyes); (2) the eyelids drag behind when the eyeball moves up and down; (3) the pupillary light reflex is slowed; (4) peripheral vision is diminished; (5) nystagmus is seen when the eyes follow a moving object; and (6) the pupils tend to be dilated.

Even though field sobriety tests existed and were regularly practiced in the United States and other countries, there was no consistency with the instruction and no validation of their reliability. In the detection of a possible DUI driver the use of non-standardized field sobriety tests therefore lead to substandard reliability and poor credibility in the court system. As a result, the Southern California Research Institute was commissioned by NHTSA in June of 1975 to study and evaluate the "field sobriety tests" that were currently being used by field officers. Armed with a battery of previous studies and their vision of the validity of some field testing, the study was designed to determine the accuracy of the tests regarding their alcohol sensitivity and evaluate a more sensitive and reliable battery of tests. This first study reportedly cost between one hundred and two hundred thousand dollars. The goal of the study was to finally "standardize" the administration of "field sobriety tests." The Research Institute was focused on developing physical coordination tests connected with DUI investigations to evaluate their relationship to intoxication and possibly driving impairment. The idea behind standardizing alcohol-sensitive tests would be to provide more reliable and consistent physical evidence in the field. Burns, Marcelline and Moskowitz. *The result was Psycho-Physical Tests for DWI Arrests.* DOT HS 802 424 (June 1977).

The researchers compiled a list of sixteen possible tests to consider, including but not limited to the Romberg balance, one leg stand, finger to nose, walk and turn, AGN, and finger count/finger dexterity, tracing, subtraction, counting backwards, and letter cancellation. In an attempt to make the chosen tests more reliable and objective the researchers worked at developing a "test battery" which would, in theory, provide some level of statistically valid and reliable indicators that a participant's breath alcohol concentration (BAC) level was at or above 0.10, rather than simply an indication of driver impairment. Stuster & Burns. *Validation of the Standardized Field Sobriety Test Battery at BAC's Below 0.10 Percent, DOTHS.* Page 28 (August, 1998)

Along the way tests were removed from contention due to their inability to be alcohol sensitive. What resulted was a pilot program that studied a six test battery that included the one leg stand, walk and turn, finger to nose, finger count, Gaze Nystagmus and tracing. There were also three alternative tests which were the Romberg balance, subtraction, counting backwards and letter cancellation. The study suggested that after review of this assortment of tests that it was not realistic to attempt to use behavioral tests to determine BAC's in a plus/minus 0.02 margin of error (based on the BAC level of 0.10 percent) or the inaccuracy when testing individuals whose BAC level was less than 0.10 percent. *Id.* According to the authors the tests were tweaked and the results were a three test battery that included the Gaze Nystagmus, the one leg stand and walk and turn test. The research concluded in 1981 and the standardization of field sobriety testing was complete. Tharp, Burns & Moskowitz. *Development and Field Tests of Psycho-Physical Tests for DWI Arrests.* DOTHS 805 864 (March 1981) The authors defined a standardized test as "[o]ne which the procedures, apparatus and scoring have been fixed so that precisely the same testing procedures can be followed at different times and locations." *Id.* at 3.

The work for the authors continued after the decision to limit the standardized field sobriety tests (SFSTs) to the aforementioned three. The three SFSTs now needed to be refined so that they could be used in a DUI setting. This refinement included standardizing the administration and scoring procedures for the three SFSTs. Tharp, Burns & Moskowitz. *Development and Field Tests for DWI Arrests.* DOTHS 805 864 (March 1981)

The 1981 study concluded that the Gaze Nystagmus could correctly identify participants at or above a BAC of 0.10 seventy-seven percent (77%) of the time, that the walk and turn test could correctly identify participants as being at or above a BAC of 0.10 sixty-eight percent (68%) of the time and the one leg stand test could correctly identify participants at or above a BAC of 0.10 sixty-five percent (65%) of the time. Further, the study stated that when the results of the Gaze Nystagmus with the walk and turn test were combined, they could accurately identify a person at or above a BAC of 0.10 level eighty percent (80%) of the time. Not to be forgotten, the authors also noted a 32% false arrest rate in the overall statistics.

Another NHTSA commissioned study was conducted in 1983. This study was to standardize practical and effective procedures for police officers to use in reaching a decision regarding the arrest of a possible DUI driver. Anderson, Schweitz & Snyder. *Field Evaluation of Behavioral Test Battery for DWI.* DOTHS 806 475 (September 1983) The results of this study echoed the statistical results of the laboratory testing summarized in 1981 by Tharp, Burns and Moskowitz in *Development and Field Tests for DWI Arrest.*

NHTSA funded yet another study to validate the SFSTs. A study conducted in Colorado in 1995 was commissioned to examine the results of arrests from seven Colorado law enforcement agencies. Burns and Anderson. *A Colorado Validation Study of the Standardized Field Sobriety Test (SFST) Battery* (1995) In this study officers were told to identify drivers who had a BAC over 0.05% (between 0.05%-0.099%) and also drivers who had a BAC over 0.10%. The study found that officers were 86% correct in their determination to arrest or release a motorist. *Id.*

In 1997 a similar SFST study was conducted in Florida. Of the 256 drivers who were studied, fifty had a BAC under 0.08 % and 206 had a BAC above a 0.08%. The study determined that of the 50 drivers with a BAC under a 0.08%, 9 were incorrectly determined to be above the legal limit, and 41 were correctly determined to be below the legal limit. The study concluded that more than 95% of the Officer's arrest decisions were correct. Burns, Marcelline Ph.D and Dioquino, Teresa. *A Florida Validation Study of the Standardized Field Sobriety Test (SFST) Battery* (1997)

In 1998 yet another study of SFSTs was conducted, this one with the San Diego Police Department in California. The research study was compiled by Anacapa Sciences, Inc., who published a final report that was submitted to the DOT and NHTSA covering the validation of the SFSTs at levels below a 0.10%. This study differed slightly from previous studies and was designed to prove that SFSTs were valid in discriminating between subjects who were below a 0.08% (or 0.10%) from those who were above.

The participating SFST-certified officers from the San Diego Police Department received a 4-hour refresher training class prior to the start of the field study. Stuster, J. and Burns, Marcelline Ph.D. *Validation Study of the Standardized Field Sobriety Test Battery below 0.10 percent* (1998) The study claimed that the officer's arrest decisions were accurate in 91% of the 297 cases, and 90% of the cases in which the BAC was estimated to be below a 0.08%.

These studies have had their critics who have complained that the results and data sections of the study were missing, that the data was generated by "volunteer" officers (hence a possible bias), that there was no actual monitoring of the data (the officers merely reported their results), and lastly the results of the study are unclear because two different arrest standards were used for .05 to 0.10 BAC and another for a BAC above 0.10.

Once the SFSTs became accepted in the policing community it became clear that the accuracy of these tests had to be monitored and reviewed. To that end the National Highway Traffic Safety Institute commissioned Jack Stuster and Marcelline Burns to review the accuracy of these tests in assisting officers in making arrest decisions for DUI at alcohol concentrations below 0.10 percent. Stuster and Burns submitted their findings to NHTSA. *Id.* The report noted:

> During the past sixteen years, NHTSA's SFSTs largely have replaced the invalidated performance tests of unknown merit that once were the patrol officers only tools in helping to make post-stop DWI arrest decisions. Regional and local preferences for other performance tests still exist, even though some of the tests have never been validated. Despite regional differences and what tests are used to assist officers in making DWI arrest decisions, NHTSA's SFSTs presently are used in all 50 states. NHTSA's SFSTs have become the standard pre-arrest procedures for evaluating DWI in most law enforcement agencies. *Id. at 3.*

NHTSA first published SFSTs manuals to be used by law enforcement agencies in 1981, with revisions to the originals in 1992 (PB 94-780228 Student Manual, PB 94-780210 Instructor Manual), 1995 (AVA-19911BB00 Student Manual, AVA-19910BB00 Instructor Manual) 2000 (AVA-20839BB00 Student Manual, AVA-20838BB00 Instructor Manual), 2002 (AVA-21135BB00 Student Manual, AVA-21134BB00 Instructor Manual), 2004 (Participant and Instructor Manuals, HS 178 R9/04), and most recently in 2006 (Student and Instructor Manuals, HS 178 R2/06). The result was a battery of three standardized field sobriety tests, namely, the horizontal gaze nystagmus (HGN), the walk and turn test, and the one-leg stand.

Horizontal Gaze Nystagmus (HGN)

The technical definition of nystagmus is that it is the rhythmic back and forth oscillation of the eyeball that occurs when there is a disturbance of the vestibular (inner ear) system or the oculomotor control of the eye. Although techniques for accurately measuring nystagmus were developed in the 20th century, nystagmus was positively linked to vestibular stimulation as early as the 19th century. Tatler, BW, Wade, NJ. *On nystagmus, saccades, and fixations.* Perception. 32(2):167-184, Page 167 (2003)

There are two major types of eye movements: pendular and jerk. Pendular nystagmus is where the oscillation speed is the same in both directions. Jerk nystagmus is where the eye moves slowly in one direction and then returns rapidly. Most types of nystagmus have the fast and slow phase (jerk nystagmus). Horizontal Gaze Nystagmus (HGN), which is the type of nystagmus used in DUI investigations, is a type of jerk nystagmus with the jerky movement toward the direction of the gaze. Adams, Raymond D. & Victor, Maurice. *Disorders of Ocular Movement and Pupillary Function.* Principles of Neurology. Ch.13, 117 (4th ed. 1991)

Like most types of nystagmus, HGN is an involuntary motion, meaning the person exhibiting the nystagmus cannot control it or is even aware of it. Forkiotis, C.J. *Optometric Exercise: The Scientific Basis for Alcohol Gaze Nystagmus.* 59 Curriculum II, No. 7 at 9 (April 1987); Good, Gregory W. & Augsburger, Arol R. *Use of Horizontal Gaze Nystagmus as a Part of Roadside Sobriety Testing.* 63 Am. J. of Optometry & Physiological Optics 467, 469 (1986); Stapleton, June M. et al. *Effects of Alcohol and Other Psychotropic Drugs on Eye Movements: Relevance to Traffic Safety.* 47 Q.J. Stud. on Alcohol 426, 430 (1986)

Critics of the horizontal gaze nystagmus test for DUI (alcohol) related purposes have argued that alcohol is not the only potential cause of nystagmus and in fact there are many different causes of nystagmus that have been observed and studied. Syndromes such as influenza, vertigo, epilepsy, measles, syphilis, arteriosclerosis, muscular dystrophy, multiple sclerosis, Korsakoff's Syndrome, brain hemorrhage, streptococcus infections, and other psychogenic disorders all have been shown to produce nystagmus. Additionally, conditions such as hypertension, motion sickness, sunstroke, eyestrain, eye muscle fatigue, glaucoma, and changes in atmospheric pressure may result in gaze nystagmus. Pangman. *Horizontal Gaze Nystagmus: Voodoo Science.* 2 DWI J. 1, 3-4 (1987)

Further, these same critics have argued that alcohol is not the only drug to cause nystagmus and that caffeine, nicotine, or aspirin also lead to nystagmus almost identical to that caused by alcohol consumption. *Id.* at 3-4. Additionally, conditions such as a person's circadian rhythms or biorhythms may affect nystagmus readings as the body reacts differently to alcohol at different times in the day. Finally, even "fatigue nystagmus" can be found in an individual but may be mistakenly interpreted as nystagmus caused by alcohol consumption. *Id.* at 3-4; Booker, J.L. *End-position nystagmus as an indicator of ethanol intoxication.* Sci Justice. 41(2):113-116. (April – June, 2001)

Walk and Turn

The walk and turn test is a "divided attention" test that is designed to determine the subject's balance, listening skills, and ability to follow instructions. In this test the participant stands in a heel-to-toe fashion with arms at their sides while a series of instructions are given by the officer. Following the instructional phase the suspect must then take nine heel-to-toe steps along a line, turn in a prescribed manner, and then take another nine heel-to-toe steps along the line, returning to the original position. All of this must be done while counting the steps aloud and keeping the arms at the sides. The individual is informed not to stop walking until the test is completed.

NHTSA warns the officer that this test requires a "designated straight line and should be conducted on a reasonably dry, hard, level, non-slippery surface." *DWI Detection and Standardized Field*

Sobriety Testing, Student Manual. NHTSA; U.S. Department of Transportation. HS 178 R2/00, Page VIII-12 (2000) Additionly, the officer is informed in the manual that original research indicated that individuals over the age of 65, and those with back, leg or middle ear problems had difficulty performing the test. Subjects wearing heels more than 2 inches high should be given the opportunity to remove their shoes. *Id.* Over the years however, some of the original instructions and provided information has been deleted from subsequent student manuals.

One Leg Stand

The one leg stand test, like the walk and turn field sobriety test, is a divided attention test that is designed to determine the subject's balance, listening skills, and ability to follow instructions. In this test the participant is required to stand on one leg while the other leg is extended in front of the person in a "stiff-leg" manner. This extended foot is to be held approximately six inches above and parallel with the ground. While this is occuring the person is instructed to stare at the elevated foot and count aloud until told to stop, by counting "one thousand and one, one thousand and two, one thousand and three," and so on.

Also like the walk and turn test this test requires a "reasonably dry, hard, level, and non-slippery surface." *DWI Detection and Standardized Field Sobriety Testing, Student Manual.* NHTSA; U.S. Department of Transportation. HS 178 R2/00, Page VIII-12 (2000) Further, the officer has knowledge that original research indicated that individuals over the age of 65, and those with back, leg or middle ear problems had difficulty performing the test. Subjects wearing heels more than 2 inches high should be given the opportunity to remove their shoes. *Id.*

General Criticisms of SFSTs

Proponents of these studies conclude that the standardization of FSTs has produced more accurate and reliable determination of possible DUI drivers. However, there have been many critics. The NHTSA studies are not peer-reviewed, thereby skipping an important review of the study itself. The peer review process enables other scientists to critique the experimental method and conclusions reached by the article's author(s). Research studies design and criterion must also meet generally acceptable scientific standards. To wit, a study such as the ones conducted to test SFSTs must include a control group and eliminate variables that can distort results. The tests relied on by NHTSA fail to do this according to NHTSA's critics.

While it is safe to assume that much of the criticism has come from criminal defense attorneys, criticism has also been scholarly. Many believe that the SFSTs are over simplified and can only relatively accurately determine that an individual's BAC is above 0.08% in cases where the actual BAC is extreme. One such critic is University of Washington professor Michael Hlastala, who states: "In the current framework, the test scores have to be quite high to provide confidence that the subject is above 0.08%, but further development could potentially improve confidence in the three test results, both singly and in combination." Hlastala, Michael P. Ph.D.; Polissar, Nayak L. Ph.D.; and Oberman, Steven J.D. *Statistical Evaluation of Standardized Field Sobriety Tests.* J Forensic Sci. Vol. 50, No. 3. Page 7 (May 2005) Further, "[t]he use of a single test performance statistic, accuracy, and the calculation of this one statistic for the entire study sample is an over-simplification of the more complex relationship between the SFST score and the MBAC level." *Id.* Hlastala also believes that "[i]t is likely that the usefulness of SFSTs will be greatest for drivers who have high-test scores."

Another criticism of the SFSTs is that they cannot be considered reliable until the mean and standard deviation of normal performance is established. Interestingly no controlled (NHTSA sponsored) studies have been completed to determine the normal range of SFST performance for sober individuals. However, there is one study that examined the concept that normal, sober individuals may be considered impaired based either on field sobriety tests or normal abilities tests. In the study, 21 sober participants (between 21-55 years of age, no known physical disabilities, and of normal weight) were videotaped while performing field sobriety tests and fourteen police officers were assigned to view their performance. Cole, S., Nowaczyk, R. *Field Sobriety Tests: Are they Designed for Failure?* Percept Mot. Skills. Page 79 (1994)

After examining the performances, the officers in the study were asked to determine if the participant was impaired. Forty-six percent of the officers declared that a sober participant in the study had "too much to drink" based on the FST performance. In this study, only 3 participants were determined to be sober by all officers, although every one of the participants was in fact, sober. *Id.*

Other arguments against the validity of the SFSTs come from those who believe that these tests do not and cannot prove that the subject was driving under the influence. Importantly no individual from NHTSA, DOT, or the NHTSA-commissioned researchers have ever claimed that the SFSTs are direct indicators of actual driving impairment. Stuster and Burns recognized the limitations and stated:

"[d]riving a motor vehicle is a very complex activity that involves a wide variety of tasks and operator capabilities. It is unlikely that complex human performance, such as that required to safely drive an automobile, can be measured at roadside. The constraints imposed by roadside testing conditions were recognized by the developers of NHTSA's SFST battery. As a consequence, they pursued the development of tests that would provide statistically valid and reliable indications of a driver's BAC, rather than indications of driving impairment. Stuster, Jack and Burn, Marcelline. *Validation of the Standardized Field Sobriety Test Battery at BACs Below .10 Percent.* DOT-HS-808-839 6. Page 28 (1998)

Another study declared that "even valid, behavioral tests are likely to be poor predictors either of actual behind-the-wheel driving." Snapper, K.J., Seaver, D.A.., Schwartz, J.P. *An Assessment of Behavioral Tests to Detect Impaired Drivers.* Final Report, DOT-HS-806-211. Pages 2-7 (1981)

Critics of the standardized field sobriety tests also included some within law enforcement. The California Highway Patrol criticizes the SFSTs and its Manual states that the "HGN is not a psychophysical test. The clues associated with HGN are not designed to be considered 'signs of impairment.'" Department of California Highway Patrol. *Driving Under the Influence Enforcement Manual.* Pages 2-12 (1995)

Critics have argued that the SFSTs are not nearly as reliable as the studies allege, that officers do not always comply with the SFST procedures, the HGN measurement is not always exact, the reliability claims of the studies were misleading, the officers in the studies were more experienced than the average officer (and these same officers were given a refresher course immediately prior to testing), and so on. Cole, S., Kulis, I., Nawaczyk, R., *NHTSA and FSTs: True Lies and False Advertising.* DWI Journal, Law & Science. 12:3. Pages 1-8. (March 1977). NHTSA attempts to address the issue of compliance with protocol by stating that "[i]f any one of the standardized field sobriety test elements is changed, the validity is compromised." NHTSA, U.S. Department of Transportation. HS 178 R2/00. *DWI Detection and Standardized Field Sobriety Testing, Student Manual.* Page VIII-3 (2000). However, critics still argue that very few of the SFSTs conducted by police officers in the field are in exact accordance with NHTSA rules. Booker JL. *End-position nystagmus as an indicator of ethanol intoxication.* Sci Justice. 41(2):113-116. Page 113 (April-June 2001)

Non-Standard Field Sobriety Tests

While the standardized field sobriety tests are now common place and regularly practiced by law enforcement when investigating a possible DUI driver, the non-standardized field sobriety tests are still used on a regular basis. Obviously the validity of these tests remain questionable.

Romberg Test

Of all the field sobriety tests that are non-standardized the best known and most commonly used is the Romberg Test. A German ear specialist by the name of Moritz Heinrich Romberg developed a balance assessment test in 1853 that could be used to diagnose diseases. This test is known as the "Romberg Test" and is widely used as a non-specific test of neurological or inner ear dysfunction. The Romberg Test has been modified for use by police officers in the performance of Field Sobriety Tests although this test is not a standardized Field Sobriety Test.

The Romberg Test is a neurological test to determine whether a subject can keep a steady standing position with the eyes closed. The basic test has an individual stand with his feet together, hands at his side, head tilted back, and eyes closed. The basic test has developed into several different variations. These different versions are commonly referred to as the "Sharpened" Romberg or the "Modified Position of Attention."

While there have been no studies validating the Romberg test in the DUI context, a number of studies have been conducted concluding that the Romberg Test when performed in the law enforcement environment is unreliable. ImObersteg, A. *The Romberg Balance Test: Differentiating Normal Sway from Alcohol-Induced Sway.* DWI Journal, Law & Science, Vol. 18, No. 5 (May, 2003) Additionally, studies have found that the increased sway found in testing can relate to things other than alcohol intoxication, such as weight, age, physical condition, exercise, sleep loss, elevated temperatures, and antihistamines. Anderson, Theodore E. et al. *Field Evaluation of a Behavioral Test Battery for DWI.* DOT-HS-806-475 (1983)

Finger to Nose

Another commonly used non-standardized field sobriety test is the finger to nose test. This test is a basic test that requires the subject to close his eyes and then touch the tip of his nose with the tip of his index finger, alternating hands. NHTSA research and studies revealed that the finger to nose test, along with the Rhomberg Test, only indicated the presence of alcohol, and "did not increase the predictive ability of testing." Sworn Testimony of Marcelline Burns in *State v. Meador*, 674 So. 2d 826, 834 (Fla. Dist. Ct. App. 1996)

Alphabet, Count Down, and Finger Count Tests

Other non-standardized field sobriety tests that are often used are the alphabet recitation, a numerical count down, and finger count tests. The alphabet test requires the subject to recite part of the alphabet (e.g., starting at a letter other than A and stopping at a letter other than Z). The count down test simply requires the subject to count aloud numbers in reverse, from highest to lowest, for example, counting backwards from 50 to 30. The finger count test requires the subject to touch the tip of the thumb to the tip of each finger on the same hand in a particular order while counting (e.g., "one, two, three, four—four, three, two, one).

These tests were considered in the initial NHTSA study in 1977 but were discarded and therefore not selected as accurate indicators of alcohol impairment. The Standardized Field Sobriety Test (SFST) Student Manual warns that these techniques are not as reliable as the SFST tests and "do not replace the SFST." NHTSA, U.S. Department of Transportation, HS 178 R2/00. *DWI Detection and Standardized Field Sobriety Testing, Student Manual.* Page VI-4 (2000)

Handwriting

Another test that is not often done by law enforcement but is occasionally used by prosecuting attorneys to indicate possible impairment is handwriting. In 2003 a researcher studied the effects of alcohol on handwriting by taking handwriting samples from 73 individuals before and after the consumption of alcohol. These samples were then evaluated under a microscope, with direct and oblique angle lighting and a video spectral comparator. The study indicates that alterations of handwriting parameters (e.g., height of upper and lower case letters, number of angularity, and number of tapered ends) increased under the effect of alcohol. The researchers concluded that handwriting changes can be observed at any level of alcohol. However, "none of the alterations in handwriting can be attributed to the effects of alcohol intake alone." Asicioglu, F, Turan, N. *Handwriting Changes Under the Effect of Alcohol. Forensic* Sci Int. 8;132(3):201-210. Page 201 (April 2003)

In an earlier study subjects provided a writing sample and provided their signature before comsuming alcohol and then again after they had BACs of over 0.12%. According to the study the average percentage of correct determinations between handwriting before and handwriting after alcohol consumption was 83.7% for sentences and 67.5% for signatures. Geller, ES, Clarke, SW, Kalsher, MJ. *Knowing When to Say When: A Simple Assessment of Alcohol Impairment.* J Appl Behav Anal. 24(1):65-72 (Spring 1991)

However, yet another study seems to dispel the validity of alcohol impairment and hand writing. The researchers concluded that handwriting could not be used in any way to measure accurately the blood alcohol concentration of a writer. Galbraith, NG. *Alcohol: Its Effect on Handwriting.* J Forensic Sci. 31(2):580-588. Page 580 (April 1986)

In summary, there is not a scientific study that has indicated that such a handwriting test has ever been evaluated for reliability as a "sobriety test" to determine alcohol influence or impairment.

Drug Recognition Experts (DRE) History and Development

A drug recognition expert or drug recognition evaluator (DRE) is a police officer who is trained to recognize impairment in drivers who are under the influence of drugs other than, or in addition to, alcohol. The International Association of Chiefs of Police (IACP) coordinates the International Drug Evaluation and Classification (DEC) Program with support from the National Highway Traffic Safety Administration (NHTSA) of the U.S. Department of Transportation.

The Los Angeles Police Department (LAPD) originated the DRE program in the early 1970s after LAPD officers noticed that many of the individuals arrested for driving under the influence had very low or zero alcohol concentrations. The officers suspected that the arrestees were under the influence of drugs but lacked the knowledge and skills to support their suspicions. As a result two LAPD sergeants collaborated with various medical doctors, research psychologists, and other medical professionals to develop a simple, standardized procedure for recognizing drug influence and impairment. Their efforts culminated in the development of a multi-step protocol and the first DRE program. The LAPD formally recognized the program in 1979.

In the early 1980s NHTSA started to take notice of the LAPD DRE. The two agencies worked together to develop a standardized DRE protocol, which led to the development of the DEC Program. During the ensuing years, NHTSA and various other agencies and research groups examined the DEC program and their studies attempted to demonstrate that a properly trained DRE can successfully identify drug impairment and accurately determine the category of drugs causing such impairment.

The development of the DRE program continued and in 1987 NHTSA initiated DEC pilot programs in Arizona, Colorado, New York and Virginia, followed by Utah, California, and Indiana in 1988. Beginning in 1989, IACP and NHTSA expanded the DEC Program across the country and currently 43 states, the District of Columbia, three branches of the military, the Internal Revenue Service (IRS), and several countries around the world participate in the DEC Program.

The governing board of the International Association of Chiefs of Police (IACP) approved the creation of the Drug Recognition Section in 1992. In 1995, IACP hosted a training conference on impaired driving in Phoenix, Arizona and since that year the IACP

Training Conference on Drugs, Alcohol and Impaired Driving has convened annually and is attended by DREs and their instructors, DUI enforcement officers, prosecutors, toxicologists, medical and school professionals, and other highway safety advocates.

The DRE protocol is, according to the literature, a standardized and systematic method of examining a Driving Under the Influence of Drugs (DUID) suspect to determine whether or not he is impaired and, if so, whether the impairment relates to drugs or a medical condition. Lastly, if the impairment is due to drugs, the DRE attempts to determine what category or combination of categories of drugs are the likely causes of the impairment. The advocates of the DRE process believe that the program is designed to be systematic because it is based on a set of observable signs and symptoms that are known, according to the program, to be reliable indicators of drug impairment.

The idea of the DRE evaluation is that a conclusion of drug impairment is not based on one particular element but instead on the totality of facts that emerge from the evaluation. Like the SFST program from NHTSA, the DRE evaluation is standardized because it is supposed to be conducted the same way, by every drug recognition expert, for every suspect whenever possible. Standardization, in theory, is important because it makes the officers better observers, helps to avoid errors, and promotes professionalism. Naturally this assumes that every DRE is done in exact accordance with the protocol outlined below. The DRE process is also being utilized by law enforcement in Canada and Australia, in addition to the United States.

Arguments against validating drug recognition experts are many and begin with the simple fact that DREs are not medically trained professionals and therefore cannot render a judgment of an individual's impairment based on the criterion provided. Further, the DRE program is usually taught by other law enforcement personnel and not by medical professionals.

Critics have also argued that the program and studies supporting the program are not peer reviewed. "Peer review, in which experts in the field scrutinize and critique scientific results prior to publication, is fundamental to scientific progress." Alberts, et. Al. *Reviewing Peer Review.* 321 Science 15 (2008) Because no such peer review exists in the DRE field, it therefore remains subject to critique.

The 12-Step DRE Protocol

The DREs utilize a 12-step process in reviewing potential drivers under the influence of drugs. The 12-step process usually requires approximately 30-45 minutes to complete however, the evaluation can take longer depending on the drug ingested. These twelve steps include the following:

1. *Breath Alcohol Test:* The arresting officer reviews the subject's breath alcohol concentration (BAC) test results and determines if the subject's apparent impairment is consistent with the subject's BAC. If so, the officer will not normally call a DRE. If the impairment is not explained by the BAC, the officer requests a DRE evaluation.

2. *Interview of the Arresting Officer:* The DRE begins the investigation by reviewing the BAC test results and discussing the circumstances of the arrest with the arresting officer, if he was not the arresting officer. The DRE asks about the subject's behavior, appearance, and driving. The DRE also asks if the subject made any statements regarding drug use and if the arresting officer(s) found any other relevant evidence consistent with drug use.

3. *Preliminary Examination and First Pulse:* The DRE conducts a preliminary examination to determine whether the subject may be suffering from an injury or other condition unrelated to drugs. Accordingly, the DRE asks the subject a series of standard questions relating to the subject's health and recent ingestion of food, alcohol and drugs, including prescribed medications. The DRE observes the subject's attitude, coordination, speech, breath and face. The DRE also determines if the subject's pupils

are of equal size and if the subject's eyes can follow a moving stimulus and track equally. The DRE also looks for horizontal gaze nystagmus (HGN) and takes the subject's pulse for the first of three times. The DRE takes each subject's pulse three times to account for nervousness, check for consistency and determine if the subject is getting worse or better. If the DRE believes that the subject **may** be suffering from a significant medical condition, the DRE will seek medical assistance immediately. If the DRE believes that the subject's condition is drug-related, the evaluation continues.

4. *Eye Examination:* The DRE examines the subject for HGN, vertical gaze Nystagmus (VGN) and for a lack of ocular convergence. A subject lacks convergence if his eyes are unable to converge toward the bridge of his nose when a stimulus is moved inward. Depressants, inhalants, and dissociative anesthetics, the so-called "DID drugs", may cause HGN. In addition, the DID drugs may cause VGN when taken in higher doses for that individual. DID drugs, as well as cannabis (marijuana), may also cause a lack of convergence.

5. *Divided Attention Psychophysical Tests:* The DRE administers four psychophysical tests: the Romberg Balance, the Walk and Turn, the One Leg Stand, and the Finger to Nose tests. The DRE can accurately determine if a subject's psychomotor and/ or divided attention skills are impaired by administering these tests.

6. *Vital Signs and Second Pulse:* The DRE takes the subject's blood pressure, temperature and pulse. Some drug categories may elevate the vital signs. Others may lower them. Vital signs provide valuable evidence of the presence and influence of a variety of drugs.

7. *Dark Room Examinations:* The DRE estimates the subject's pupil sizes under three different lighting conditions with a measuring device called a pupilometer. The device will assist the DRE in determining whether the subject's pupils are dilated, constricted, or normal. Some drugs increase pupil

size (dilate), while others may decrease (constrict) pupil size. The DRE also checks for the eyes' reaction to light. Certain drugs may slow the eyes' reaction to light. Finally, the DRE examines the subject's nasal and oral cavities for signs of drug ingestion.

8. *Examination for Muscle Tone:* The DRE examines the subject's skeletal muscle tone. Certain categories of drugs may cause the muscles to become rigid. Other categories may cause the muscles to become very loose and flaccid.

9. *Check for Injection Sites and Third Pulse:* The DRE examines the subject for injection sites, which may indicate recent use of certain types of drugs. The DRE also takes the subject's pulse for the third and final time.

10. *Subject's Statements and Other Observations:* The DRE typically reads *Miranda,* if not done so previously, and asks the subject a series of questions regarding the subject's drug use.

11. *Analysis and Opinions of the Evaluator:* Based on the totality of the evaluation, the DRE forms an opinion as to whether or not the subject is impaired. If the DRE determines that the subject is impaired, the DRE will indicate what category or categories of drugs may have contributed to the subject's impairment. The DRE bases these conclusions on his training and experience and the DRE Drug Symptomatology Matrix. While DREs use the drug matrix, they also rely heavily on their general training and experience.

12. *Toxicological Examination:* After completing the evaluation, the DRE normally requests a urine, blood and/or saliva sample from the subject for a toxicology lab analysis.

Drug Categories Evaluated by a DRE

The DRE categorization process is premised on the belief championed by physicians that different types of drugs affect people differently. Accordingly drugs may be categorized or classified according to certain shared symptomatologies or effects, and these drugs are divided into one of seven categories: Central Nervous System (CNS) Depressants, CNS Stimulants, Hallucinogens, Phencyclidine (PCP) and its analogs, Narcotic Analgesics, Inhalants, and Cannabis. It is believed that drugs from each of these seven categories can possibly affect a person's central nervous system and impair a person's normal faculties, and in the DUI field, affect a person's ability to safely operate a motor vehicle.

1. *Central Nervous System (CNS) Depressants:* CNS Depressants slow down the operations of the brain and the body. Examples include alcohol, barbiturates, anti-anxiety tranquilizers (e.g . Valium, Librium, Xanax, Prozac, Thorazine), GHB (Gamma Hydroxybutyrate), Rohypnol and many other anti-depressants (e.g., Zoloft, Paxil).

2. *CNS Stimulants:* CNS Stimulants accelerate the heart rate and elevate the blood pressure and "speed-up" or over-stimulate the body and include Cocaine, "Crack", Amphetamines and Methamphetamine.

3. *Hallucinogens:* Hallucinogens cause the user to perceive things differently than they actually are. Examples include LSD, Peyote, Psilocybin and MDMA (Ecstasy).

4. *Dissociative Anesthetics:* Dissociative Anesthetics are drugs that inhibit pain by cutting off or dissociating the brain's perception of the pain. PCP and its analogs are examples of Dissociative Anesthetics.

5. *Narcotic Analgesics:* Narcotic analgesics relieve pain, induce euphoria and create mood changes in the user. Examples include Opium, Codeine, Heroin, Demerol, Darvon, Morphine, Methadone, Vicodin and OxyContin.

6. *Inhalants:* Inhalants include a wide variety of breathable substances that produce mind-altering results and effects. Examples of inhalants include Toluene, plastic cement, paint, gasoline, paint thinners, hair sprays and various anesthetic gases.

7. *Cannabis:* Cannabis (marijuana) is a popular drug and is frequently found to have been consumed by drivers in the DUI context. The active ingredient in cannabis is delta-9 tetrahydrocannabinol, or THC. This category includes cannabinoids and synthetics like Dronabinol.

CHAPTER 6

The History of Determining Blood Alcohol Concentration (BAC)

History is not a science; it is a method.
—Charles Seignobos

Determining the amount of alcohol or drugs in an individual's system can be accomplished by a number of different ways. In the DUI realm the law may permit the discovery of the BAC by breath, blood, urine, saliva, and sweat. This chapter will focus more on the evolution of breath testing as this practice remains the work horse in DUI field. Proponents have advocated that breath testing remains a relatively reliable form of obtaining the BAC from an individual and furthermore, it remains a relatively inexpensive manner of evidenciary testing. Naturally there is also much criticism regarding the relability of breath testing and that will be examined too.

The study of human breath is not a 20th century phenomenom. As far back as 1774 French chemist Antoine Lavoisier conducted studies regarding respiration, but his contribution to the field of breath testing involves his invention, the "gasometer." This invention was the first instrument to make relatively accurate measurements of respiration gases. Lavoisier used a piston in his gasometer to hold gas pressure constant while measuring the volume of gases used in his experiments. Lavoisier's work was limited for he was later branded a traitor during the Reign of Terror by French Revolutionists, was tried, convicted, and guillotined in 1794, at the age of 50.

William Henry formulated a chemical equation in 1803, later known as "Henry's Law," that has had significant impact on the evolution of the measurement of human breath. Henry's Law describes the mechanism of exchange in the lungs, which is influenced by physiological factors. Henry's law directly explains the volume of alcohol in a simulator's vapor. The "Law" also states that in a closed system, at any given temperature, the concentration of a volatile substance in the air above a fluid is proportional to the concentration of the volatile substance in the fluid. Jones, A.W. *Physiological Aspects of Breath Alcohol Measurement, Alcohol, Drugs and Driving.* 6(2):1-24, Page 12 (1990) Specifically, Henry's Law states:

> At a constant temperature, the amount of a given gas dissolved in a given type and volume of liquid is directly proportional to the partial pressure of that gas in equilibrium with that liquid.

Henry's law has since been shown to apply for a wide range of dilute solutions, not merely those of gases.

More than fifty years after Lavoisier's gasometer device British and Australian physician John Hutchinson adapted the design and invented the first "spirometer," which was used for measuring the volume of a patient's breath. In 1852 Hutchinson published a paper describing his water spirometer and the measurements he had taken of over 4,000 subjects, describing the relationship between lung capacity and height. Hutchinson, John. *The Spirometer, the Stethoscope and the Scale Balance.* London: John Churchill (1852)

In 1874, British physician Francis Anstie actually trapped human breath and applied colorimetric analysis to study alcohol in the body. Anstie, FE: *Final experiments on the elimination of alcohol from the body.* Practitioner 13:15 (1874) In addition to his study of the excretion of alcohol from the breath, Dr. Anstie also had a "rule" named after him, namely "Anstie's Limit" which refers to the daily amount of alcohol that the average drinking individual can consume without risk of deterioration of health. Further research by Dr. Anstie was halted as he died the year this paper was published. Crow, K., Batt, R. *Human Metabolism of Alcohol, Volume I; Pharmacokinetics, Medicolegal Aspects, and General Interests*, CRC Press. (1977)

Another significant early study of alcohol and breath analysis was by Arthur Cushny who predicted that like Henry's Law, the concentration of alcohol in blood could be predicted from the concentration in alveolar air. Cushny, A.R. *On the exhalation of drugs by the lungs.* J Physiol 46:17 (1910)

In 1927 Dr. Emil Bogen reported measuring blood alcohol concentration (BAC) by analyzing a person's breath. Bogen, Emil M.D. *The Diagnosis of Drunkenness – A Quantitative Study of Acute Alcoholic Intoxication.* California and Western Medicine: Vol. XXVI, No. 6. Los Angeles (June 1927) Dr. Bogen's paper was awarded the State Association Research Prize of one hundred and fifty dollars at the Fifty-Sixth Annual Session of the California Medical Association in April, 1927.

Dr. Bogen suggested that extreme intoxication is relatively easy to observe and diagnose but those people who "may be under the influence of alcohol to an extent that seriously affects his powers and behavior, especially in such a responsible situation as driving an automobile, without presenting the entire common syndrome of drunkenness," pose a different problem when it comes to accurate visual diagnosis. As such additional tests were thought to be necessary to prove an individual's level of intoxication.

Dr. Bogen's study concerned itself with the correlation of the concentration of alcohol in and the data obtained from clinical examinations from the first one hundred persons suspected of alcohol impairment who were brought to the Los Angeles General Hospital during the latter half of the year in 1926. The study resembled a rather crude version of a modern DUI investigation including questioning the individual as to quantity and variety of liquor consumed and the time of their last drink; if there was an odor of alcohol when the patient exhaled deeply; the size of the individual's pupils; if the patient's face appeared flushed; if the patient staggered or reeled when walking unassisted across a hallway; if the patient could stand with feet together and eyes closed without swaying (Romberg test); if the patient could touch the tip of his nose with an outstretched forefinger with eyes closed (Coordination test); if the patient could speak clearly, without slurring or mixing up syllables (the phrase "Methodist Episcopal" was often used in the test); if any aberration of conduct or behavior were noted, especially "garrulousness, boisterousness or pugnacity;" if there was any complicating injury or disease present; and any other information which might be of value. *Id*. Finally, a specimen of urine was obtained on admission and placed in a sealed test tube on ice until examined for alcoholic content. *Id*.

After obtaining the above results a sample of expired air was taken from the patient and directly exhaled into the bladder of a football and immediately tested for alcoholic content. In order to give the test some level of credibility Dr. Bogen stated that "numerous checks and control tests (were) performed to insure accuracy and reliability." *Id*. The concentration of alcohol was determined in the breath by requesting that the patient blow up a football having a capacity of about 2000 cc.

In the same year as Bogen's study was completed, Dr. Gorsky, a police surgeon in Britain testified at an early "DUI" trial regarding the "drunkenness" of the defendant. Dr. Gorsky testified that in addition to the usual tests for drunkenness available at the time, he had the defendant blow into a football (soccer) bladder thereby inflating it. The doctor analyzed the contents of the bladder and, combined with witness reports, led Dr. Gorsky to conclude that the defendant was "50 per cent drunk." Mitchell, C. Ainsworth *Science and the Detective*. The American Journal of Police Science (Northwestern University) 3 (2): 169–182 (March/April 1932). The defendant was convicted largely based on the evidence provided by Dr. Gorsky. *Id*.

The first analytical breath testing machine that had some practicality (although it was hardly portable) was invented by Professor Rolla N. Harger in 1938. Appropriately called the "Drunk-o-meter," it was intended to be used by police to collect evidence of intoxication and to be used in courts of law. Using this new invention, Dr. R. L. Holcomb conducted his own research in 1938 into the risks associated with consuming alcohol and then driving. His study concluded that the risk of causing an accident increased six times at a blood alcohol concentration (BAC) of 0.100 and 25 times at 0.150. Holcomb, R.L. *Alcohol in Relation to Traffic Accidents.* JAMA, 1076-1085 (1938)

Professor Harger was among those involved in a training course on breath alcohol testing that began in 1948. The week-long courses were sponsored by the National Safety Council's Committee on Tests for Intoxication and were held at Indiana University. http://www. borkensteincourse.org/history.html Helping Professor Harger teach the classes were Dr. Kurt Dubowski, Ph.D., Dr. Robert B. Forney, Sr., Ph.D., Lloyd Shupe and Lt. Robert F. Borkenstein of the Indiana State Police. *Id.*

Erik M. P. Widmark (1889-1945) was a pioneer in the field of alcohol kinetics and his work assisted the legal community in developing traffic safety legislation and statutory levels of impairment at the beginning of the automobile era. Andreasson, R, and Jones, AW. *The Life and Work of Erik M. P. Widmark.* Am J Forensic Med Pathol. 17(3):177-190. Page 177 (1996)

The early studies in the absorption, distribution, and elimination of alcohol in the body by Widmark enabled him to develop a mathematical formula for predicting alcohol levels after alcohol consumption. The formula is based on the concept that alcohol distributes in the body based on the water content of the tissues into which it is being distributed. Therefore weight and gender are key factors in his formula. In addition to distribution factors, the formula takes into account the dynamics of elimination, by adjusting the theoretical maximum concentration by the elimination rate over time.

The legal theory that emerged following the research of Professor Widmark in the 1930s was "retrograde extrapolation." Retrograde extrapolation is the mathematical process by which an individual's blood alcohol concentration at the time of driving is estimated by projecting backwards from a later chemical test. Effectively, this involves estimating the absorption and elimination of alcohol in the interim between driving and testing. The rate of elimination in the average person is commonly estimated at .015 to .020 percent per hour, although again this can naturally vary from person to person and in a given person from one moment to another. Metabolism can be affected by numerous factors, including such things as body temperature, the type of alcoholic beverage consumed, and the amount and type of food consumed.

As one would expect, Widmark's Formula and retrograde extrapolation have both believers and non-believers. The non-believers argue that retrograde extrapolation is imprecise, requires too many unknown and variable facts, and that it is virtually impossible or useless in the forensic setting. Believers would argue that scientists apply scientific principles of toxicology, metabolism, physiology, pharmacology, and biology in assessing the validity of claims made in research papers promoting the theory and therefore the theory is credible and supported by science. Either way the debate will rage on.

The 1940s saw further development of breath test machinery and most notable was Dr. Glenn C. Forester's "Intoximeter" in 1941. The Intoximeter used an acidified potassium permangate solution to detect the level of alcohol in an individual's breath. Following World War II, Michigan enacted the first statewide breath testing program using an early model of the Intoximeter. Thereafter, Dr. Forester founded a company called Intoximeter, Inc., which remains a player in the breath testing machine business. http://www.intox.com/

Around the same time as the Intoximeter was designed another breath testing device was being developed. Professor Leon Greenberg, Associate Director of the Department of Applied Physiology at Yale University, developed the Alcometer in 1941, the same year as the Intoximeter. The Alcometer utilized a process which involved the use of iodine vapor, starch and potassium iodide. The chemicals in the machine then reacted with a person's breath sample and subsequently changed color depending on the level of alcohol present.

The next significant development in breath testing coincided with the implementation of the New York implied consent law. In 1954 Robert Borkenstein, a retired Captain in the Indiana State Police who had been the Director of the Police Laboratory, filed for US Patent Number 2824789, "Apparatus for analyzing a gas." He had invented the Breathalyzer breath testing instrument.

The device was designed so that a driver would breathe into a rubber hose and the air sample would go into a cylinder that had a handle controlling its valves. A light went on when the cylinder was full and turning the handle again released the air sample into a solution which then analyzed and recorded the results on a meter after the color change was analyzed. The Breathalyzer was a significant improvement over all previous designs and dominated sales of breath testing machines in the United States for nearly 20 years. An improved version of the original device still remains in use in a few jurisdictions more than 50 years after its introduction.

Borkeinstein later taught forensic studies at Indiana University and his class on alcohol and highway safety was frequently attended by police officers and later given the name, appropriately "the Borkeinstein course." Borkeinstein was a busy man indeed and also invented a coin-operated breath analysis machine in 1970. This machine was to be placed in drinking establishments (ie. Bars/Taverns) and after an individual blew into a straw the machine would analyze the breath for a small fee (a quarter). The machine would then flash, "Be a safe driver," "Be a good walker" or "You're a passenger," depending on the level of alcohol content on the person's breath. Predictably, this machine became less of a safety or warning device and more of a game. Dr. Borkeinstein died in August of 2002 at age 89.

In the 1960s gas chromatography (GC) became the method of choice for forensic analysis of alcohol. Tagliaro, F, Lubli, G, Ghielmi, S, Franchi, D, Marigo, M. *Chromatographic methods for blood alcohol determination*. J Chromatog Biomed Appl 580;

161-190 (1992) Gottried Machata pioneered the technique of headspace gas chromatography for measuring alcohol and other volatiles in body fluids in the 1970s. Machata, G. *The advantages of automated blood alcohol determined by headspace analysis.* Z Rechtsmed 75; 229-234 (1975) This technique permitted thousands of specimens to be analyzed on a single GC column without risk of contamination or deterioration. Furthermore the HS-GC sampling system was done automatically which, according to researchers, substantially improved the accuracy and precision of the analytical results. Jones, A.W, Schuberth, J. *Computer-aided headspace gas chromatography applied to blood-alcohol analysis: Importance of on-line process control.* J Forensic Sci 34: 1116-1127 (1989)

The next advance in breath alcohol analysis came in 1971 when the technique of infrared spectrometry was incorporated into a bench-top instrument for breath-alcohol analysis. The machine that brought this into reality was the Intoxilyzer. Harte, R. *An instrument for the determination of ethanol in breath in law enforcement practice.* J. Forensic Sci. 16: 493-510 (1970) Since then, infrared absorption at wavelengths of 3.4 microns or 9.5 microns or both has become the primary analytical technology for measuring alcohol in the breath for evidentiary purposes. Dubowski, KM. *The technology of breath-alcohol analysis.* US Department of Health and Health Services, DHHS Publication No. (ADM) 92-1728. Pages 1-38 (1992); Gullberg, RG. *Methodology and quality assurance in forensic breath alcohol analysis.* Forensic Sci Rev 12, 49-68 (2000)

The typical IR-based breath machine will have an IR detector at the end of the chamber which converts the IR energy to electrical energy. In the breath testing procedure the machine generally analyzes ambient air to determine a baseline voltage output. When the subject's breath is measured, there is a resultant voltage decrease and it is this drop that is measured and converted to a numerical result.

With IR technology the breath testing machines do not specifically identify ethanol because they only identify the absorption of a particular bond or functional group. Since there are many organic molecules that contain similar bonds or functional groups, breath machines can never be totally specific or actually identify the entire molecule of ethanol. As a result certain devices combine IR and electrochemical cell detection to assist in identifying a limited number of possible interfering substances, such as acetone (i.e. the Intoximeter 3000 and the BAC DataMaster). However, one potential problem with this type of technology is that other substances may not be identified and may render innaccurate results. Bell, C.M. *Attaining Specificity in the Measurement of Ethanol in Breath.* Acta Med Leg Soc. (Liege) (1990)

Another problem with IR devices is that particles in the breath chamber that are not ethanol or other interfering substances, can scatter the light and keep some light from reaching the detector. Any substance that decreases the amount of light that reaches the detector increases the apparent BAC reading. This is called the "Tyndall Effect," named after scientist John Tyndall (1820-1893).

An example of this effect is if there is loose dirt in the breath chamber then fine particles can be blown in during sampling and will scatter light. This may occur if the driver of a vehicle has been involved in an accident and the vehicle's airbag has been deployed. The fine particles of talc and cornstarch that are within an airbag can get blown into the machine and lead to an erroneous reading. Nichols, D.H., Whited, F.K. *The Tyndall Effect: Its Relation to Evidential Breath Testing.* Drinking/Driving Law Letter (2000)

During the 1970s hand-held breath test devices that incorporated electrochemical fuel cell sensors for oxidation of alcohol began to appear and were proving suitable as roadside screening tests for alcohol impairment. Jones, AW. *Electrochemical measurements of breath-alcohol concentration; precision and accuracy in relation to blood-alcohol.* Clin Chim Acta 146; 175-183 (1985)

The National Highway Traffic Safety Administration (NHTSA) published the "Standards for Devices to Measure Breath Alcohol" in 1974 and listed devices which met the Federally mandated criteria. Thereafter state programs that applied for Highway Safety Funding were restricted to using only the breath testing equipment listed as meeting the Federal criteria. *Highway Safety Programs; Standards for Devices to Measure Breath Alcohol.* DOT, NHTSA. Federal Register, Volume 39. 41399 (1974)

The 1974 NHTSA publication for breath test devices renamed the list "Model Specifications for Evidential Breath Testing Devices" and in 1984 included a "Conforming Products List." Unlike the 1974 version state programs no longer were restricted to using devices listed as meeting the Federal criteria, though most states continue to limit their consideration to equipment on the list. *Highway Safety Programs; Model Specifications for Devices To Measure Breath Alcohol.* DOT, NHTSA. Federal Register, Volume 49. 48864 (1984)

NHTSA modified their specifications again in 1993 and changed the levels at which the machines were calibrated (0.020%, 0.040%, 0.08% and 0.160% instead of 0.050%, 0.101% and 0.151%) and also added a test for acetone detection. This version of the publication further expanded their definition of "alcohol" to included low molecular weight alcohol such as methanol and isopropanol. *Highway Safety Programs; Model Specifications for Devices To Measure Breath Alcohol.* DOT, NHTSA. Federal Register, Volume 58. 48705 (1993)

There is little debate in the DUI community that breath testing is an inferior method of testing an invidivual's blood alcohol concentration in comparison to blood. However, it is equally agreed that breath testing does have some advantages over a blood draw, those primarily being that it is cheaper, is faster, gives immediate results, and is less invasive.

The biggest disadvantage that a breath test has over a blood test is reliability. Since the 1970s, researchers have warned scientists and those who use breath testing devices of factors that can affect a reliable breath alcohol (BAC) reading. Mason, M., Dubowski, K., *Breath-Alcohol Analysis: Uses, Methods, and Some Forensic Problems.* Review and Opinion. J Forensic Sci. (January, 1976) The primary factors that can potentially affect the accuracy of a breath testing machine include physiological factors, machine characteristics, and administrative practices.

Preliminary Breath Testing Devices (PBTs)

The majority of the preliminary breath test machines (handheld units) utilize an electrochemical fuel cell technology that fits in the smaller and more compact handheld units. The disadvantage of these units is that they are less reliable and accurate than the larger table top versions that use IR technology. Despite issues over reliability and accuracy these hand held screening devices are popular for use as a screening tool to detect the presence of alcohol.

There are a number of different PBT models in use for DUI purposes. The more popular models include the Intoxilyzer S-D2 and Intoxilyzer S-D5 (both manufactured by CMI Inc.), and the AlcoSensor III and AlcoSensor IV PBT Device (both manufacturedby Intoximeters Inc. of St. Louis, Missouri).

The arguments against the fuel cell technology are many. The first is that this technology is not specific to ethanol only and as a result a PBT reading can provide innaccurate results. One study found that an "Alcolmeter Pocket Model" reacted positively to ethanol but it also reacted to acetaldehyde, methanol, isopropanol, and n-propranolol. Jones, Alan W. and Goldberg, L. *Evaluation of Breath Alcohol Instruments I: In Vitro Experiments with Alcolmeter Pocket Model.* 12 Forensic Science International 1 (1978)

Other issues with fuel cell technology and their accuracy and reliablity is that the devices are susceptible to weather extremes. NHTSA issued the following warning regarding the AlcoSensor IV without a heated cell:

If the ambient air is cold enough, and if the hand held breath tester is unheated, it is possible for the moisture in the breath to condense onto the airway surface of the tester, and cause alcohol present to condense with it. It has been pointed out to NHTSA that if this condensation occurs, it is possible for alcohol in one test to carry over to a second test, which would cause a false positive result. U.S. Dept. of Transp. NHTSA. *Special Testing for Possible Carry Over Effects Using the Intoximeters Inc. Alco Sensor IV at 10 Degrees Centigrade*. DOT HS 809 424 (March 2002)

In the United States, NHTSA maintains a "Conforming Products List" of breath alcohol devices approved for preliminary screening use. *Highway Safety Programs; Conforming Products List of Screening Devices to Measure Alcohol in Bodily Fluids*. DOT, NHTSA. Federal Register, Volume 72, No. 20 (January, 2007) Similarly, in Canada, a preliminary non-evidentiary screening device can be approved by Parliament as an approved screening device.

Evidentiary Breath Test Devices

Drunkometer

Arguably the first practical analytical breath testing machine was the appropriately named "Drunk-o-meter." The device was invented by Professor Rolla N. Harger in 1938. Professor Harger was the Chair of the Department of Biochemistry at the Indiana University School of Medicine and his idea had its origins in 1931. The "Drunk-o-meter" was intended from the beginning to be used by police and was a very elementary device that required an individual to blow into a balloon that was inside the machine. The breath sample was then transferred through an acidified potassium permanganate solution. If the solution changed color there was alcohol in the breath sample. The greater the color change, the more alcohol there was present in the breath. In addition to the fact that the machine was crude, it was also cumbersome. It looked like a portable laboratory and lacked the practicality and relative reliability of later machines. Tilstone, William J., Savage, Kathleen A., and Clark Leigh A. *Forensic science: an encyclopedia of history, methods, and techniques*. ABC-CLIO (2006)

Alcometer

In 1941 Professor Leon Greenberg, who was the Associate Director of the Department of Applied Physiology at Yale University, developed a breath testing device with the ability to measure alcohol called the "Alcometer." The Alcometer employed a process where iodine vapor, starch and potassium iodide reacted with the breath of a subject and thereafter changed color depending on the level of alcohol present. The Alcometer was described as "a portable automatic laboratory" and would advance law enforcement in that:

> [t]he police can now easily distinguish between the man who should be prosecuted for drunkenness and the man who appears to be inebriated but is actually suffering from sober shock and should be rushed to the hospital. Burgheim, Richard A. *Yale Center of Alcohol Studies Investigates Drinking Habits of Carefree Undergraduates.* The Harvard Crimson (November 21, 1953)

Intoximeter

In 1941 Professor Glen Forester from St. Louis, Missouri, developed the "Intoximeter." The Intoximeter's roots are that of a field testing device. This original machine consisted of a mouthpiece, a check valve, a balloon, a tube with permaganate-sulphuric acid, a tube with magnesium perchlorate and an ascarite tube. Since its inception there have been upgrades and several models known as the Intoximeter sold and utilized in the United States.

The original "field testing" Intoximeter used magnesium perchlorate to absorb carbon dioxide from the subject's breath sample. From there the alcohol was distilled from the perchlorate solution, and the amount of alcohol was determined by the colorimetric procedures. Once the sample was received it was analyzed in the laboratory where the increase in weight of the ascarite tube was determined and thereafter the volume of the breath sample was calculated based upon an assumption that deep lung, or alveolar air of each person tested contained 5.5% carbon dioxide by volume.

This type of technology for breath test purposes died in the late 1960s when the National Safety Council recommended discontinuance of the use of any instrument which based alcohol analysis upon the carbon dioxide content of the breath sample. The retirement of this technology was due to the discovery that the carbon dioxide content of expired deep lung air among subjects was too variable to allow carbon dioxide to be used as a calculation for the volume of the breath sample. National Safety Council Committee on Alcohol and Drugs, *A Model Program for the Control of Alcohol for Traffic Safety* (1967); National Safety Council, Committee on Alcohol and Drugs, *Recommendations of the Ad Hoc Committee on Testing and Training* (1968)

The photoelectric Intoximeter replaced the original Intoximeter and is similar to the Breathalyzer in that they both utilize a photometer. This new unit measured alcohol in a specified amount of breath using the wet chemical oxidation reaction. This newer machine collected two breath samples, using two cylinders and in the first cylinder, the breath passed into the ampoule where the chemical reaction takes place. In the second cylinder, the breath is trapped by magnesium perchlorate and then stored for future analysis.

Not surprisingly the photoelectric Intoximeter had similar problems as the Breathalyzer. However, surprisingly the photoelectric Intoximeter is still in use in some states.

Breathalyzer

In 1954 Dr. R. F. Borkenstein invented the Breathalyzer. The invention of the breathalyzer provided law enforcement with a non-invasive test providing immediate results to determine an individual's BAC at the time of testing. The Breathalyzer machine measures the percent weight by volume of blood alcohol using photometric measurement of a quantity of alcohol and a measured sample of deep lung air (alveolar air). The Breathalyzers were manufactured by Smith & Wesson in Springfield, Massachusetts until July, 1984, until the Breathalyzer division was sold to National Draeger, Inc., an American subsidiary of a German manufacturing company.

Like all photometers the Breathalyzer Model 900 worked by using a measured quantity of alveolar that is then bubbled through a solution contained in a glass jar called a test ampoule. The solution is a mix of potassium dichromate and sulphuric acid in water which acts with a catalyst known as silver nitrate. When the alcohol mixes with the solution, it becomes oxidized to acetic acid. The potassium dichromate is then reduced in proportion to the quantity of alcohol that is oxidized and this reduction results in a loss of color to the solution. This loss of color allows more light from a source on one side of the ampoule to pass through onto a surface on the other side. The resulting amount of light that passes through is proportional to the amount of color change and the amount of alcohol present.

During the test two ampoules are used and each ampoule is chemically identical. Within the unit there is a lamp that is located on a movable carriage between the ampoules. The lamp directs light through each ampoule and onto a distant surface. This carriage is then adjusted so that the light on the two surfaces is identical. The second ampoule however, is considered a "reference ampoule" and is never exposed to any chemicals and as a result, never changes color. Once the test ampoule is exposed to the breath sample and reacts, the amount of light that passes through the two ampoules is compared a second time. The difference is then measured and converted to a measurement of blood alcohol concentration. That figure is then multiplied by the 2100 to 1 ratio to give the blood alcohol concentration.

The potential number of sources of errors in the Breathalyzer are many. For instance, the reagent which detects ethyl alcohol will also react with any other reducing agent that it comes into contact with. This is a concern since there are a number of interfering substances which can potentially affect the reagent, including acetone, methanol, acetaldehyde, among others, none of which are "alcohol." Additionally, if the ampoule is broken it is possible that anything adjacent (ie. foreign substances on the operator's clothing or body) may make their way into the ampoule, thereby affecting the test. Further, things such as smoke, paint, or any other foreign substance can also be transferred from the bubbler tube into the reagent.

Another issue with the Breathalyzer is acquiring a breath sample of sufficient concentration. If the sample is not of sufficent concentration it could lead to innaccurate readings. Further, the temperature of the chamber may also result in readings that are either too high (when the chamber is too cool) or too low (when the chamber is too hot).

Breathalyzer 2000

Smith & Wesson, the original manufacturers of the Breathalyzer, began production of a new unit in 1981. The Model 2000 was the company's first attempt at a breath alcohol machine using the principle of infrared absorption. The Model 2000 also contains a "microprocessor" which programs the machine through a sequence of internal controls during the course of the test.

The machine uses a "balanced light concept" similar to the original Breathalyzer models which is designed to assure that changes in power line voltage should not affect BAC readings. As a result the Model 2000 has both a dual channel design and a split channel design which is used in an attempt to guarantee some measure of specificity for ethyl alcohol and to isolate energy changes which result from the presence of ethyl alcohol in a sample. Unlike the original Breathlyzer model the Model 2000 contains no moving parts, except for the mechanical printout assembly. Both the light filters and the temperature are fixed.

Compared to the original Breathalyzer models the Model 2000 is a sophisticated machine and it is this relative sophistication that is the source of some of its problems. Infrared analysis is a physical measurement and as such it is a non-chemical means of analying a breath sample.

Other potential problems with the Model 2000 is that it may be susceptible to radio frequency interference (RFI) and humidity. Interestingly, prior to the sale of the company to National Draiger the humidity detector was removed from all of its machines. A possible error would be if there was too much humidity in the breath sample a false high reading may result.

Intoxilyzer

Like the Breathalyzer 2000 the Intoxilyzer is an infrared breath test analyzer. The machines were once manufactured by CMI, Inc. but are now manufactured by MPD, Inc. of Owensboro, Kentucky. The breath testing device was developed in 1971 by Richard A. Harte of Omicron Systems Corporation of Palo Alto, California, and was originally called the "Omicron Intoxilyzer." Varying models of the "Intoxilyzer" are in use in more than 35 states, and nearly 30 states have it as their sole breath testing device. It is by far the most widely used breath testing device in the United States.

All Intoxilyzers measure the amount of infrared light absorbed by ethyl alcohol in a subject's breath sample. Every Intoxilyzer works on the same basic premise except for the Intoxilyzer 5000, which uses a computerized mode. Problems with the Intoxilyzer have included the machine's issues with acetone detection and other IR related problems as experienced with the IR Breathalyzer devices.

BAC Verifier

Verax Systems, Inc. originally manufactured the BAC Verifier but eventually sold the rights to the to National Patent Analytical Systems.

The BAC Verifier traps a larger breath sample than other breath analyzers which allows for duplicate analysis testing. It also allows for the trapping of a sufficient volume of air so that two separate samples of the same breath can be analyzed. As a result, two separate tests can be performed on the same breath sample.

Like other machines (the Intoxilyzer 5000, the Intoximeter 3000, and the Breathalyzer 2000) the BAC Verifier uses an infrared analysis and a microprocessor to minimize operator intervention and manipulation.

There are many potential sources of error in the BAC Verifier, which include problems with specificity and that the machine may be susceptible to radio-frequency interference (RFI). Interestingly, many breath testing machines were tested in late 1982 by NHTSA to determine susceptibility to RFI but the BAC Verifier was one of the machines not tested. The manufacturer claims that the machines have spray coating which shields them from any RFI but there is no independent testing to prove this.

DataMaster

The DataMaster evolved from the BAC Verifier. The operation of both machines is very much the same although the casing of the machine, the printer, the layout of the printed circuit boards, the software, the mounting of the breath tube, the circuitry, and the simulator are different. The casing for the DataMaster is all metal which is supposed to eliminate certain radio frequency interference, while the casing for the Verifier is plastic.

Another problem the Verifier had was with its central processing unit (CPU) board which was located underneath the machine and caused some maintenance problems due to its location. The DataMaster design attempted to resolve this issue and included nine printed circuit boards which supposedly result in easier maintenance, removal, and replacement. Additionally, the manufacturer claims that the printed circuit boards are a superior electrical design because the different circuits are isolated. Because the original Verifier had problems with electrical interference within the circuitry of the CPU, the CPU board was changed in the DataMaster.

Also changed in the DataMaster design was the detector circuitry. The DataMaster has a variable resister while the Verifier had a fixed resistor. The variable resistor in the DataMaster was designed so that the resistance value can be adjusted thereby increasing the stability of the signal produced by the detector.

The most important change in the DataMaster however was the updated software. Software is constantly changing and being improved and advanced and the Verifier could not adapt to these changes. The Verifier had limited RAM data storage capability while the DataMaster has expanded RAM data storage capacity and as such could accommodate additional software. The mathematical formula used to calculate the presence of acetone in breath samples was also changed in the new DataMaster software.

Yet another difference betwee the older Verifier and the DataMaster is that the DataMaster uses a different simulator. The Verifier uses the Smith & Wesson simulator, while the DataMaster uses a Guth simulator. The last notable change between the two machines is the breath tube mounting. In the DataMaster the breath tube can be adjusted when placed in the mounting pivots while on the Verifier the breath tube, once attached, is fixed in one position.

Despite the changes between the Verifier and the DataMaster there are several reported problems with the DataMaster devices. Most of these problems have originated in the State of Washington and have included repair and maintenance problems, problems with the meter valve (instability producing imprecise readings, or failing to produce readings), problems with zeroing, instability of infra-red lamps, improper display of interferents (generally acetone), problems with displaying results to three decimal points, and problems with lack of specificity for ethanol. Another problem occurred in 2007/2008 in Washington State where BAC results using DataMaster and DataMaster CDM machines were suppressed in many courts due to procedural and ethical violations by the State Toxicology Laboratory. The fallout resulted in the resignation of the long standing State Toxicologist Dr. Barry Logan (Dr. Logan now serves on the faculty at the Borkenstein Course at Indiana University). Additionally, as is the case with computer-controlled machines (ie. the Intoximeter 3000, Intoxilyzer 5000, and the Verifier) the DataMaster is subject to "transient error." Transient error occurs when the computer will not function properly for a period of time until it corrects itself.

The New DataMaster "DMT"

In 2004 National Patent Analytical Systems began marketing a modernized version of the standard DataMaster. This new device, DataMaster Transportable (DMT) evolved from the standard DataMaster and in many respects operates similarly yet contains a variety of new features and updates. The DMT comes with a new user interface, internal circuitry, CPU, sample chamber size and naturally, software. The device is also smaller in size and the metal case contains fewer openings, thereby theoretically removing the possibility of radio frequency waves interfering with test results, although quietly admitting that the older (but still used) DataMaster may be prone to RFI.

The new DMT and the older DataMaster differ in many significant ways. The new DMT uses newer computer technology, a full color touch screen graphics LCD display, can operate on 90 to 240 VAC, or from a 12 VDC power source which allows for mobile applications, permits voice commands, has a bar code reader/scanner, is USB Capable, has external or screen operated keyboard, a 1000 test storage capability (more with memory expansion), has a wet bath or dry gas simulation, and has a single point calibration and temperature controlled simulator and breath tubes.

With all of the advances promised by the DMT it is rather surprising to learn that few jurisdictions have considered ordering the new technology to replace the old. Perhaps the reason is money. It would be very costly to purchase the new machinery en masse and even more expensive to train all the officers and technicians to operate and maintain it.

CHAPTER 7

The History of Alcohol/Drug Evaluations and Treatment

The only thing new in the world is the history you don't know.
—Harry S Truman

In the context of driving under the influence, alcohol and drug use is front and center. While the great majority of DUI offenders are not substance abusers who require treatment, for those who are there exists another very real dilemma, reoffending. As a result most courts will order the defendant charged with DUI to undergo an alcohol/drug evaluation to determine whether they suffer from substance dependency. Moreover, advocates such as MADD vigorously campaign for mandatory alcohol or drug evaluations in the court environment.

Many pundits have claimed that substance use disorders are a significant public health problem in many countries. Further, the most commonly abused substance is alcohol. Gabbard: *Treatments of Psychiatric Disorders.* Published by the American Psychiatric Association: 3rd edition (2001) As an example, the number of 'dependent drinkers' in the United Kingdom was calculated at over 2.8 million in 2001. *Global Status Report on Alcohol 2004.* WHO European Ministerial Conference on Young People and Alcohol. World Health Organization: Department of Mental Health and Substance Abuse. Geneva (2004) Additionally, the World Health

Organization (WHO) estimates that about 140 million people throughout the world suffer from alcohol dependence. *Id.*

The legal system in America is designed to provide more severe penalties on repeat DUI offenders than first time offenders. However, despite the threat of enhanced penalties for repeat offenders there are a group of individuals who continue to drink then drive. This group is considered the "hard core drinking driver" (HCDD) and according to some, is an individual who despite education, threats, and punishments, drives frequently after consuming alcohol. Simpson, H. M., Beirness, D. J., Robertson, R. D., Mayhew, D. R., & Hedlund, J. H. *Hard core drinking drivers*. Traffic Injury Prevention. 5(3), 261-269 (2004) This group is in the minority of all impaired drivers but they are a concerning minority to be sure. Recent surveys suggest that 3% of all licensed drivers account for 80% of the total number of impaired driving incidences. *Id.* Because this activity poses relatively high threats to public safety the legal system has attempted to identify individuals in this highest risk category and develop special monitoring and management strategies based on their unique characteristics. Voas, R. B., & Fisher, D. A. *Court procedures for handling intoxicated drivers*. Alcohol Research and Health. 25(1), 32-42 (2001)

One of the problems with identifying this group of HCDDs is that they share many characteristics with the larger pool of DUI offenders. Arstein-Kerslake, G., & Peck, R. C. *Typological analysis of California DUI offenders and DUI recidivism correlates*. In Proceedings of the Section on Alcohol, Drugs and Traffic Safety: 34th International Congress on Alcoholism and Drug Dependence (Pages 115-140). August 4-10. Calgary, Alberta, Canada (1985) However, a profile has been created of the HCDD that includes the majority being male (90-95 percent), aged 25 to 45 (more than 75 percent are under age 40 and only 10 percent over age 50), with 12 grades or less education, employed in a non-white-collar occupation (with a history of occupational instability), and lower socioeconomic status. Simpson, H. M., Beirness, D. J., Robertson, R. D., Mayhew, D. R., & Hedlund, J. H. *Hard core drinking drivers*.

Traffic Injury Prevention. 5(3), 261-269 (2004)

Additional characteristics of HCDDs include a longer and more sustained substance use history and when compared to the larger pool of DUI offenders, HCDDs are more likely to have a family history of alcohol and other drug problems, including family modeling of drinking and driving. Gulliver, P., & Begg, D. *Influences during adolescence on perceptions and behaviour related to alcohol use and unsafe driving as young adults.* Accident Analysis and Prevention. 36(5), 773-781 (2004) According to one study, individuals reporting onset of drinking before age 14 are seven times more likely to be in an alcohol-related crash than those who begin drinking after age 21. Hingson, R., Heeren, T., Levenson, S., Jamanka, A., & Voas, R. *Age of drinking onset, driving after drinking, and involvement in alcohol related motor-vehicle crashes.* Accident Analysis and Prevention. 34(1), 85-92. (2002)

Interestingly the HCDD seems to have other addiction issues which include the early onset of smoking, the amount of smoking (more than 30 cigarettes per day), high intensity of nicotine craving, smoking within five minutes of waking up, and lack of attempts to cut down or quit. John, U., Meyer, C., Rumpf, H. J., & Hapke, U. *Probabiltiies of alcohol highrisk drinking, abuse or dependence estimated on grounds of tobacco smoking and nicotine dependence.* Addiction, 98(6), 805-814 (2003) Finally, HCDDs often report prior treatment for alcohol or other drug problems, but records reveal noncompliance with sentencing conditions and treatment and moreover, interviews with HCDDs reveal the perception that treatment was a "waste of time." Peck, R. C., Arstein-Kerslake, G. W., & Helander, C. J. *Psychometric and biographical correlates of drunk-driving recidivism and treatment program compliance.* Journal of Studies on Alcohol. 55(6), 667-678 (1994); Timken, D. *What Works: Effective Interventions with DUI Offenders.* LaCrosse, WI: International Community Corrections Association (1999)

Defining Alcoholism

Attempts to define alcoholism have been met with uncertainty, conflict, and ambiguity. Definitions have evolved from classical-historical times to the present, reflecting the prevalent cultural, religious, and scientific biases. Today the word "alcoholism" simultaneously denotes competing conceptions of the nature and causes of alcohol addiction. These conceptions include moral, legal, medical, behavioral, psychological, and sociological models of alcoholism.

The multiplicity of definitions for alcoholism has proven a barrier to communication among clinicians and researchers, and according to many professionals, a hindrance to effective treatment. Accurate diagnosis is the first step in predicting the course and outcome of a disease, in planning for its treatment, and in comparing the effectiveness of different kinds of treatment. Accurate diagnosis requires unambiguous terminology.

Although they differ in detail and emphasis, most definitions of alcoholism recognize the condition of people who cannot help repetitively drinking quantities of alcohol, usually enough to cause intoxication, which harm them. Before the invention of the term "alcoholism," this condition was designated by a variety of terms, including intemperance, inebriety, and habitual drunkenness.

In 1849, Dr. Magnus Huss, a Swedish physician, first used the term "alcoholism" to describe a diseased condition resulting from excessive alcohol consumption. Coombs, Robert H. *Addiction Counseling Review: Preparing for Comprehensive, Certification, and Licensing Examinations.* Routledge Pub. Page 84 (2004) In 1866, a French doctoral candidate, M. Gabriel, first used the term in its modern sense, as a disease "manifested by a loss of control over alcohol intake, leading to excessive alcohol consumption—what we would now refer to as an addiction." *Id.* He also designated alcoholism a public health problem. The use of "alcoholism" to designate a disease identified by the symptom of excessive alcohol intake promptly caught on and was adopted into most modern languages.

Alcoholism was first recognized as a disease in 1785, by the

Philadelphian Dr. Benjamin Rush, signer of the Declaration of Independence and first physician-general of George Washington's Continental Army. In his widely distributed essay on "the effects of ardent spirits," Rush explicitly called intemperance a disease and, explicitly, an addiction. *Id.* Throughout the 19th century, American physicians considered and treated alcoholism (then termed intemperance or inebriety) as a disease. Such examples are included the medical journal essays of Dr. J.H. Kain (1828) and Dr. R. Hills (1849). Equally relevant is the founding of special hospitals for the treatment of this disease, as well as special journals for its explication. Among these journals are the *Quarterly Journal of Inebriety* (U.S., 1876-1913), and the *British Journal of Inebriety*, now the *British Journal of Addiction* (1884-present).

Despite the scientific view among many professionals that alcoholism was indeed a disease, there remained widespread doubt, especially among those who attached a moralistic conception of alcoholism. This may best be illustrated by the Reverend J.E. Todd's 1882 essay, *Drunkenness a Vice, Not a Disease*. The essay is replete with quotes connecting alcoholism and sin and here is but one example: "If there is any man on earth who deserves the abhorrence of mankind and the curse of God it is the drunkard." Todd, J.E. Rev. *Drunkenness a Vice, Not a Disease*. Hartford, CT: Case, Lockwood & Brainard. Page 11 (1882) Regardless, the vast majority of physicians, as represented through medical organizations, continue to regard alcoholism as a disease.

Alcohol addiction was recognized in the Standard Classified Nomenclature of Disease produced in 1933 with the explicit approval of the American Medical Association, the American Psychiatric Association (APA), the Association of American Physicians, the American Public Health Association, and the American Hospital Association. Alcoholism is listed in The Manual for Coding Causes of Illness, published by the U.S. Public Health Service in 1944. Logie, H.B., ED. *A Standard Classified Nomenclature of Disease*. New York: Commonwealth Fund (1933)

Diagnostic Criteria for Alcoholism

Like the evolution of the definition of alcoholism the diagnostic criteria for alcoholism has similarly evolved. By definition medical diagnostic criteria for alcoholism assumes that alcoholism is actually a "disease." Therefore, these criteria acknowledge that alcoholism is an addiction, recognized by such symptoms of addiction as withdrawal and increased tolerance. Different sets of criteria place more or less emphasis on these symptoms and many medical definitions and criteria refer to a variety of medical, social, or other adverse consequences associated with alcoholism.

In 1960, E.M. Jellinek noted that some people "who never become addicted" to alcohol were being labeled alcoholics. Jellinek, E.M. *Alcoholism, a genus and some of its species.* Canadian Medical Association Journal 83:1341-1345 (1960); *The Disease Concept of Alcoholism.* Highland Park, NJ: Hillhouse Press. (1960) Jellinek began experimenting with a definition of alcoholism as "any use of alcoholic beverages that causes any damage to the individual or society or both," but immediately noted that this definition was too vague. *Id.* He therefore proceeded to adopt a family of Greek-letter designations for subtypes of alcoholism, only two of which (gamma and delta) refer to true alcohol addiction, and therefore to alcoholism as a disease. Essentially, gamma alcoholism refers to loss of control during drinking bouts, while delta alcoholism refers to inability to abstain (i.e., craving between bouts). The remaining three categories (alpha, beta, and epsilon) are designed to describe the condition of problem drinkers but not those individuals who suffer from the disease of alcoholism.

DSM-I and DSM-II (1952 and 1968)

The Diagnostic and Statistical Manual of Mental Disorders (DSM), published by the APA, is a diagnostic guide for psychiatric, including addictive, disorders. Subsequent versions of the initial model are still in use today to diagnose those individuals who are obtaining alcohol and drug evaluations for court purposes.

The first edition (DSM-I) defined alcoholism as alcohol addiction. American Psychiatric Association, *Diagnostic and Statistical Manual of Mental Disorders* (DSM-I). Washington, DC (1952) The second edition (DSM-II) divided alcoholism into three subcategories, only one of which was characterized as alcohol addition; the other two categories related to "excessive drinking," or what one might call "problem drinking." American Psychiatric Association. *Diagnostic and Statistical Manual of Mental Disorders*, Second Edition (DSM-II). Washington, DC (1968) The DSM-II definition of alcoholism was based on the definition appearing in the International Classification of Diseases. World Health Organization. *Manual of the International Statistical Classification of Diseases, Injuries, and Causes of Death*. 8th Revision (ICD-8). Geneva: the Organization (1967)

The Feighner Criteria (1972)

In response to perceived deficiencies in DSM-II, a group of researchers at the Washington University School of Medicine in St. Louis published diagnostic criteria for 14 psychiatric illnesses, including alcoholism. Their approach was collectively referred to as the Feighner Criteria. Feighner, J.P. *Diagnostic criteria for use in psychiatric research. Archieves of General Psychiatry* 26(1):57-63 (1972) Alcoholism was defined in this study in part on the basis of withdrawal symptoms and loss of control over drinking. Other criteria included medical, legal, occupational, and social problems resulting from alcohol intake.

National Council on Alcoholism (1972-1976)

In addition to the "Feighner Criteria," the National Council on Alcoholism (NCA) defined alcoholism as a disease process consisting of a pathologic dependence on alcohol. Criteria Committee of the National Council on Alcoholism, *Criteria for the diagnosis of alcoholism. American Journal of Psychiatry* 129(2):127-135 (1972) The proposed diagnostic criteria emphasized psychological problems and the concepts of Alcoholics Anonymous, but also placed heavy emphasis on symptoms of dependence and tolerance.

In 1976, NCA joined with the American Medical Society on Alcoholism (AMSA) and defined alcoholism as a "chronic, progressive, and potentially fatal disease characterized by tolerance and physical dependence or pathologic organ changes, or both, as the direct or indirect consequences of the alcohol ingested."

DSM-III and DSM-III-R (1980 and 1987)

The third edition of the DSM model defined alcohol dependence in much the same way as Jellinek had defined gamma alcoholism. American Psychiatric Association. *Diagnostic and Statistical Manual of Mental Disorders*, Third Edition (DSM-III) Washington, DC (1980). DSM-III criteria for alcoholism requires evidence of either tolerance or withdrawal symptoms, along with evidence of either loss of control, or social or physical problems due to alcoholism. These criteria were kept as consistent as possible with the ninth revision of the ICD. World Health Organization. *Manual of the International Statistical Classification of Diseases, Injuries, and Causes of Death*, 9th Revision (ICD-9). Geneva (1977)

The study and treatment of alcohol dependence continued to evolve and the 1987 revision of DSM-III (DSM-III-R) incorporated a broadened conception of dependence derived from the alcohol dependence syndrome as defined by G. Edwards. Edwards, G. *The alcohol dependence syndrome: A concept as stimulus to enquiry.* British Journal of Addiction 81(2):171-183 (1986).

Alcohol dependence, as defined in the DSM-IV, is a "psychiatric diagnosis and depicts a physical dependence on alcohol." For a person to meet criteria for Alcohol Dependence within the criteria listed in the DSM-IV, they must meet 3 of a total 7 possible criteria within a 12 month period of time.

The first two criteria listed in the DSM-IV are related to physiological dependence: to wit, tolerance and withdrawal. The third and fourth criteria establish a pattern of losing control of drinking by breaking rules/laws or failing at attempts to restrain from drinking. The fifth and sixth criteria are indicative of a progression of addiction as more and more time is spent drinking and the subsequent lifestyle changes that result. The seventh criteria for alcohol dependence is achieved when an individual continues to drink despite being conscious that their drinking is causing or aggravating a particular psychological or physiological problem(s).

Importantly, because only three of seven criteria are required to be diagnosed with alcohol dependence, not everyone evaluated and diagnosed with alcohol dependence meets the same criteria. Therefore not all have identical symptoms and problems connected to drinking. Alcohol dependence is differentiated from alcohol abuse by the presence of symptoms such as tolerance and withdrawal.

The DSM-IV (the standard for diagnosis in psychiatry and psychology) defines alcohol abuse as "repeated use despite recurrent adverse consequences." VandenBos, Gary R. ed. APA *Dictionary of Psychology*. 1st Ed. Washington: American Psychological Association (2007) It further defines alcohol dependence as alcohol abuse combined with tolerance, withdrawal, and an uncontrollable drive to drink.

The DSM models have not been without critics. The most fundamental criticism of the DSM concerns the validity and reliability of its diagnostic categories and criteria. Kendell, R. and Jablensky, A. *Distinguishing between the validity and utility of psychiatric diagnoses.* Am J Psychiatry (2003); Baca-Garcia, E, Perez-Rodriguez, M.M., Basurte-Villamor, I, Fernandez del Moral, A.L., Jimenez-Arriero, M.A., Gonzalez de Rivera, J.L., Saiz-Ruiz, J, and Oquendo, MA. *Diagnostic stability of psychiatric disorders in clinical practice.* Br J Psychiatry. (2007); Pincus et al. *Clinical Significance and DSM-IV.* Arch Gen Psychiatry (1998) Further, critics have argued that the DSM models lack hard science. Criticism has even come from some of the earlier contributors to the DSM, scientists, mental health professionals, and from politicians.

The next version of the DSM is DSM-V and is tentatively scheduled for publication in 2012. *DSM-V: The Future Manual.* This as yet unpublished manual has already received criticism. Robert Spitzer, the head of the DSM-III task force, has publicly criticized the American Psychiatric Association for mandating that DSM-V task force members sign a nondisclosure agreement, effectively conducting the whole process in secret: "When I first heard about this agreement, I just went bonkers. Transparency is necessary if the document is to have credibility, and, in time, you're going to have people complaining all over the place that they didn't have the opportunity to challenge anything." Carey, Benedict. *Psychiatrists Revise the Book of Human Troubles.* New York Times (December 17, 2008)

"Neuroadaptation" (1980)

Arguably the most dramatic proposal for changing the definition of alcoholism was made by the group of specialists who met at the invitation of WHO in Geneva in August 1980. Edwards, G.; Arif, A.; and Hodgson, R. *Nomenclature and classification of drug- and alcohol-related problems: A WHO memorandum.* Bulletin of the World Health Organization (1981) The group proposed a new term, "neuroadaptation," to replace "dependence." The advantage of the term "neuroadaptation" over addiction, as well as over dependence, is that it locates the site of the disorder (in the central nervous system) and indicates the cause: adaptation (learning). However, this term did not gain wide acceptance, therefore the word "alcoholism" has remained the most commonly used term, with occasional deference to "alcohol addiction" or "alcohol dependence."

American Society of Addiction Medicine (1990)-ASAM

The new kid on the block in defining and treating addiction is the American Society of Addiction Medicine. American Society of Addiction Medicine. *Disease definition of alcoholism revised. Addiction Review* 2(2):3 (1990) In 1990 ASAM proposed a definition which incorporated many of the then contemporary ideas, namely:

Alcoholism is a primary, chronic disease with genetic, psychosocial, and environmental factors influencing its development and manifestations. The disease is often progressive and fatal. It is characterized by continuous or periodic impaired control over drinking, preoccupation with the drug alcohol, use of alcohol despite adverse consequences, and distortions in thinking, most notably denial.

The ASAM Patient Placement Criteria -ASAM-PPC

The American Society of Addiction Medicine Patient Placement Criteria (ASAM-PPC) was developed to provide a standardized treatment matching tool that has been in use since the early 1990's. The ASAM criteria allows a "clinician to systematically evaluate the severity of a patient's need for treatment along six dimensions, and then utilize a fixed combination rule to determine which of four levels of care a substance abusing patient will respond to with the greatest success." Turner, W. M., Turner, K. H., Reif, S., Gutowski, W. E., & Gastfriend, D. R. *Feasibility of multidimensional substance abuse treatment matching: Automating the ASAM Patient Placement Criteria.* Drug and Alcohol Dependence (1999) The four levels of care are: Outpatient Treatment (level 1), Intensive Outpatient/Partial Hospitalization (level 2), Medically Monitored Intensive Inpatient Treatment (level 3), and Medically Managed Intensive Inpatient Treatment (level 4).

Many have questioned the validity and effectiveness of the ASAM-PPC under normal clinical settings. One such group was commissioned in 1997 to study the predictive validity of the ASAM-PPC for inpatient versus intensive outpatient care. *McKay, J.R., Cacciola, J.S., Mclellan, A.T., Alaterman, A.I. and Wirtz, P.W. An initial evaluation of the psychosocial dimensions of the American Society of Addiction Medicine criteria for inpatient versus intensive outpatient substance abuse rehabilitation.* J. Stud. Alcohol 58 (1997) Using ASAM-PPC criteria the study determined whether the level of care received by 159 cocaine-dependent and 133 alcohol-dependent male patients was correctly matched. While there were some positive results when looking at short-term outcomes the authors felt that the overwhelming evidence did not support the predictive validity of the ASAM-PPC with regards to differentiating level 2 or level 3 treatment. Interestingly, and most applicable to the DUI setting, alcohol patients determined by the ASAM-PPC in need of inpatient care had no better results than those mismatched to outpatient care. The authors do point out that the ASAM-PPC is an improvement over previous matching protocols in promoting more cost-effective treatments. However, they feel that in regard to the specific population studied, the criteria for inpatient care may still be too broad.

In 2002, another study was performed that examined the effectiveness of the ASAM-PPC in a substance abuse treatment program which tried to minimize barriers to treatment. Kosanke, N., Magura, S., Staines, G., Foote, J., & DeLuca, A. *Feasibility of matching alcohol patients to ASAM levels of care.* American Journal on Addictions, 11. (2002) The study took place at a treatment center that accepted both public and private insurance coverage and the authors assessed the amount of mismatches in treatment placement and whether patients received overtreatment or under treatment. According to the study clients were matched correctly 72% of the time and interestingly the reasons given for overtreatment were the availability of Medicaid coverage for inpatient treatment, referral sources, philosophy of gradually "stepping down" from inpatient detoxification, social pressures on patients, and mandated treatment. The study did not make mention of overtreatment possibly being the result of the treatment facility wanting to cash in on insurance availability (thereby padding the pockets of the business owners). The reasons for under treatment, according to the study, were work schedule conflicts, patient reluctance, insurance coverage and interference with family or personal responsibilities.

Another concern many experts had was based on whether the complexity of the ASAM criteria would yield acceptable results when administered by the average clinician. A study in 1999 evaluated a computerized decision-making algorithm that automatically performs the complex information integration required by the ASAM-PPC criteria. Turner, W. M., Turner, K. H., Reif, S., Gutowski, W. E., & Gastfriend, D. R. *Feasibility of multidimensional substance abuse treatment matching: Automating the ASAM Patient Placement Criteria.* Drug and Alcohol Dependence (1999) One variable in determining the effectiveness of any assessment tool is how consistently each counselor performs the screening. The idea suggested in the study was if a computerized ASAM-PPC was shown to be as effective as one given by a trained intake counselor, hypothetically this would remove the human element which traditionally has lead to occasionally inconsistent results when determining the level of care. According to the authors, "the algorithm showed acceptable discrimination between each of three ASAM Levels of Care across numerous clinical subscales." The authors concluded that the computerized model succeeded in integrating diverse clinically relevant factors within the level of care designations.

Another study that was completed in 2003 examined the predictive validity of the ASAM PPC for matching alcoholism patients to different levels of care. Magura, S., Staines, G., Kosanke, N., Rosenblum, A., Foote, J., DeLuca, A., & Bali, P. *Predictive validity of the ASAM patient placement criteria for naturalistically matched vs. mismatched alcoholism patients.* The American Journal on Addictions, 12 (2003) The data obtained supported the original hypotheses (matching to level of care is optimal, under treatment is clinically harmful and overtreatment is a waste of resources). The authors concluded that in general the ASAM-PPC was effective in reducing both under treatment and overtreatment.

The initial Patient Placement Criteria (PPC) of the American Society of Addiction Medicine (ASAM) was generally designed for programs that offered only addiction treatment services. However, a weakness in the original program was that the ASAM PPC seemingly paid little attention to the existence of co-occurring mental health problems in populations of persons with substance use disorders. That is why the inclusion of Dimension 3, Emotional, Behavioral Conditions and

Complications, as one of the six assessment dimensions, in 1991, emphasized the need for programs and practitioners to address a person's mental health needs.

It was not until the revised second edition, Patient Placement Criteria for the Treatment of Substance-Related Disorders, ASAM PPC-2R that the ASAM Criteria went further to help practitioners determine the appropriate type of treatment services to match the severity/stability of mental health problems. Mee-Lee, D. Shulman, G. D., Fishman, M., Gastfriend, D. R., & Griffith, J. H. (Eds.) *ASAM patient placement criteria for the treatment of substance-related disorders, second edition-revised (ASAM PPC-2R)*. Chevy Chase, MD: American Society of Addiction Medicine, Inc. (2001)

The ASAM PPC-2R adopted the increasingly used term "Co-Occurring Mental and Substance-Related Disorders." This term is also consistent with the Diagnostic and Statistical Manual of Mental Disorders of the American Psychiatric Association, DSM-IV-TR, (APA, 2000). The ASAM PPC-2R model also refers to the term "dual diagnosis" because it still has the widest recognition nationally. One significant change in ASAM PPC-2R was to expand the understanding of Dimension 3 to Emotional, Behavioral, or Cognitive Conditions and Complications.

Alternative Treatment Practices

In addition to the "standardized" and accepted forms of diagnosis and treatment for substance abuse, there are additional practices that have followers. While some of the following forms of treatment may work for many and therefore cannot be dismissed, the concern in the legal environment is whether different forms of diagnosis and treatment would be accepted in the court setting. This creates a quandary because the goal of evaluations and treatment is to cure the addiction. Hence, it seems counter productive that some forms of treatment that may work for certain types of individuals are rejected by Courts simply because it is not on a list of accepted agencies in the court's file.

Self Reporting

There are several tools that are used by treatment providers to detect whether an individual has substance abuse issues or may potentially have substance abuse issues. One such tool involves self reports, typically in the form of questionnaires.

The CAGE questionnaire is one such example and has been extensively validated for use in identifying alcoholism. The CAGE questionnaire is an acronym so named for the four questions it asks, namely: 1. Have you ever felt you needed to **C**ut down on your drinking?; 2. Have people **A**nnoyed you by criticizing your drinking?; 3. Have you ever felt **G**uilty about drinking?; 4. Have you ever felt you needed a drink first thing in the morning (**E**ye-opener) to steady your nerves or to get rid of a hangover? Ewing, John A. *Detecting Alcoholism: The CAGE Questionnaire.* JAMA 252: 1905-1907 (1984) The CAGE questionnaire has been studied and validated for use in identifying alcoholism. Kitchens, J.M. *Does this patient have an alcohol problem?* JAMA 272 (22): 1782-7 (1994) One such study determined that CAGE test scores had a sensitivity of 93% and a specificity of 76% for identifying people with alcohol problems. Bernadt, M.W., Mumford, J., Taylor, C., Smith, B., Murray, R.M. *Comparison of questionnaire and laboratory tests in the detection of excessive drinking and alcoholism.* Lancet 6 (8267): 325-8 (1982) Importantly, it is not valid for diagnosis of other substance use disorders, although somewhat modified versions of the CAGE are frequently implemented for such a purpose.

Another example of self reporting is the Alcohol Dependence Data Questionnaire which is a more sensitive diagnostic test than the CAGE test. This particular test helps distinguish a diagnosis of alcohol dependence from one of heavy alcohol use.

Yet another self reporting aid is the Michigan Alcohol Screening Test (MAST). This test is used as a screening tool for alcoholism and is used by courts in many jurisdictions to determine the appropriate sentencing for people convicted of alcohol-related offenses. Vaillant, GE. *A 60-year follow-up of alcoholic men.* Addiction. 98: 1043–51 (2003)

The World Health Organization developed its own screening questionnaire called the Alcohol Use Disorders Identification Test (AUDIT). This test is unique in that it has been validated internationally and is commonly used in six countries. Ewing, JA. *Detecting alcoholism. The CAGE questionnaire.* JAMA : The Journal of the American Medical Association 252 (14): 1905–7 (October 1984) Similar to the CAGE questionnaire, it uses a simple series of questions and a resulting high score earns a more thorough investigation of potential issues and dependency.

The last self reporting test of note is the Paddington Alcohol Test (PAT) which was developed to screen for alcohol related problems for those who have been admitted into a hospital (or emergency situation) due to injury or trauma. It is very similar to the AUDIT questionnaire but with one very significant difference, it is administered far quicker (one-fifth of the time needed for the AUDIT questionnaire). This is an obvious need for individuals who maybe injured or in a trauma like condition.

Rationing and Moderation

There are many who believe that complete abstinence from alcohol is not the appropriate or realistic remedy to alcoholism. There exits rationing and moderation programs such as "Moderation Management" and "DrinkWise" that do not mandate complete abstinence. A 2002 U.S. study by the National Institute on Alcohol Abuse and Alcoholism (NIAAA) showed that 17.7% of individuals diagnosed as alcohol dependent returned to low-risk drinking. However, this group showed fewer initial symptoms of dependency. Dawson, D.A., Grant, B.F., Stinson, F.S., Chou, P.S., Huang, B, and Ruan, W.J. *Recovery from DSM-IV alcohol dependence: United States, 2001-2002".* Addiction (Abingdon, England) 100 (3): 281– 92. (March 2005) However, a subsequent study, using the same NESARC subjects that were judged to be in remission in 2001-2002, examined the rates of return to problem drinking in 2004-2005. The major conclusion made by the authors of this NIAAA study was "abstinence represents the most stable form of remission for most recovering alcoholics". Dawson, D.A., Goldstein, R.B., and Grant, B.F. *Rates and correlates of relapse among individuals in remission from DSM-IV alcohol dependence: a 3-year follow-up.* Alcoholism, clinical and experimental research. 31 (12): 2036–45. (December 2007)

Medications

In addition to traditional forms of treating alcohol and drug dependencies, namely treatment and abstinence, medication is also used to help cure addiction. A variety of medications may be prescribed as part of treatment for alcohol and drug addiction.

Antabuse (also known as disulfiram) is a commonly used substance that prevents the elimination of acetaldehyde, a chemical the body produces when breaking down ethanol. Acetaldehyde itself is the cause of many hangover symptoms from alcohol use. As a result, if the user consumes alcohol while taking antabuse the resulting effect is severe discomfort, namely an extremely fast-acting and long-lasting uncomfortable hangover. This negative side effect is designed to discourage an alcoholic from drinking in significant amounts while they take the medicine. A 9-year study found that incorporation of supervised disulfiram and a related compound carbamide into a comprehensive treatment program resulted in an abstinence rate of over 50%. Krampe, H, Stawicki, S, Wagner, T, *et al. Follow-up of 180 alcoholic patients for up to 7 years after outpatient treatment: impact of alcohol deterrents on outcome.* Alcoholism, clinical and experimental research 30 (1) (January 2006)

Naltrexone is an antagonist for opioid receptors and has been observed to effectively block the body's ability to use endorphins and opiates. Naltrexone is used in two very different forms of treatment. The first form of treatment uses naltrexone to decrease cravings for alcohol and encourage abstinence, while the second form of treatment, called pharmacological extinction, combines naltrexone with normal drinking habits in order to reverse the endorphin conditioning that causes alcohol addiction. Naltrexone comes in two forms, an oral naltrexone (a pill that must be taken daily to be effective) and the second form is a time-release formulation (named Vivitrol) that is injected in the buttocks once a month.

Acamprosate (also known as Campral (produced by Forest Labs)) is believed to stabilize the chemical balance of the brain that would otherwise be disrupted by alcoholism. The Food and Drug Administration (FDA) approved this drug in 2004, saying "[w]hile its mechanism of action is not fully understood, Campral is thought to act on the brain pathways related to alcohol abuse... Campral proved superior to placebo in maintaining abstinence for a short period of time..." *FDA Approves New Drug for Treatment of Alcoholism.* http://www.fda.gov; FDA Application No. (NDA) 021431. Alternatively, other studies have found no benefit in using acamprosate to treat alcohol dependency. *Naltrexone or Specialized Alcohol Counseling an Effective Treatment for Alcohol Dependence When Delivered with Medical Management.* http://www.niaaa.nih.gov

Topiramate (brand name Topamax) is a derivative of the naturally occurring sugar monosaccharide D-fructose and has been found effective in assisting alcoholics with stopping or reducing the amount of alcohol they consume. One study found that heavy drinkers were six times more likely to remain abstinent for a month if they took the medication, even in small doses. Johnson, B.A., Ait-Daoud, N, Bowden, C.L., *et al. Oral topiramate for treatment of alcohol dependence: a randomised controlled trial.* Lancet 361 (9370): 1677–850 (May 2003); Swift, R.M. *"Topiramate for the treatment of alcohol dependence: initiating abstinence".* Lancet 361 (9370): 1666–7 (May 2003) In another study, those who received topiramate had fewer heavy drinking days, fewer drinks per day and more days of continuous abstinence than those who received the placebo. Johnson BA, Rosenthal N, Capece JA, *et al. Topiramate for treating alcohol dependence: a randomized controlled trial.* JAMA : the journal of the American Medical Association 298 (14): 1641–51 (October 2007) Topiramate works by reducing dopamine so that drinkers no longer get any pleasure from consuming alcohol and is the only medication shown to be effective for persons who are still drinking.

The Weird and Unusual

The evolution of treating "alcoholism" has been slow. It has only been since the middle of the twentieth century that government has dedicated serious money to the study of the diagnosis and treatment of this disease. Prior to this time however, there were still many groups and individuals who were attempting to find cures and treatment for alcoholism. Many of these attempts were legitimate and many were undoubtedly versions of snake-oil salesmen.

In the late 19th and early 20th centuries, physical methods of treating alcoholism found some acceptance within American medicine. This period saw the introduction of drug therapies, mechanical manipulation, surgical alteration, natural therapies (water, air, sunlight), and chemical and electro-convulsive therapies.

Shockingly, one form of treatment for alcoholism was sterilization. The law in Iowa in 1913 gave administrators and officers of asylums discretionary power to sterilize those people who in their judgment "would produce children with tendency to disease, deformity, crime, insanity, feeble-mindedness, idiocy, imbecility, or alcoholism." Reilly, Philip R. *The Surgical Solution: A History of Involuntary Sterilization of the United States*. Baltimore: The Johns Hopkins U. P. Page 53 (1991)

The sterilization of alcoholics was performed in the United States but found its zenith in Nazi Germany. It has been estimated that between 20,000 and 30,000 German alcoholics were subjected to forced sterilization during the Nazi reign. Kevles, D.J. *In the Name of Eugenics: Genetics and the Uses of Human Heredity*. New York: Alfred A. Knopf. (1985)

A far more humane form of treatment came by way of natural therapeutics. Dr. Henry Lindlahr, the author of the 1919 text entitled "Natural Therapeutics", described this approach to alcoholism treatment:

The active treatment of alcoholism must include everything that is good in natural methods. Of primary importance is a strict vegetarian diet, alternating between raw food, dry food, milk diet and fasting regimen. Tonic cold water treatments, massage, Swedish movements, neurotherapy, curative gymnastics, air and sun baths and everything else conducive to a thorough regeneration of the system must be applied systematically. Lindlahr, H. *Practice of Natural Therapeutics*. Chicago: Lindlahr Publishing Company (1919)

Water and its relationship to alcohol abuse has a long history in America. In his 1774 essay, "The Mighty Destroyer Displayed," Anthony Benezet recommended using water to progressively dilute alcoholic drinks as a way of weaning alcoholics from the habit. Benezet, Anthony. *The Mighty Destroyer Displayed*. Joseph Crukshank Pub. Philadelphia (1774) Dr. Benjamin Rush, during the same period recommended cold showers in the treatment of alcoholism and cold water as an alternative to alcohol.

In the late 19th and early 20th centuries drug therapies started to be used for the treatment of alcoholism. One of the most unusual of the drug therapies for alcoholism was the substitution of opiates for alcohol. By far the most outspoken advocate of this approach was Dr. J.R. Black, who, in an 1889 article in the *Cincinnati Lancet-Clinic*, advocated incurable alcoholics to morphine. Black urged the "substitution of morphine instead of alcohol for all to whom such a craving is an incurable propensity." Black, J. *Advantages of Substituting the Morphia Habit for the Incurably Alcoholic*. The Cincinnati Lancet-Clinic. 22:540 (1889)

Yet another interesting and perplexing treatment for alcoholism was "convulsive therapy." This therapy for alcoholism originated in 1934 after Dr. J. L. Meduna observed that agitation and depression in a patient subsided following a seizure. During 1935 and 1936, seizures were induced through the use of a drug such as metrazol or cardiazol, in an effort to achieve this effect. This practice was discontinued when patients complained of the extreme terror they experienced just before onset of the seizure.

A ghastly surgical method that was eventually attempted on alcoholics in an attempt to cure their addiction was the lobotomy. Psychosurgery as a treatment for alcoholism stopped primarily due to consistent reports that such procedures had only a "negligible" effect on the alcoholic's drinking behavior. Talbot, B., Ellis, E. and Greenblatt, M. *Alcoholism and Lobotomy*. AJSA, 12(3): 386-394 (1951)

Other physical treatment for alcoholism employed in the latter half of the 19th century and first half of the 20th century included the application of electrical current that was believed to stimulate the growth of damaged nerve tissue, exposing alcoholics to hot-air boxes and light boxes that mimicked the climatic conditions of the equator, where alcoholism was rare, massage treatments and vibrating machines, treatments involving oxygen inhalation and injections of calcium salts, treatments involving spinal puncture, and finally there were institutions that reported treating alcoholics with "typhoid fever therapy" and "colonic irrigation therapy." Ashworth, W. *Rambling Thoughts About Whiskey and Drug Addiction*. Virginia Medical Monographs. 58:678 (1932); Voegtlin, W.L., & Lemere, F. *The treatment of alcohol addiction*. A review of literature. Quarterly 10. Journal of Studies on Alcohol. 2. Page 772 (1942); Corwin, E. H. L., and Cunningham, E. V. *Institutional Facilities for the Treatment of Alcoholism*. New York: The Research Council on Problems of Alcohol. Pages 11-85 (1944)

Perhaps the most unusual treatment was proposed by a physician in a 1900 medical journal. Based on his observation that alcoholics lost interest in drinking while suffering from an active case of gonorrhea, the physician suggested inoculating alcoholics with gonorrhea as an economical alternative to institutional treatment. *Gonorrhea, A Cure for Inebriety*. Canadian Practice. 25:170 (1900) Not surprisingly this form of treatment never caught on.

ALCOHOL AND DRUG SUPPORT ORGANIZATIONS

Alcoholics Anonymous

Alcoholics Anonymous (AA) is a worldwide fellowship of men and women who share a common desire to stop drinking alcohol. *The Twelve Traditions.* The A.A. Grapevine (Alcoholics Anonymous) 6 (6) (November 1949) The goal is for members to completely abstain from alcohol, attend meetings regularly, and follow its program to help each other with their common purpose; to "stay sober and help other alcoholics achieve sobriety." *Alcoholics Anonymous' Alcoholics Anonymous: the story of how many thousands of men and women have recovered from alcoholism* (4th edition ed.). New York, NY: Alcoholics Anonymous World Services (June 1, 1976)

AA's history begins with Bill Wilson whose promising Wall Street career was threatened because of his constant intoxication. Bill was introduced to the idea of a spiritual cure for his alcoholism by Ebby Thacher, an old drinking buddy. Ebby had become a member of the Oxford Group, a "first century Christian movement." Wilson was treated at Charles B. Towns hospital by Dr. William Silkworth, who personally promoted a disease concept of alcoholism. While in the hospital, Wilson underwent what he believed to be a spiritual experience and he was able to stop drinking.

Although Wilson successfully remained sober for an extended period of time, while on a 1935 business trip to Akron, Ohio, he felt the urge to drink again. In an effort to stay sober he sought another alcoholic for help. Wilson was introduced to Dr. Bob Smith and the two co-founded AA with a word of mouth program to help alcoholics. Smith's last drink was on June 10, 1935 and this date is considered by members to be the founding date of AA. *Pass It on: The Story of Bill Wilson and how the A.A. Message Reached the World.* New York, NY: Alcoholics Anonymous World Services, Inc. Pages 131–149 (December 1984) According to Wilson and Smith, by 1937 they had helped 40 alcoholics get sober. In 1939 AA had approximately 100 members and in an effort to expand the program Wilson wrote a book entitled *Alcoholics Anonymous*, which then became the name of the organization. The book (also known as "The Big Book") introduced the twelve-step program which involved the admission of powerlessness over alcohol, moral inventory, and asking for help from God. In 1941 book sales and membership increased after radio interviews and favorable articles in national magazines, particularly by Jack Alexander in *The Saturday Evening Post.*

In 1946 Wilson wrote the guidelines for non-coercive group management that eventually became known as the "Twelve Traditions." This writing was the result of significant membership growth and the resulting confusion and disputes within groups over practices, finances, and publicity. AA truly came of age in 1955 when Wilson turned over the stewardship of AA to the General Service Conference at their 1955 St. Louis convention. *Pass It on: The Story of Bill Wilson and how the A.A. Message Reached the World.* New York, NY: Alcoholics Anonymous World Services, Inc. Page 359 (December 1984) In the 1950s AA also began its international expansion, and by 2006 there were 1,867,212 members in 106,202 AA groups worldwide. "AA Fact File." *Alcoholics Anonymous website.* http://www.aa.org.

A member of AA who accepts a service position or works in an organizing role is considered a "trusted servant." The terms of such positions are rotating and limited with the typical period lasting from three months to two years and determined by group vote. Each AA group is a self-governing entity and AA World Services acts strictly in an advisory capacity. AA is served entirely by those who are or have been alcohol dependant (alcoholics). The only exception is that there are seven "nonalcoholic friends of the fellowship" on the twenty-one member AA Board of Trustees. "AA Fact File." *Alcoholics Anonymous website.* http://www.aa.org/

AA is a non-profit organization and members pay no dues or membership fees. However, individual groups often rely on member donations, and are collected to pay for expenses such as room rentals, refreshments, and literature. Importantly, AA has a policy of not rejecting any member due to their inability to financially contribute and no one is turned away for lack of funds.

AA's philosophy is to have its members change their drinking habits and encourage its members to improve their moral character and spiritual well-being. Humphreys, Keith and Kaskutas, Lee A. *World Views of Alcoholics Anonymous, Women for Sobriety, and Adult Children of Alcoholics/Al-Anon Mutual Help Groups.* Addiction Research & Theory 3 (3): 231-243 (1995) AA encourages its members to help with duties and service work in the organization, attend AA meetings regularly, and remain in contact with fellow AA members. *A Newcomer Asks pamphlet.* http://www.alcoholics-anonymous.org

In addition to changing one's moral behavior members are encouraged to find an experienced fellow alcoholic within the organization (referred to as a "sponsor") to help them understand and follow the AA program. Some members suggest the sponsor is preferably one that has maintained sobriety for at least a year and is of the same sex as the member. Zemore, S. E., Kaskutas, L. A., & Ammon, L. N. *In 12-step groups, helping helps the helper.* Addiction 99 (8): 1015–1023 (August 2004) The philosophy behind the sponsor program is that with help the member's new behaviors will result in improved abstinence and thereby lowering the probability of binge drinking.

In a typical AA meeting, the chairperson starts by calling the meeting to order and offering a short prayer, meditation, and/or period of silence (practice varies by meeting). Then, a section from the book Alcoholics Anonymous may be read aloud, usually the beginning of Chapter Five, entitled "How It Works". Announcements from the chairperson and group members follow. Many groups celebrate newcomers, visitors, and sobriety anniversaries with rounds of applause. Depending on the type of meeting, a talk by a speaker relating their personal experience with alcoholism and AA or a discussion session with topics chosen by the chairperson, the speaker, or the attendees follows. When a member decides to share he/she is expected to begin with the statement, "My name is

_____ and I am an alcoholic (or visitor, or friend)". Meetings typically end with a prayer, usually the Serenity Prayer and the Lord's Prayer.

The study of AA effectiveness has found many polarized views. A *Cochrane Review* of eight studies, published between 1967 and 2005, measuring the effectiveness of AA found no significant difference between the results of AA and twelve-step facilitation approaches compared to other treatments. The report stated that "[n]o experimental studies unequivocally demonstrated the effectiveness of AA or TSF approaches for reducing alcohol dependence or problems." Ferri, M, Amato, L, Davoli, M. *Alcoholics Anonymous and other 12-step programmes for alcohol dependence.* Cochrane Database of Systematic Reviews. Issue 3. (2006) To further determine the effectiveness of AA, the authors suggested more studies comparing treatment outcomes with control groups were necessary.

In 1989 AA authorized an internal report to determine the attrition rate of its members. The report evaluated five different surveys and estimated that of those who attended AA meetings for the first time, nearly one third (31.5%) left the program after one month. The report stated that by the end of the third month, just over half (52.6%) had left and of those who remained after three months, about half (55.6%) will continue with the program until the twelfth month. *Comments On A.A. Triennial Surveys.* Alcoholics Anonymous World Services. (Dec. 1990); Alcoholics Anonymous UK: Legal Professionals. *Alcoholics Anonymous UK website.* The study concluded that if members remained with the program for a period of time of more than one year, the rate of attrition slowed.

AA has not examined why the attrition rate is what it is. However, there remains a significant involvement in the program by individuals who may not wish to participate. For example, AA receives 11% of its membership from court ordered attendance. Humphreys, Keith. *Alcoholics Anonymous and 12-Step Alcoholism Treatment Programs.* Recent Developments in Alcoholism. 16. Springer US. Pages 149–164 (2002) The willingness of its participants, or lack thereof, would surely also be attributable to the high attrition rate.

AA does acknowledge that not all drinkers are alcoholics, but advocates total abstinence for those who are. Peele, Stanton. *The Diseasing of America*. Lexington, MA: Lexington Books (1989); Shute, Nancy. *The drinking dilemma: by calling abstinence the only cure, we ensure that the nation's $100 billion alcohol problem won't be solved*. U.S. News & World Report 123 (9): 54–64 (September 1997) There are some critics who argue that some AA groups apply the disease model to all problem drinkers, whether or not they are full-blown alcoholics, and believe that more options should be available to problem drinkers who can manage their drinking with the right treatment. Dawson, DA, Grant, BF, Stinson, FS, Chou, PS, Huang, B, Ruan, WJ. *Recovery from DSM-IV alcohol dependence: United States, 2001-2002*. Addiction. 100(3):281-92 (2005); Dawson, DA, Goldstein, RB, Grant, BF. *Rates and correlates of relapse among individuals in remission from DSM-IV alcohol dependence: a 3-year follow-up*. Alcohol Clin Exp Res. (12):2036-45 (2007)

One scribe wrote of the perceived negative effects of twelve-step philosophy and concluded that AA uses many methods that are also used by cults. Levinson, D. Galanter, Marc. ed. *Current status of the field: An anthropological perspective on the behavior modification treatment of alcoholism*. Recent Developments in Alcoholism (New York: Plenum Press) 1: 255–261. (1983) However, another study concluded that AA's program bore little semblance to a religious cult because the techniques used appeared beneficial. Wilcox, D.M. *Chapter 7: Language, Culture, and Belief System. Alcoholic thinking: Language, culture, and belief in Alcoholics Anonymous*. Westport, CT: Greenwood Publishing Group. Pages 109–124 (1998)

Narcotics Anonymous

Modeled after Alcoholics Anonymous (AA), Narcotics Anonymous (NA) is a twelve-step program of recovery from drug addiction and is the second-largest 12-step organization in the world. The organization describes itself as a nonprofit "fellowship or society of men and women for whom drugs had become a major problem." Narcotics Anonymous World Services, Inc., ed. *N.A. White Booklet.* *Narcotics Anonymous World Services, Inc.* "N.A. History Workshop." (1976/1986) Like AA the NA program is group-oriented, and is based on the Twelve Steps and the Twelve Traditions as introduced by AA.

The only requirement NA demands for its members is "a desire to stop using," and members "meet regularly to help each other stay clean." NA defines "clean" as complete abstinence from all mood and mind altering substances (including alcohol). *Id.* Membership in N.A. is free, and there are no dues or fees.

Narcotics Anonymous developed out of the Alcoholics Anonymous Program of the late 1940s, and was co-founded by Jimmy Kinnon and others. Meetings began in the Los Angeles area of California in the early fifties and NA was officially founded in 1953. "History and Origins (draft)". *Narcotics Anonymous Way of Life.* N.A. Foundation Group; http://www.na-history.org; *U.S. Public Health Service: Public Affairs Pamphlet #186;* page 29 (September, 1952) This group attempted to form a fellowship or network of groups that would be mutually supporting. Throughout the summer of 1953 the founding members debated the bylaws of the organization in an attempt to find common ground. The first documented meeting occurred August 17, 1953 and on September 14, 1953 official notice from the leadership of AA gave permission to the organization to use the A.A. steps and traditions, but not the A.A. name. Henceforth the organization became known as Narcotics Anonymous. In 1954, NA released its first publication called the "Little Yellow Booklet" which contained the 12 steps.

The initial years of NA were not met with much fanfare. Truth be told there were considerable problems that had to be addressed before the organization could grow. The initial group had difficulty finding places that would allow them to meet, and often the group had to meet in people's homes. One of the most difficult places for NA to become established was in the State of New York. The Rockefeller drug laws in New York had made it a crime for drug addicts to meet together for any reason, making N.A. effectively illegal. It was, therefore, many years before NA became recognized as a beneficial organization.

Toward the end of the 1950s NA meeting participation began to decline. Then in the early 1960s NA enjoyed a renaissance of sorts and meetings began to form again and grow. In 1962 the "White Booklet" was written and published by NA and this became the foundation for all subsequent NA literature. This booklet was republished in 1966 as the NA White Book, and included the personal stories of many addicts.

During the 1970s NA experienced significant growth in its membership. In 1970 there were only 20 regular weekly meetings and all of these were in the United States. Within two years there were 70 regular weekly meetings and the organization had spread to Germany, Australia, and Bermuda. By 1976, there were 200 regular weekly meetings (including 83 in California alone), and NA had found a foothold in Brazil, Canada, Colombia, India, the Republic of Ireland, Japan, New Zealand, and the United Kingdom. A year later, in 1976, NA opened its World Service Office. Five years later, there were 1100 different meetings all over the world. *A Guide to World Services in N.A.* Narcotics Anonymous World Services, Inc. Pages 1–5 and 37 (2004)

Al-Anon/Alateen

Al-Anon and Alateen are both international organizations which are jointly referred to as the Al-Anon Family Groups. Al-Anon is for adults within the program whereas Alateen is for young people (ages 12 to 20). Al-Anon was formed in 1951 by Lois Wilson, wife of Alcoholics Anonymous (AA) co-founder Bill Wilson. Ms. Wilson recognized the need for such an organization to support family members living with AA members as they began to identify their own issues that were associated with their family members' alcoholism. Today membership consists of over half a million men, women and teens and the organization provides a twelve-step program of recovery for friends and family members of alcoholics. Haaken, Janice, *From Al-Anon to ACOA: Codependence and the Reconstruction of Caregiving.* Signs: Journal of Women in Culture and Society 18 (2): 321–345 (1993) In the USA, Al-Anon is organized as a 501(c)(3) non-profit organization in many states.

Cocaine Anonymous

Cocaine Anonymous (CA) is another twelve-step program patterned very closely after Alcoholics Anonymous, although the two groups are unaffiliated. CA is a program for people who seek recovery from drug addiction, specifically for those who have been addicted to cocaine, crack, speed or similar substances. *And All Other Mind-Altering Substances.* Cocaine Anonymous (2007)

Cocaine Anonymous was founded on November 23rd, 1982 in Hollywood, California. The founding members where Johnny S, Ray G, and Gilbert M, all of whom were from the Los Angeles area. In August 1982, prior to the official founding, Tom Kinney the owner of the entertainment industry sober living facility called "Studio 12," recognized the need for a type of meeting where cocaine addicted people could share about their struggles and sobriety. Tom Kinney arranged for a local AA meeting to be held and to allow the topic of that meeting to be specifically about cocaine addiction. Two days after this meeting another meeting was held and the name Cocaine Anonymous was officially used for the first time. Cocaine Anonymous. *Hope, Faith and Courage: Stories from the Fellowship of Cocaine Anonymous.* Los Angeles, California: Cocaine Anonymous World Services (January 1993); Cohen, Sidney. *The Substance Abuse Problems.* New York, New York: Haworth Press (1985) Presently CA reports more than 700,000 members world-wide, in 38 countries, with more than 2,000 individual meetings. www.ca.org.

CA uses the book *Alcoholics Anonymous* as its basic text, with additional resources including, *Hope, Faith and Courage: Stories from the Fellowship of Cocaine Anonymous.* Los Angeles, California: Cocaine Anonymous World Services (January 1993); Alcoholics

Anonymous *Twelve Steps and Twelve Traditions.* Hazelden (2002)

Marijuana Anonymous

Like AA (and the other spin offs from AA), Marijuana Anonymous (MA) is a fellowship of men and women who share their experiences and support with each other so that they may help themselves and others cure their marijuana addiction. It utilizes the same 12-Step program, as developed by Alcoholics Anonymous. Wetzstein, Cheryl. *Addicted to weed, boomers abandon life-ruining `herb': Marijuana Anonymous tries to help.* Washington Times. (November 12, 1997)

The organization grew out of frustration from those who attended other 12-step programs, such as Alcoholics Anonymous and Narcotics Anonymous, who felt that those programs did not take "marijuana addiction" seriously. Rees, Vaughan, Copeland, Jan and Swift, Wendy. *A brief cognitive-behavioural intervention for cannabis dependence: Therapists' treatment manual.* University of New South Wales (1998)

In June of 1989, delegates from Marijuana Smokers Anonymous (Orange County, California), Marijuana Addicts Anonymous (the San Francisco Bay area), and Marijuana Anonymous (Los Angeles County) met to establish a unified twelve-step recovery program for marijuana addicts. A smaller Marijuana Anonymous group in Seattle had been unable to send delegates because of the cost, and another small Marijuana Addicts Anonymous group in New York, was heard from after the fact. That first conference was held in Morro Bay, halfway between San Francisco and Los Angeles. At this conference one group, Marijuana Anonymous, was born. Shortly after the unification of the US programs, MA was contacted by another Marijuana Anonymous organization in New Zealand. This was the beginning of a worldwide organization. *A Brief History of Marijuana Anonymous.* The Literature Committee of Marijuana Anonymous World Service Conference (2001)

Crystal Meth Anonymous

Like its "Anonymous" brethren, Crystal Meth Anonymous (CMA) is a twelve-step fellowship but is for recovered and recovering methamphetamine addicts. Participants meet in local groups of varying sizes in order to stay clean and help others recover from methamphetamine addiction. Like AA, CMA encourages complete abstinence from methamphetamine, alcohol, inhalants, and all other drugs not taken as prescribed. Some of its members use the Alcoholic's Anonymous' "Big Book" as a guide for their program while others use the "Basic Text" of Narcotics Anonymous or that of other 12-step fellowships.

CMA was founded on September 16th, 1994 in West Hollywood, California. The first meeting was attended by 13 people and the group recognized the need for meetings independent from AA that focused on the specific care and treatment for crystal meth. *Id.*

CMA membership steadily grew across the United States and meetings in Canada and Australia followed thereafter. CMA now has a presence in over 100 metropolitan areas of the United States, as well as parts of Canada, Australia, and New Zealand. http://www.crystalmeth.org/. The first CMA World Service Conference was held in Park City, Utah from October 17th - 19th, 2008 and at that convention, the CMA Charter was adopted.

The growth of CMA membership reflects the rapid increase in use of Methamphetamines. In 2002, the United States Department of Health and Human Services estimated 12 million people, age 12 and over, had used methamphetamine, while 600,000 claimed to be current users. Further, the United States Department of Health and Human Services estimates that Methamphetamine use had a growth rate of approximately 300,000 new users per year. Lee, Steven. *Crystal Methamphetamine: Current Issues in Addiction and Treatment.* Paradigm (Spring 2006)

CHAPTER 8

The History of DUI Organizations

History is not history unless it is the truth.
—Abraham Lincoln

The history of the crime of driving under the influence would not be complete without reference to some of the major players. The significant organizations can generally be divided into three groups, although admittedly the lines between the first two groups are often blurred and their goals are not dissimilar. The first group is law enforcement or governmentally funded organizations (ie. NHTSA, IACP), the second group is organized to solicit community and political support on behalf of its agenda (ie. MADD), and the third and smallest group advocates on behalf of those accused of DUI (ie. NCDD) Each of these three groups serve a different purpose and each has had a role in shaping the field of driving under the influence.

Some significant organizations such as the National Association of Police Organizations (NAPO) and International Police Association (IPA) have been intentionally omitted from this chapter. This is not to make light of their impact in law enforcement but rather these organizations focus on areas such as union support and brotherhood rather than the active practice of law enforcement and in particular, the crime of driving under the influence.

National Highway Traffic Safety Administration (NHTSA)

The National Highway Traffic Safety Administration (NHTSA) is an agency of the Executive Branch of the United States Government and part of the Department of Transportation. According to the agency its mission is to "[s]ave lives, prevent injuries, reduce vehicle-related crashes." www.nhtsa.dot.gov No other entity, save the government itself, has had a greater influence in the field of DUI in the United States than NHTSA.

NHTSA's primary role within the government is to write and enforce safety, theft-resistance, and fuel economy standards for motor vehicles (under the banner of the Corporate Average Fuel Economy (CAFE) system). In addition to these roles NHTSA also licenses vehicle manufacturers and importers, allows or blocks the import of vehicles and safety-regulated vehicle parts, administers the VIN system, develops the anthropomorphic dummies used in safety testing, as well as the test protocols themselves, and provides vehicle insurance cost information.

Another of NHTSA's significant activities is the creation and maintenance of the data files maintained by the National Center for Statistics and Analysis. In particular, the Fatality Analysis Reporting System (FARS) has become a resource for traffic safety research in the United States and other countries. NHTSA has a lot on its plate in addition to its role in vehicle safety and in particular DUI law.

In 1966 the United States Department of Transportation was born (on October 15, 1966). Around this time other government agencies were created which would eventually join to become NHTSA, including the National Traffic Safety Agency, the National Highway Safety Agency, and the National Highway Safety Bureau. NHTSA was officially established in 1970 by the Highway Safety Act of 1970. In 1972, the Motor Vehicle Information and Cost Savings Act expanded NHTSA's scope to include consumer information programs.

Presently NHTSA has an annual budget of US $815 Million (2007) and the agency classifies most of its spending under the "driver safety" heading, with a minority spent on "vehicle safety," and a smaller amount on environmental matters of which it is in charge (i.e. vehicular fuel economy). NHTSA's impact in the DUI field has been significant, and of particular note has been their role in DUI investigations and the standardization of FSTs. (Also see Chapter 5)

The International Association of Chiefs of Police (IACP)

The International Association of Chiefs of Police (IACP) is headquartered in Alexandria, Virginia and as of 2006 had more than 20,000 members and 130 staff members. The organization, which was founded in 1893, is represented by three divisions – the State and Provincial Police Division, the International Policing Division and the State Associations of Chiefs of Police – and sixteen sections, including Police Psychological Services and Public Transit Policing sections.

The association's goals are to advance the science and art of police services; to develop and disseminate improved administrative, technical, and operational practices and promote their use in police work; to foster police cooperation and the exchange of information and experience among police administrators through the world; to bring about recruitment and training in the police profession of qualified persons; and to encourage adherence of all police officers to high professional standards of performance and conduct. Since its inception the IACP has played a major role in shaping law enforcement. Professionally recognized programs such as the FBI Identification Division and the Uniform Crime Records system can trace their origins back to the IACP. Greene, Jack R. Editor. *The Encyclopedia of Police Science*. Third Edition. Volume 1. Routledge (October 23, 2006)

The IACP President William Berger specifically addressed driving under the influence in his speech at the organization's annual conference in 2001 at Toronto, Canada. Chief Berger, on October 31, 2001, spoke of seven important "initiatives" that concerned him and that he would directly and aggressively involve the organization. "Initiative 5" dealt with driving under the influence, to which Chief Berger stated the following:

> It troubles me greatly when I hear state superintendents of police tell me that on any given day, there are hundreds of individuals who have had five or more convictions for D.U.I. still driving on the streets of their community. That is appalling. Who better than our Fifth Vice President Lonnie Westphal, Chief of the Colorado State Patrol, to be charged with reviewing our current state of enforcement of both D.U.I. and D.R.E. programs. I'm asking Lonnie to reach out to the state patrols and the world to establish data on the state of D.U.I. and D.R.E. to provide to our membership. With ecstasy being sold in this country in record volumes and becoming the #1 drug among our youth, replacing alcohol, it is imperative that we strengthen our D.R.E. programs which unfortunately, due to costs and training requirements, have eroded over the past several years.

Berger, William. *Inauguration Speech 10-31-2001*. International Association of Chiefs of Police Annual Conference. Toronto, Canada (2001)

The National District Attorneys Association (NDAA)

The National District Attorneys Association (NDAA) professes to be the oldest and largest professional organization that represents criminal prosecutors in the world. http://www.ndaa.org/ The membership comes from the offices of district attorneys, state's attorneys, attorneys general and county and city prosecutors with responsibility for prosecuting criminal violations in every state and territory of the United States. *Id.*

The NDAA was formed in 1950 by local prosecutors to give a focal point to advance their causes and issues at the national level. NDAA representatives regularly meet with the Department of Justice, members of Congress and other national associations to represent the views of prosecutors to influence federal and national policies and programs which impact law enforcement and prosecution.

The NDAA is governed by a board of directors which is made up of state directors appointed to the board by the prosecuting associations of the states, current and past officers of the association. NDAA is headquartered in Alexandria, Virginia, along with the training, research and development division. The training and education division and the National Advocacy Center are located in Columbia, South Carolina.

One of the purposes enumerated in the literature of the NDAA is to operate the training, research and development division of the corporation.

The mission of the institute is to support the objectives of NDAA by providing to state and local prosecutors knowledge, skills and support to ensure that justice is done and the public safety and rights of all are safeguarded. To accomplish this mission, the institute serves as a nationwide, interdisciplinary resource center for training, research, technical assistance, and publications reflecting the highest standards and cutting-edge practices of the prosecutorial profession. *Id.*

In addition to training and research that is afforded prosecuting attorneys, a manual specific to the prosecution of DUI offenders is also made available at no cost. The manual, *Prosecution of Driving While Under the Influence*, includes an overview of field sobriety testing, an explanation of the physiology of alcohol, a discussion of common DUI defenses and how to respond to each of them. There is no information available to determine how many of the country's prosecuting attorneys actually receive a copy of this resource.

Mothers Against Drunk Driving (MADD)

Mothers Against Drunk Driving, or MADD, is a Texas based non-profit organization founded in 1980 by Candice Lightner after her 13-year-old daughter was killed by a drunk driver in California.

MADD supports education, advocacy and victim assistance in the DUI legal realm. It also strongly advocates maintaining the per se blood alcohol content level of .08% and stronger sanctions for DUI offenders, including mandatory jail sentences, treatment for alcoholism and drug dependency issues, the installation of ignition interlock devices, and license suspensions. http://www.madd.org/ In 1983 a television movie about Lightner and the organization resulted in publicity for the group and at about the same time the group attracted the attention of the United States Congress. This publicity launched MADD as a major advocate in favor of stricter drunk driving laws.

Arguably MADD's greatest success occurred in 1984 with the introduction of the National Minimum Drinking Age Act. This federal law mandated a federal penalty (initially a 5% loss of federal highway dollars, later raised to 10%) for states that failed to raise the legal age for the purchase and possession of alcohol to 21 years of age. South Dakota, a state that permitted 19-year-olds to purchase beer containing up to 3.2% alcohol, sued to challenge the law, naming Secretary of Transportation Elizabeth Dole as the defendant because her office was responsible for enforcing the legislation. The law was upheld by the United States Supreme Court in the 1987 case of *South Dakota v. Dole*, 483 U.S. 203 (1987) and by 1988 every state and the District of Columbia had capitulated.

In 1990 MADD introduced its "20 by 2000" which was a goal to reduce the proportion of traffic fatalities that are alcohol-related by 20 percent by the year 2000. MADD announced that this goal was met in 1997, three years early. That same year, MADD Canada was founded. http://www.madd.ca/english/about/index.html In 1999, MADD's National Board of Directors voted to change the organization's mission statement to also include the prevention of underage drinking.

Another focus of MADD had been to lobby governmental officials to promote the reduction of the legal limit for blood alcohol concentration 0.10 to BAC 0.08. In 2000 Congress passed a law standardizing the per se BAC limit to 0.08 and by 2005 every state was in compliance.

MADD also advocates the mandatory attendance at a victim impact panels (VIP) for those charged with a DUI, the installation of ignition interlock devices for those convicted of DUIs, conducting "sobriety checkpoints" and "saturation patrols," maintaining the legal age of drinking in the United States at 21 years of age, additional taxes on the purchase of beer, and even for lowering the per se BAC limit again to a figure less than the current and accepted limit of 0.08.

There have been many who have applauded the roll of MADD in the field of DUI prevention. Certainly they have used their sphere of influence to persuade the public and law makers. To that end, in 1994 the Chronicle of Philanthropy released the results of a study of charitable and non-profit organization popularity and credibility. The study concluded that MADD was ranked as the most popular charity/ non-profit in America of over 100 charities researched. *The Charities Americans Like Most And Least.* The Chronicle of Philanthropy, (December 13, 1996)

However, the admiration of MADD is not unanimous. As with many organizations that advocate strong public policy, they have faced much criticism. The late William F. Buckley, Jr., a conservative activist who had criticized MADD from time to time, commented in 2001 on MADD's movement to maintain the legal drinking age at 21 years of age and restrict youth drinking: "We all know that up until the counter-Woodstock anti-alcohol putsch of a generation ago, drinking was permitted in most states after age 18. What seemed to happen simultaneously was that our lawmakers resolved (a) to forbid drinking until age 21, and (b) to permit voting at age 18," Buckley wrote. Buckley Jr., William F. *On the Right.* Universal Press (June 5, 2001)

Radley Balko, a writer for *Reason Magazine*, has been critical of MADD, it's targeting the social drinker, and its advocacy of random roadblocks to find drivers who have been drinking. In a 2002 article, Balko while giving credit to MADD's original mission argued that MADD's policies were becoming increasingly overbearing. "In fairness, MADD deserves credit for raising awareness of the dangers of driving while intoxicated. It was almost certainly MADD's dogged efforts to spark public debate that effected the drop in fatalities since 1980, when Candy Lightner founded the group after her daughter was killed by a drunk driver," Balko wrote. "But MADD is at heart a bureaucracy, a big one. It boasts an annual budget of $45 million, $12 million of which pays for salaries, pensions and benefits. Bureaucracies don't change easily, even when the problems they were created to address change." Balko, Radley. *Targeting the Social Drinker Is Just MADD.* CATO Institute (December 2002)

Balko continued his criticism in 2009 after President Obama's nomination of MADD's CEO Chuck Hurley to head up the National Highway Traffic Safety Administration (NHTSA). Balko, Radley. *Putting MADD in Charge of America's Highways.* Reason Magazine (April 24, 2009) Balko further stated that "[w]ith Hurley in charge, MADD's goals will become NHTSA's goals. That's troubling because at heart, MADD is an activist organization. The group's once-admirable goal of raising public awareness about drunk driving has over the last several years morphed into a zealous, evangelical teetotaling campaign." *Id.* Later, President Obama withdrew the nomination of Hurley for the head of NHTSA.

Besides criticism of MADD's policies and their increasing political input, there has been much negative attention focused on their fundraising and the dollars they have procured. Daniel Borochoff, the executive director of the American Institute of Philanthropy criticized MADD for the amount of money it spends on fundraising efforts and management. O'Donnell, Jayne. *"MADD enters 25th year with change on its mind."* USA Today (September 28, 2005). Even the American Institute of Philanthropy was critical of MADD giving it a "D" rating, which is considered "unsatisfactory." http://

www.charitywatch.org/criteria.html

Criticism of MADD has not been restricted to outsiders. For example, former President of MADD, Glynn Byrch, criticized MADD's policies with respect to underage drinking in a letter to the editor of the *Washington Post. Addressing Life's Perilous Pleasures.* The Washington Post. Letters to the Editor section. (Monday, August 15, 2005)

Finally, MADD founder Candy Lightner, who left the organization in 1985, has even been critical of the organization. In a 2002 interview published in the *Washington Times* she stated that "[MADD] has become far more neo-prohibitionist than I had ever wanted or envisioned ... I didn't start MADD to deal with alcohol. I started MADD to deal with the issue of drunk driving." Bresnahan, S. *"MADD struggles to remain relevant."* Washington Times (August 6, 2002)

Students Against Destructive Decisions (SADD)

SADD was founded as "Students Against Driving Drunk" in 1981 in Wayland, Massachusetts (now located in Marlborough, Massachusetts) and is a peer-to-peer youth education organization, focused on substance and alcohol use and abuse prevention. The organization currently has over 10,000 chapters in middle schools, high schools, and colleges in the USA and New Zealand. http://www.sadd.org/history.htm The organization eventually adopted the new name "Students Against Destructive Decisions."

Originally, SADD's message to young people was to say "No" to drinking and driving and cocaine consumption. In 1997, SADD expanded its mission to preventing the consumption of alcohol or illegal drugs and other related problems. After the name change the organization shifted their focus to the prevention of all destructive behaviors and attitudes that are potentially harmful to young people, including underage drinking, substance abuse, impaired driving, violence, and suicide.

SADD is also known for developing the "Contract for Life,"

which is a document that is signed by both parents and student. The document stipulates that the student will attempt their best to avoid drinking and driving, if, importantly, parents agree to do the same. Parents also agree to pick up their child at a party upon request, with no questions asked, if the student calls the parents after seeing harmful substances being used. http://www.sadd.org/contract.htm This contract is still in use today and has been updated to reflect the expanded scope of the Students Against Destructive Decisions mission.

National College for DUI Defense (NCDD)

Individuals charged with the crime of DUI did not have an organizational advocate on a national level until 1995 when the National College for DUI Defense, Inc. was started by twelve DUI defense attorneys from a number of different states. The group, headquartered in Montgomery, Alabama, incorporated as a non-profit organization in 1995 after organizational meetings in Atlanta and Chicago. Currently there are over 950 defense attorney members who are active members. www.NCDD.com

The college states that "[i]n sum, the mission of the College is to vindicate the promise of the United States Constitution, that a citizen accused has the right to the effective assistance of his or her counsel." As part of this mission, the College regularly hosts 3-day seminars for the profession, often in conjunction with the National Association of Criminal Defense Lawyers. These seminars educate and train DUI defense attorneys in all areas of DUI law and provide updates to the members on changes in the law and evidentiary changes in the field of DUI practice.

In 1999 the college recognized member lawyers with "board certification" who exemplify the program's standards, and who meet the criteria established by the board. In 2003 the American Bar Association recognized DUI defense law as a specialty area in the practice of law, and awarded its "Certificate of Accreditation" to the board certification program. The NCDD is currently the only organization in the country accredited to certify lawyers as DUI defense law specialists.

National Association of Criminal Defense Lawyers (NACDL)

The National Association of Criminal Defense Lawyers (NACDL) is an American criminal defense organization. Their stated mission is to advance "the mission of the nation's criminal defense lawyers to ensure justice and due process for persons accused of crime or other misconduct." http://www.nacdl.org Members of this organization include private criminal defense lawyers, public defenders, active U.S. military defense counsel, law professors, judges, and defense counsel in international criminal tribunals.

The NACDL was founded in 1958 and is now headquartered in Washington, D.C., and has more than 12,800 direct members and 94 state, local, and international affiliate criminal defense lawyer organizations with a total of about 35,000 members. *Id.*

The organization has a regular journal called *The Champion* which offers timely, informative articles written for and by criminal defense lawyers, featuring the latest developments in DUI/DWI law, and many more areas of criminal defense. NACDL forms an alliance with the NCDD and helps to co-host several large scale training seminars annually.

CHAPTER 9

The History of Prevention and Reoccurrence Programs

History does not usually make real sense until long afterward.
—Bruce Catton

Since drinking and driving was rendered illegal, society has employed legal threats against committing the crime. The familiar statutory formula of first offense, second offense, third offense to felony offense, has been a basic feature of the legal landscape since the 1930s. King, J. and Tipperman, M. *Offense of Driving While Intoxicated: The Development of Statutes and Case Law in New York.* Hofstra Law Review 3:541-604 (1975) Additionally, because DUI is a criminal offense there is always the threat of jail, often significant jail and frequently, depending on the state the DUI is committed, the jail time is mandatory. Therefore the deterrence model presently being employed against drinking and driving is not new. However, the deterrence model is continually evolving, embracing new technology, and bowing to public pressure.

The basic idea behind prevention and reoccurrence programs is to deter people from drinking and driving, to punish them if they do, and to stop them from committing the act again. Advocates of these programs include the state and federal government, law enforcement, social advocacy groups such as MADD, and undoubtedly, certain business owners (ignition interlock companies, alcohol/drug treatment centers, towing companies, and so on).

NHTSA's *Guide to Sentencing DUI Offenders* (1996b) lists five keys to lowering DUI recidivism: 1. Evaluating offenders for alcohol-related problems and recidivism risk; 2. Selecting appropriate sanctions and remedies for each offender; 3. Including provisions for appropriate alcoholism treatment in the sentencing order for offenders who require treatment; 4. Monitoring the offender's compliance with treatment; 5. Acting swiftly to correct noncompliance. National Highway Traffic Safety Administration and National Institute on Alcohol Abuse and Alcoholism. *A Guide to Sentencing DUI Offenders.* (Technical Report DOT HS 808 365). Washington, DC: (1996b)

Mandatory Alcohol/Drug Evaluations

Mandatory alcohol/drug evaluations and treatment of DUI offenders to address potential substance abuse problems has support in law enforcement, in the judiciary, and organizations such as MADD. The idea is that if the offender is evaluated, found in need of treatment, and thereafter is treated for substance abuse issues then the chance of repeating the crime of DUI is diminished. Wells-Parker, E., Bangert-Drowns, B., McMillen, R. & Williams, M. *Final results from a meta-analysis of remedial interventions with DUI Offenders.* Addiction. 90:907-926 (1995)

MADD also suggests that an evaluation and treatment are not enough to correct future problems with drinking and driving and are not a replacement for other sanctions. MADD states that "[t]reatment works best when coupled with sanctions like administrative license revocation or vehicle impoundment." *Id.*; www.madd.org There are too many critics of this approach to mention in this book.

A unique approach to alcohol treatment is an optional (not mandatory) program afforded defendants in Washington State. In Washington State individuals charged with DUI are given an opportunity to utilize alcohol (or drug) treatment as a means to have their DUI dismissed. The program is called "deferred prosecution" and is unique to that State. Deferred prosecution permits those who are alcohol or drug dependent (or suffer from mental health issues) to enter into a two year treatment program in exchange for a complete dismissal of the charge (or charges) in five years, no jail, no fines, and no loss of license. Revised Code of Washington (RCW) 10.05

The Washington legislature has recognized that some people who are charged with criminal offenses are not necessarily criminal by nature but suffer from a problem that needs treatment. Jolly, David N. *The DUI Handbook For The Accused.* Outskirts Press. Pages 124-125 (2007) The legislature has recognized that the best way to keep an alcoholic (or drug addict) from driving drunk (or affected by drugs) is to get him or her to stop drinking or abusing drugs. *Id.* From this belief came the deferred prosecution statute. *Id.*

In order to qualify for deferred prosecution the defendant must obtain an evaluation from a state approved treatment agency. The treatment facility conducts a detailed assessment and if it concludes that the criminal conduct was the result of alcoholism, drug addiction or mental health problems and that the individual is amenable to treatment then the court will permit the petition (application) for deferred prosecution. Washington State only permits an individual to use this program once in a lifetime.

The program consists of a statutorily required two-year treatment program which is broken down to a demanding three phase schedule. The first phase is typically three or four nights a week (sometimes five nights a week depending on the provider) for the first three months (seventy -two hours of treatment in the first 90 days) or can involve an inpatient program. Phase two involves weekly treatment and counseling for six months. Phase three, the least rigorous of the three phases, requires counseling once a month for the balance of the two-year program. Additionally, two Alcoholics Anonymous or other self-help meetings per week are required for the full two years. Complete abstinence is required and the individual must be in total compliance or faces the risk of having the program revoked.

Ignition Interlock Device

The ignition interlock device (IID, or breath alcohol ignition interlock device (BIID)) is gaining popularity in governmental circles, court systems, and advocates against the crime of driving under the influence. The device is a breath test type apparatus that is connected to the vehicle's dashboard, or more correctly to its ignition mechanism. The instrument requires the driver to provide a breath sample before allowing the vehicle to start. If the breath sample renders a clean result (i.e. a blood alcohol concentration reading below the permitted amount (usually, 0.00, 0.02, or 0.04 per cent)) the vehicle's engine will start. Alternatively, if the driver provides a breath sample that is over the required amount then the vehicle will not turn over and the failed attempt will be reported to the governing agency.

While the vehicle is in motion (or the engine is turned on) the IID will randomly require the driver to provide another breath sample. The time between required breath samples is dependant on the calibration of the unit, however typically random breath samples are required every 10 to 20 minutes while the vehicle is in operation. The purpose behind the random breath sample is to prevent a driver from having a "sober" friend blow into the device starting the vehicle. If the requested breath sample is not provided or exceeds the required limit, the device will record the incident, warn the driver and then start up an alarm (e.g., lights flashing, horn honking, etc.) until the ignition is turned off, or a clean breath sample has been provided.

A common, but inaccurate belief is that interlock devices will turn off the vehicle's engine if alcohol is detected. Due to the fact that this would then create an unsafe or dangerous driving situation that would expose interlock manufacturers to substantial liability, a vehicle's engine does not turn off if a breath sample detects too much alcohol on a driver's breath. It is physically impossible for an interlock device to turn off a running vehicle.

Most of the ignition interlock devices in use today use an ethanol-specific fuel cell for a sensor. This type of sensor is an electrochemical device where alcohol undergoes a chemical oxidation reaction on a catalytic electrode surface, typically made of platinum, to generate an electric current. This current is then measured and converted to an alcohol equivalent reading. Fuel cell technology is not nearly as accurate or reliable as the infrared spectroscopy technology used in evidentiary breathalyzers. However, IDs are obviously substantially cheaper and smaller and therefore more practical for widespread use.

The devices keep a running record of the activity on the unit and this record, or log, is printed out or downloaded each time the device's sensors are calibrated, commonly at 30, 60, or 90-day intervals. In the DUI realm these records are provided to the courts for probation review and to the Department of Licensing in some instances. If the court still has jurisdiction and a violation is detected the court may require the driver to re-appear and possibly face addition sanctions.

Most states in the U.S. now permit judges to order the installation of an IID as a condition of probation. There are also many states that mandate that an IID be installed for repeat offenders and in some states for first offenders. Forty-three States have laws allowing the installation of alcohol ignition interlocks on the vehicles of offenders. (AK, AR, AZ, CA, CO, DC, DE, FL, GA, IA, ID, IL, IN, KS, KY, LA, MA, MD, MI, MO, MS, MT, NC, ND, NE, NH, NJ, NM, NV, NY, OH, OK, OR, PA, RI, SC, TN, TX, UT, VA, WA, WI, WV). Fell, James C., Voas, Robert B., McKnight, A. Scott, and Levy, Marvin. *A National Survey of Vehicle Sanction Laws for Alcohol-Related Driving Offenses in the United States: Preliminary Findings*. Pacific Institute for Research & Evaluation, Calverton, MD National Highway Traffic Safety Administration, Washington, DC. Seattle, Wa. (2007) A list of federally-approved IID devices is maintained by the National Highway Traffic Safety Administration's NHTSA Conforming Products List.

In addition to the United States many other countries are requiring the ignition interlock as a penalty for drivers who are convicted of DUI. This is particularly the case for repeat DUI offenders. In the United States MADD launched a highly publicized campaign which aggressively advocated mandatory IID installation for all first offenders. Politicians in the United States, Sweden, Japan, Canada, among others, have also campaigned for such devices to be installed as standard equipment in all motor vehicles sold.

In the United States advocacy of mandatory installation of an IID in all new cars has been championed by MADD. To that end, Glynn Birch, the former President of MADD stated that "[t]he main reason why people continue to drive drunk today is because they can." *MADD: Device Key to Keep Drinkers off Road*. Newsday (November 21, 2006)

To support the advocacy of the installation of IIDs there is research that suggests that drivers who have interlocks installed have lower recidivism rates while the device is in use, but that recidivism rates rise after interlock removal. Voas, R.B.; Marques, P.R.; Tippetts, A.S.; and Beirness, D.J. *Alberta Interlock Program: The evaluation of a province-wide program on DUI recidivism.* Addict 94(12):1849-1859 (1999); Tashima, H.N., and Helander, C.J. *1999 Annual Report of the California DUI Management Information System.* Sacramento, CA: California Department of Motor Vehicles Research and Development Section. (1999) Further, there are even a few studies that have reported that recidivism was significantly reduced both during interlock installation and after removal. Weinrath, M. *Ignition interlock program for drunk drivers: A multivariate test.* Crime Delinquency 43(1):42-59 (1997); Beck, K.H.; Rauch, W.J.; Baker, E.A.; and Williams, A.F. *Effects of ignition interlock license restrictions on drivers with multiple alcohol offenses: A randomized trial in Maryland.* Am J Public Health 89(11):1696-1700 (1999)

There have been concerns that the installation of IID is in fact, dangerous. One study observed that "the risk of a subsequent crash was higher for drivers installing an IID by 84 percent." DeYoung, D.J., Tashima, H.N., and Masten, S.V. *An Evaluation of the Effectiveness of Ignition Interlock in California.* California Department of Motor Vehicles. Presentation at the 84th Annual Meeting of the Transportation

Research Board. Washington, D.C. Page 10 (January 11, 2005) This finding is not surprising considering the device demands drivers provide breath samples periodically while driving.

Other concerns are that false positives can occur in an IID. In one study a man who was attempting dramatic weight loss and who was on a very low calorie diet had his IID fail to start. *International Journal of Obesity*. 31 559-561. (August 8, 2006) The IID company Smart Start states that the following items can cause their device to fail: spicy foods, certain mouthwashes, some chocolate mints, Altoids, Dentyne and other gums, cinnamon rolls and donuts (the sugar and active yeast can combine to create a low level alcohol fail) and smoke (if blown directly into the unit). www.smartstartinc.com The debate regarding their value and their need shall continue.

Secure Continuous Remote Alcohol Monitor (SCRAM)

The "Secure Continuous Remote Alcohol Monitor system," or more commonly known as SCRAM, is a water and tamper-resistant Bracelet that collects, stores and transmits measurements of an individual's blood alcohol content (BAC). The SCRAM device is made by a company named AMS, was developed in 1991, first introduced in 2003, and now is used in more than forty states.

The device is considered a transdermal alcohol sensor and measures alcohol that is lost through the skin from sweat. The device utilizes three technologies that work simultaneously, yet separately, namely the Transdermal Alcohol Content (TAC) for alcohol detection, as mentioned, thermometer for determination of body temperature of the subject, and infrared signal system for detection of distance from the skin to the SCRAM unit. The gadget, worn as an ankle Bracelet, "sniffs" every 30 minutes and transfers data via a wireless connection to a probation officer or other law-enforcement official. The device can also detect tampering. This device is used frequently in courts where Judges impose conditions of release after an arraignment or preliminary hearing or by probation departments after sentencing.

Not surprisingly there are critics of these devices and the technology. Opponents have argued that there is the possibility of radio, electrical, or other electromagnetic interference at the location of an alleged violation. Hlastala, M.P., and Barone, P.T. *Identification of Transdermal Ethyl Alcohol.* DWI Journal: Law & Science: Vol. 22, No. 11, Page 5 (November, 2007)

There is also a possibility that cologne/perfume applied to the skin can contaminate the area and interfere with the SCRAM device's determination of alcohol presence. This theory has been kept alive by a study that found alcohol does not necessarily absorb directly into the skin but can remain on or near the surface of the skin for a considerable time. Giles, H.G., Meggiorini, S., Renaud, G.E.. *Determination of Gas Sensor Instruction and Relationship with Plasma Concentration.* Alcohol, Clinical and Experimental Research. Vol. 11, No. 3, Pages 249-253 (1987)

Another possible source of error according to one study is that the SCRAM device calculation of skin alcohol concentration could be up to 19 % higher than the actual measurement in the blood. Buono, M.J. *Sweat Ethanol Concentrations are Highly Correlated with Co-Existing Blood Values in Humans.* Experimental Physiology. Vol. 84, Pages 401-404 (1998) Yet another possible problem with the device concerns its sensitivity to temperature, both the internal body temperature and external skin temperature on the user. Phillips, M. *Sweat-Patch Test for Alcohol Consumption: Rapid Assay with an Electrical Detector.* Alcoholism, Clinical and Experimental Research. Vol. 6, No. 4. Pages 532-534 (1982)

Sobriety Checkpoints/Check Stops

Previously addressed in Chapter 5, sobriety checkpoints involve law enforcement officials positioning themselves on a road way and stopping every vehicle, or random vehicles and investigating the possibility that the driver is under the influence of alcohol or drugs. The primary advocates for sobriety checkpoints have been NHTSA, law enforcement, and MADD.

DUI Victim Panel

MADD has advocated for many years the mandatory attendance at a victim impact panel (VIP) for those charged with a DUI. A DUI VIP is an event in which the attendees listen to presentations made by relatives of victims or victims of DUI incidents and/or accidents. These victims or relatives relate their experiences to the attendees. Most DUI VIPs charge for participation and some of the money collected from fees paid by participants eventually find its way back to MADD. In fact the organization collected $4,436,481 in 2006 from VIPs.

There have been mixed reviews over the years regarding the value of the DUI VIP. According to the John Howard Society, some studies have shown that allowing victims to give testimony is psychologically beneficial to them and aids in their recovery and in their positive opinion of the criminal justice system. *Victim Impact Statements.* John Howard Society of Alberta (1997) In the alternative, a New Mexico study suggested that DUI VIPs tended to be perceived as confrontational by multiple offenders. According to the study such offenders then had a higher incidence of future offenses. Woodall, W.G., Delaney, H., Rogers, E. & Wheeler, D.R. *A Randomized Trial of Victim Impact Panels' DWI Deterrence Effectiveness.* Center on Alcoholism, Substance Abuse, and Addictions (CASAA), University of New Mexico (2000) Overall the effects and value of victim impact panels on recidivism has been mixed. Shinar, D., and Compton, R.P. *Victim impact panels: Their impact on DWI recidivism.* Alcohol Drugs Driv 11(1):73-87, (1995); Fors, S.W., and Rojek, D.G. *The effect of victim impact panels on DUI/DWI rearrest rates: A twelve-month follow-up.* J Stud Alcohol 60(4):514-520 (1999); C'de Baca, J., Lapham, S.C., Paine, S., and Skipper, B.J. *Victim impact panels: Who is sentenced to attend? Does attendance affect recidivism of first-time DWI offenders?* Alcohol Clin Exp Res 24(9):1420-1426 (2000)

License Suspensions

Certain studies have concluded that laws permitting administrative license suspensions (ALS) at the time of an arrest for DUI have been found to reduce both alcohol-related fatality accidents and repeat DUI offenses. Voas, R.B., Tippets, A.S., and Fell, J. *The relationship of alcohol safety laws to drinking drivers in fatal crashes.* Accid Anal Prev 32:483-492 (2000); Voas, R.B., Tippetts, A.S., and Taylor, E.P. *Impact of Ohio administrative license suspension.* In: 42nd Annual Proceedings: Association for the Advancement of Automotive Medicine. Des Plaines, IL: AAAM. (1998) A study of an Ohio ALS law found that first-time and repeat DUI offenders who had their licenses immediately confiscated had significantly lower rates of DUI offenses, moving violations, and crashes during the following two years compared with DUI offenders convicted before the ALS law went into effect. *Id.* Although research shows that license suspensions reduce repeat DUI offenses, there is also evidence that up to 75 percent of suspended drivers continue to drive.

A license suspension received in one state may then be entered into a database called the U.S. Interstate Drivers License Compact. The Drivers License Compact is an agreement between 45 participating states to share information about drivers and their Department of Licensing (DOL/DMV) records that include, but are not limited to, infractions, convictions, driver's license suspensions, license restrictions, revocations, DUI charges, accidents, and eligibility for license reinstatement. Jolly, David N. *The DUI Handbook For The Accused.* Outskirts Press (2007) Both the Drivers License Compact and the Non-Resident Violator Compact are in the process of being merged into one database titled the National Driver Register. *Id.* The main purpose of the NDR database is to share information on drivers who have committed a serious infraction or violation in a state other than where they are licensed to drive. The five states that are not currently members and do not participate in sharing DUI and licensing record information are Georgia, Massachusetts, Michigan, Tennessee and Wisconsin.

Another collateral consequence of a DUI and a resulting license suspension is additional insurance. This insurance in the United States is termed "SR-22," which is an administrative form that attests to an insurance company's coverage, or the posting of a personal public bond in the amount of the state's minimum liability coverage for the licensed driver or vehicle registration. SR-22s are typically filed with the respective State's Department of Licensing (DOL) / Department of Motor Vehicles (DMV) and in some States must be carried by the licensed driver, or in the registered vehicle (particularly if the licensee has been cited for coverage lapses, DUI or other administrative infractions). SR-22s may attest coverage for a vehicle regardless of operator (owner liability coverage), or cover a specific person regardless of the specific vehicle operated (operator liability coverage).

Vehicle Impound

Another penalty or sanction that many states have at their disposal is to impound the vehicle of the DUI offender. Eleven States have laws permitting impoundment for DUI related offenses (AK, CA, CT, FL, IA, KS, MO, MS, OR, VA, WA) and this does not include state laws where the impoundment is temporary (hours) to prevent impaired offenders from driving after release from arrest. Fell, James C., Voas, Robert B., McKnight, A. Scott, and Levy, Marvin. *A National Survey of Vehicle Sanction Laws for Alcohol-Related Driving Offenses in the United States: Preliminary Findings.* Pacific Institute for Research & Evaluation, Calverton, MD National Highway Traffic Safety Administration, Washington, DC. Seattle, Wa. (2007)

A NHTSA funded study of vehicle sanctions in 1997 evaluated the deterrent effect of a 30-day vehicle impoundment law for unlicensed driving implemented in California. DeYoung, D.J. *An evaluation of the specific deterrence effect of vehicle impoundment on suspended, revoked and unlicensed drivers in California.* Report No. DOT HS 808 727. Washington, DC: National Highway Traffic Safety Administration. (1997) Prior to the study in the United States a similar study was completed in 1989 in the Province of Manitoba that evaluated a 30-day (first-offense), 60-day (second-offense) DWLS vehicle impoundment program. Beirness, D. J., Simpson, H. M., Mayhew, D. R., and Jonah, B. J. *The impact of administrative licence suspension and vehicle impoundment for DWI in Manitoba.* (1997) Both studies concluded that subsequent DWLS offenses were reduced as a direct result of the vehicle impoundment programs. However, what these studies did not affirmatively address was if this program directly reduced further DUI offenses by these individuals. As a result, in the DUI context, lengthy vehicle impoundment appears to be primarily punitive.

Vehicle Immobilization

Another tool to prevent DUI offenders from driving is immobilizing their vehicle. This is done by using a bar-type locking device ("club") on the steering wheel or locking device on a wheel ("boot"). Thirteen States have laws permitting vehicle immobilization as a sanction for impaired driving offenses (FL, IA, IL, KS, MI, MS, NM, OH, OR, SC, VA, VT, WI). Fell, James C., Voas, Robert B., McKnight, A. Scott, and Levy, Marvin. *A National Survey of Vehicle Sanction Laws for Alcohol-Related Driving Offenses in the United States: Preliminary Findings.* Pacific Institute for Research & Evaluation, Calverton, MD National Highway Traffic Safety Administration, Washington, DC. Seattle, Wa. (2007)

One such immobilization device is the "Denver Boot" which is manufactured by Clancy Systems International Inc. The Denver Boot was invented in 1953 by Frank Marugg. http://www.clancysystems. com. Marugg was a friend to many politicians and police department officials in Denver and the Denver Sheriff's Department asked him for help with their parking enforcement problem. Marugg and the Sheriff decided to build a device to immobilize vehicles whose owners didn't pay their outstanding parking tickets. He subsequently invented and patented the Denver Boot. The Marugg family later sold the company in 1986 to Clancy Systems.

In Ohio researchers conducted a field test to study the deterrent effects that a combined impoundment and immobilization program had on accidents and violations for multiple DUI and suspended license offenders. Voas, RB, *et al.*, *Effectiveness of the Ohio Vehicle Action and Administrative License Suspension Laws.* Washington, DC: NHTSA (2000) From September 1993 to September 1995, the vehicles of nearly 1,000 offenders were impounded and then immobilized. The recidivism rates of these offenders were compared to eligible offenders who did not receive any vehicle sanctions. The study determined that offenders whose vehicles were impounded and immobilized had lower rates of DUI recidivism both during and after the termination of the sanctions. Similar findings were obtained in Hamilton County, where only vehicle impoundment was used. Voas, R.B., Tippetts, A.S., and Taylor, E. *The Effect of Vehicle Impoundment and Immobilization on Driving Offenses of Suspended and Repeat DWI Drivers.* 40th annual proceedings of the Association for the Advancement of Automotive Medicine. Vancouver, British Columbia (1996); Voas, R.B., Tippetts, A.S., and Taylor, E. *Evaluation of the Vehicle Immobilization Law in Franklin County (Columbus) Ohio.* Proceedings from Lifesavers 15, Orlando, Florida. (1997)

Special License Plates or Plate Markings

This sanction includes placing special markings or designations on the license plate that alert police that a convicted DUI offender is in a family or group that drives that vehicle. The special license plate or plate marking sanction permits other family members access to the vehicle, but prohibits the convicted offender from driving it. Six States have laws permitting special license plates for impaired driving offenses (GA, HI, MI, MN, NJ, OH). Fell, James C., Voas, Robert B., McKnight, A. Scott, and Levy, Marvin. *A National Survey of Vehicle Sanction Laws for Alcohol-Related Driving Offenses in the United States: Preliminary Findings.* Pacific Institute for Research & Evaluation, Calverton, MD National Highway Traffic Safety Administration, Washington, DC. Seattle, Wa. (2007)

Ohio was the first state to use modified license plates on vehicles and in 1967, Ohio issued special license plates to DUI offenders and gave judges discretion to enforce this law. However judges rarely enforced the plates and as a result the special plate law was mandated by state law to all DUI offenders in 2004. Dyer, Bob. *DUI plates are another Ohio flop.* Akron Beacon Journal. (June 19, 2007) Unlike Ohio's standard-issue plates (which as of 2008 are red and blue on white), the DUI plates are yellow with red writing with no registration stickers or graphics. They are sometimes known as "party plates." Dyer, Bob. *DUI plates are another Ohio flop.* Akron Beacon Journal. (06/19/2007) In Minnesota, DUI plates are referred to as "whiskey plates." Youso, Karen. *Fixit: Whiskey plates' indicate a DUI.* Minneapolis Star Tribune. (March 23, 2007)

For several years, a Minnesota law permitted judges to confiscate the license plates of repeat offenders, specifically violators with three DUI violations in five years or four or more DUI violations in ten years. However, like in Ohio, very few judges actually used this method for controlling the driving of these offenders. Ross, H.L., Simon, S, Cleary, J. *License plate confiscation for persistent alcohol impaired drivers. Accident; analysis and prevention* (1996). As a result discretion was removed and in 1991 the law was changed to provide for administrative confiscation of the license plates at the time of arrest. Rodgers, A. *Effect of Minnesota's license plate impoundment law on recidivism of multiple DWI violators.* Alcohol, Drugs, and Driving. Vol. 10. Pages 127-134 (1994) According to NHTSA the study found a 50-percent decrease in recidivism over a two-year period (when compared with DUI violators who did not experience impoundment). NHTSA. *Traffic Safety Facts Laws - Vehicle and License Plate Sanctions.* DOT HS 810 880 (January 2008)

Back in the 1990s neighboring states Oregon and Washington enacted what was coined the "Zebra Tag" law. This law allowed police officers to take the driver's vehicle registration when apprehending a driver who did not have a valid license. NHTSA. *Traffic Safety Facts Laws - Vehicle and License Plate Sanctions.* DOT HS 810 880 (January 2008). In each case, the driver was given a temporary registration certificate, and a striped ("Zebra") sticker was placed over the annual sticker on the vehicle's rear license plate. During the program the Zebra Tag law was applied to approximately 7,000 offenders in Washington and 31,000 in Oregon. The study in Oregon concluded that suspended DUI offenders at risk of being "tagged" if caught driving were found to have fewer moving violations and accidents under the Zebra Tag law than were reinstated DUI offenders not at risk for "driving while licensed suspended" (DWLS) or being tagged. Presumably the drivers were in fear of being watched more closely so they drove more carefully. Additionally, the study found that those DWLS offenders in Oregon who had their vehicle plates tagged had lower rates of DUI offenses, moving violations, and repeat DWLS offenses than similarly eligible offenders whose vehicle plates were not tagged. NHTSA believed that "tagging the vehicle had a specific deterrent effect that reduced illegal driving." Conversely, according to NHTSA the law did not have a significant impact in Washington. Voas, Robert and A. Scott Tippetts, A.S. "Unlicensed Driving by DUIs – A Major Safety Problem?" TRB ID No. CR077. Paper presented at the 73rd Annual Meeting, Transportation Research Board, Landover, MD (January 9-13, 1994)

Vehicle Sanctions In Other Countries

The drafters of *A National Survey of Vehicle Sanction Laws for Alcohol-Related Driving Offenses in the United States: Preliminary Findings,* indicated that they made contact with officials in Australia, Belgium, Canada, Denmark, New Zealand, Norway, Spain, Sweden, and the United Kingdom to determine what vehicle sanctions were typically used when punishing the DUI driver. What they concluded was that with the exception of alcohol ignition interlock programs, vehicle sanctions were rarely used. The writers found that vehicle impoundment and forfeiture were generally considered too harsh in these aforementioned countries and too much of a hardship for family members. The one exception they found was New Zealand which has a comprehensive vehicle impoundment and confiscation program that is in use. *A National Survey of Vehicle Sanction Laws for Alcohol-Related Driving Offenses in the United States: Preliminary Findings.* Pacific Institute for Research & Evaluation, Calverton, MD National Highway Traffic Safety Administration, Washington, DC. Seattle, Wa. (2007)

In regards to the use of alcohol ignition interlocks, these devices have become particularly popular in Canada and Australia with both countries conducting significant research into their implementation. The criminal code in Canada has been amended to enable provinces and territories to begin interlock programs and as a consequence the majority of Canadian provinces have mandated them. In Australia the five largest states (New South Wales, Victoria, Queensland, Western Australia and South Australia) have all begun interlock programs. In Europe, Sweden has instituted a small interlock program and other countries have undertaken feasibility or pilot studies in coordination with the European Union. Marques, P., Bjerre, B., Dussault, C., Voas, R. B., Beirness, D. J., Marples, I. R., & Rauch, W. R. *Alcohol ignition interlock devices—I: Position paper.* Oosterhout, Netherlands (November, 2001)

Anti-Plea Bargaining

Another policy that MADD advocates is "anti-plea bargaining." This practice prohibits plea bargaining or reducing any alcohol-related offense to a non-alcohol related offense. There are sixteen (16) states and territories with anti-plea bargaining laws, and they are as follows: California, Colorado, Florida, Georgia, Hawaii, Kansas, Kentucky, Michigan, Mississippi, Nevada, New Jersey, New Mexico, New York, Oregon, Pennsylvania, and Wyoming. Jolly, David N. *The DUI Handbook For The Accused.* Outskirts Press (2007)

DUI Emphasis Campaigns

Educating the public about the dangers of drinking and driving and the penalties that would be imposed has made its way into society since the early 1980s in the United States and earlier in other countries. These "public service announcements" (PSAs) are done at a local level, in schools, and by organizations advocating against the activity (ie. MADD). However, the most active participant in the United States has been the "Ad Council." The U.S. Department of Transportation and NHTSA have partnered with the Ad Council since 1982 with "Drunk Driving Prevention" campaigns. http://www.adcouncil.org/ During the 1980s the original "tagline" for the campaign was "Drinking & Driving Can Kill A Friendship," and evolved into the 1990s tagline, "Friends Don't Let Friends Drive Drunk." Interestingly, and topical, Michael Jackson donated his Grammy-award winning song "Beat It" for use in television and radio PSAs in campaigns against drinking and driving. *Id.* (Michael Jackson passed away weeks prior to this book being published)

In Australia the drinking and driving campaigns are aggressive and graphic – far more so than their counter parts in the United States. The Victorian Traffic Accident Commission (TAC) has advertised in the media since the late 1980s depicting the dangers of drinking and driving; in many commercials showing car accidents and dead bodies. Besides advertising in the media TAC has also been an active player in advertising in the sporting arena. TAC has promoted its "Drink, drive, bloody idiot" campaign directly on the jerseys of professional Australian Rules Football (AFL) teams. The TAC had lucrative contracts with several teams in the AFL but unfortunately all of these contracts were rescinded due to breaches made by players at these clubs (players were arrested for drinking and driving). Most notable was the loss of the contract with the Richmond Football Club after it had been sponsored by TAC for 16 years, and to a lesser extent the loss of the contract with the Collingwood Football Club. TAC Terminates Richmond Sponsorship; Media Release. Victorian Traffic Accident Commission (April 1, 2005); Collier, Karen and

Warner, Michael. *Collingwood loses its TAC sponsorship after new drink-drive charge.* Herald Sun Newspaper. (January 09, 2008) This author easily remembers the slogan "Don't Drink and Drive over 0.05" in the 1970s in Australia. Moreover, after reviewing black and white video from the 1973 Australian Football League Grand Final (Championship game) the slogan is visible throughout the stadium and on the main scoreboard.

What is striking is that all of these advertising campaigns use catchy slogans that attempt to either shock or be memorable, such as: "Drunk Driving. Over the Limit. Under Arrest" (NHTSA); "Sober or Slammer" (Minnesota); "Booze It & Lose It" (North Carolina/ Tennessee); "Drink. Drive. Go to Jail" (NHTSA); "Looks like someone had too much holiday spirit" (NHTSA); "Don't Get Cuffed & Stuffed" and "'Get Out of Jail Free' cards don't work in real life"(Washington State).

CHAPTER 10

The Future of DUI

History teaches everything, even the future.
—Alphonse de Lamartine

The evolution of the legal and clinical practice of driving under the influence has been slow. Clearly, the trained professionals and the rules that guide them have not kept pace with other criminal technology and technological advances in western civilization as a whole. The field of DUI practice relies on subjective opinions of police officers who have only an elementary understanding of the science and history of the testing procedures they are using, as well as scientific evidence gathered from devices that are based on technology developed several decades earlier. It is seemingly unacceptable that this area of the law has been slow to evolve despite the fact that politicians have expended great energy and even greater amounts of money emphasizing law enforcement patrols and laws to rid society of this potentially dangerous activity.

There is good news in the field of driving under the influence and that is the number of DUI related deaths has been on the decline (although no statistics reveal whether this decline is a result of behavioral changes or improvements in vehicle safety). According to the National Highway Traffic Safety Administration (NHTSA) in 2008, 11,773 individuals lost their lives in motor vehicle accidents in the United States involving a driver with a BAC of 0.08 or higher, yet this number was down 9.7% from the previous year (there is no indication in the report as to the "at-fault" driver). *Traffic Safety Facts: 2008 Traffic Safety Annual Assessment - Highlights*. NHTSA. DOT HS 811 172 (June 2009) According to NHTSA, as far back as 1982 fatal accidents involving alcohol in the driver's system accounted for 35% of all traffic fatalities in the United States, but by 2005 the number had been reduced to 20%. Dang, Jennifer N. *Statistical Analysis of Alcohol-Related Driving Trends, 1982-2005*. NHTSA. DOT HS 810 942 (May 2008)

Despite the decline in the number of deaths involving drivers under the influence the field of practice has much room for improvement. The improvement must start with the education and training of law enforcement personal. The education and training that a law enforcement officer receives prior to being permitted to stop, arrest, and process a suspect for DUI is not acceptable. The amount of time that police academies spend training officers in traffic control and specifically DUI investigations is limited to hours, not weeks or semesters. Considering the focus and money spent on enforcing DUIs officers should be better educated, and to suggest the contrary is to support mediocrity.

The issue of education and training for law enforcement has been an issue for the past century. More than forty years ago the *Report of the President's Commission on Law Enforcement and the Administration of Justice* attempted to address the issue of producing "better-educated police officers" by stating that the ultimate aim of all police departments should be that all personnel with general enforcement powers have baccalaureate degrees. Katzenbach, Nicholas deB. *United States President's Commission on Law Enforcement and Administration of Justice. Task Force on the Police.* Washington, D.C.: Govt Print Off. (1967) More than forty years later this goal remains unrealized.

In addition to improved training law enforcement also deserve better tools for use in their trade. The field sobriety testing that is primarily relied on by officers, the horizontal gaze nystagmus, the walk and turn and the one leg stand, were standardized by a series of studies completed over 30 years ago. However, these NHTSA sponsored studies and resulting standardized tests were not ground breaking as these series of tests, or tests very much like them, had already existed for decades. Additionally, law enforcement also regularly uses the Romberg Balance Test, which was developed by Moritz Romberg in 1853 to diagnose diseases, not indicate impairment by alcohol or drugs. Do we not have any better testing available to us or is there not enough research and study dedicated toward this practice area? Either way, the current set of field sobriety testing is archaic, not well understood by the practitioners, and has not advanced significantly in the last 50 years. In the twenty-first century law enforcement deserve a better mouse trap than field sobriety tests that were first used more than half a century earlier.

Law enforcement is not alone in training deficiencies however. In truth the majority of attorneys practicing in the DUI field, both prosecuting and defense attorneys alike, do not understand the law and science of driving under the influence as well as they should. Similarly, Judges deserve better training in the nuances of this area of law, as well as the accepted protocol and procedures in driving under the influence.

The most dramatic change in the practice of DUI will be in technological advancements for devices that measure blood alcohol concentration. When the history of driving under the influence is examined it is clear that technology will move this field into a different sphere of practice. I have no doubts that breath testing will be slowly removed as the primary evidentiary test of blood alcohol concentration and will be replaced by a more advanced, sophisticated and accurate measurement system.

One potential replacement for the traditional breath test is a saliva test. In 2008, scientists announced that more cost effective saliva tests could eventually replace some blood tests, as saliva contains 20% of the proteins found in blood. Denny, Paul, Hagen, Fred K., Hardt, Markus, et al. *The Proteomes of Human Parotid and Submandibular/Sublingual Gland Salivas Collected as the Ductal Secretions.* Journal of Proteome Research (March 25, 2008) Researchers in the United States have identified all 1,116 unique proteins found in human saliva glands, and it is this discovery that could usher in a wave of convenient, spit-based diagnostic tests that do not require an invasive blood draw. Such tests are already used to detect HIV and hepatitis and could be used to detect BAC levels of drivers in the future.

There are numerous studies that were conducted prior to recent developments in saliva testing and protein mapping and those studies generally found that saliva is comparable to breath as an analytical specimen. McColl, K.E., Whiting, B., Moore, M.R., Goldberg, A. *Correlation of Ethanol Concentrations in Blood and Saliva.* Clin Sci (Lond) 56(3):283-286 (March 1979); Bates, M.E., Brick, J., and White, H.R. *The Correspondence Between Saliva and Breath Estimates of Blood Alcohol Concentration: Advantages and Limitations of the Saliva Method.* J Stud Alcohol. 54(1):17-22 (January 1993) However, as with breath testing, mouth alcohol contamination would remain a valid concern in gathering such evidence.

The saliva test has been tested in several jurisdictions. In Australia, the State of Victoria has thoroughly tested the viability of saliva testing. The Victorian government approved saliva testing for drug screening (similar to PBTs) so long as: the preliminary roadside screening test take no longer than five minutes to complete, only saliva is tested, the device that collects the saliva sample must not be overly intrusive, and the test subject must receive a portion of the second saliva sample. Thiessen, Brian. *Roadside technology combats drug driving.* Blue Line Magazine. (June/July 2006) The Victorian government approved two devices for saliva testing, the Securetec Drugwipe II and Cozart Rapiscan, as they were assessed as reliable and accurate, according to their studies. *Id.* Similar studies have been conducted in Canada and Europe.

Another possible replacement for breath testing in the distant future is fingerprint testing. A company in New Mexico, named Lumidigm has developed a fingerprint sensor that detects blood alcohol content (BAC). The technology is a light-based scanner that takes three-dimensional images of fingerprints. Additionally, the sensors can be adjusted to test for the presence of alcohol being excreted from the skin. Lumidign has field tested this handheld equipment with the assistance of the Bernalillo County Sheriff's Department in New Mexico. http://www.lumidigm.com/

Prevention programs in the area of DUI will also continue to evolve, improve and will be an area of focus and undoubtedly controversy. In recent years ignition interlock devices have been used to prevent a driver from driving under the influence but have only been installed when ordered by a Judge or as a prerequisite to having a driver's license reinstated. However, the use of similar devices may become mandatory, if you believe organizations such as MADD and certain politicians.

A similar device to the ignition interlock has been developed by the automobile manufacturer, Saab. They have developed a device called the "Alco-key," which is a miniature alcohol-sensing apparatus that would be built into the car's key fob and work in conjunction with the car manufacturer's already-existing anti-theft technology. Similar to an ignition interlock device, when the driver unlocks the vehicle the device would demand a breath sample. The breath sample passes down a small inner tube containing a semi-conductor sensor the size of a pin-head. The sample is then analyzed and a small green or red light on the fob lights up. If the reading is higher than the pre-programmed threshold then the anti-theft engine immobilizer activates and the car cannot be operated until an acceptable sample is received. Saab believes the primary use for this device will be on cars owned by companies and parents of young drivers. Birchard, John. *Sweden's Saab Holds Key to Stemming Drunk Driving Fatalities.* UTC (2004)

Saab is not alone in their work designing alcohol sensing units that can be installed in vehicles. Nissan has been examining the possible implementation of a similar system that is designed to prevent an engine from starting when a certain amount of alcohol is detected on the driver's breath. Additionally, the system Nissan is designing may be combined with a camera that monitors the driver for drowsiness (the latter system is already in place in some Mercedes

Benz models). Volvo and Toyota have also heavily invested in related anti-drink and drive technology. http://mdn.mainichi-msn.co.jp

There is other technology that is being introduced that may be used in preventative programs and these include breath testing devices in mobile phones. A mobile phone with a breath analyzer has been garnering support in Japan with transport companies. The system was developed by major mobile phone operator NTT DoCoMo Inc, and has been introduced to dozens of companies in Japan. Bus and transport companies are also considering using the device. http://www.upi.com The ever popular Apple iphone now has an application for detecting an individual's BAC. Called the "ibreath," the device connects to an iphone or itouch and costs $79. Chmielewski, Dawn C. *The accessory's maker hopes the iPod's cool factor will overcome any stigma of being responsible and using a breathalyzer.* Los Angeles Times (December 19, 2008)

Another preventative device contemplated by some jurisdictions is an arm patch that measures alcohol. The use of this device would potentially be of benefit for courts monitoring probation of those convicted of alcohol related offenses. Similar to a SCRAM Bracelet, the patch senses trace amounts of the enzyme secreted in sweat and turns red if it detects the particular enzyme. Fitzpatrick, Michael. *www.NewScientist.com* (2007)

Despite the increase in preventative programs and public campaigns there are those drivers who, regardless of the warnings, will drive while under the influence. These drivers will most certainly face increasingly harsh penalties in the future. The years ahead will probably see more states enacting felony DUI statutes and lower thresholds when a felony DUI can be charged. Additionally, it is foreseeable that there will be more severe penalties for those DUI drivers who have passengers in their vehicle, particularly in cases involving children. Further, drug specific DUI laws are already law in some states and on the books in many others. This area will see tremendous growth as government and law enforcement learn more about drugs and their impact on driving.

An interesting debate that will continue, and in my estimation escalate, will be the desire of many in government to lower the per se BAC from 0.08 to 0.05. In many countries throughout the world the per se limit has been 0.05 or lower for decades, yet the United States only mandated a uniform 0.08 law in 1999 (and enacted later than that). It is highly probable that at some point in the next 25 years most states in America, if not all, will reduce the per se BAC to a figure lower than the currently uniform 0.08.

The law as it pertains to driving under the influence will continue to evolve and the interpretation of the Constitution of the United States will continue. Government and law enforcement will continue to push the limits of the Constitution and argue that society's interest in reducing drinking and driving outweighs any perceived minor personal infringements. Those who oppose such infringements will point to individual rights and their protection by way of the United States Constitution. The debate will continue throughout and beyond my lifetime.

As mentioned in the introduction of this book, the future of driving under the influence will be an interesting journey that will see conflict, controversy, billions of dollars of government funding, and great tragedy, not unlike its first 100 years.

ALSO BY David N. Jolly

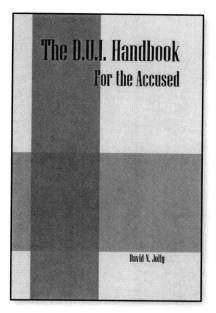

The D.U.I. Handbook

Driving Under the Influence of alcohol or drugs (DUI) is a very serious offense with potentially extreme consequences. A DUI conviction will result in jail, fines, higher insurance costs, the installation of an ignition interlock device, loss of license, and may also include loss of job, and even deportation if you are not a U.S. citizen. The DUI Handbook For the Accused details the DUI process from beginning to end, including discussing police DUI procedures, the court process, how to hire a qualified DUI attorney, how your attorney will, or should, defend your case, possible defenses to a DUI, and how to avoid a DUI entirely. This book is designed to help simplify a very complicated area of law. View the following websites for more information: www.WashDUI.com

**Learn more at: www.outskirtspress.com/
theDUIhandbook**

DATE DUE

	GAYLORD		PRINTED IN U.S.A.

CPSIA information can b
Printed in the USA
BVOW000005050713

324996BV00003B/143/P

9 781432 746223